CAPTA... 'S
M...

Ann Hulme

Nottinghamshire County Council

NOTTINGHAMSHIRE COUNTY COUNCIL
LEISURE SERVICES

WITHDRAWN FOR RE-SALE

Leisure Services/Libraries

MILLS & BOON LIMITED
ETON HOUSE   18-24 PARADISE ROAD
RICHMOND   SURREY   TW9 1SR

All the characters in this book have no existence outside the imagination of the Author, and have no relation whatsoever to anyone bearing the same name or names. They are not even distantly inspired by any individual known or unknown to the Author, and all the incidents are pure invention.

All Rights Reserved. The text of this publication or any part thereof may not be reproduced or transmitted in any form or by any means, electronic or mechanical, including photocopying, recording, storage in an information retrieval system, or otherwise, without the written permission of the publisher.

This book is sold subject to the condition that it shall not, by way of trade or otherwise, be lent, resold, hired out or otherwise circulated without the prior consent of the publisher in any form of binding or cover other than that in which it is published and without a similar condition including this condition being imposed on the subsequent purchaser.

First published in Great Britain 1989
by Mills & Boon Limited

© Ann Hulme 1989

Australian copyright 1989
Philippine copyright 1989
This edition 1989

ISBN 0 263 76485 0

Set in Times Roman 10½ on 12 pt.
04-8907-71360 C

Made and printed in Great Britain

CHAPTER ONE

'You'll get half a dozen petticoats for them kids off this, Miss Grey. Scarlet be all right for you? We got the same in white.' The draper paused with his scissors poised above the roll of flannelette on his counter.

'The scarlet would be much better, Mr Simpson,' Rachel assured him. 'Children love a pretty colour. Besides,' she added honestly, 'not all of the mothers are enamoured of the wash-tub and white, you know...'

'Ah,' said Mr Simpson, beginning to cut through the cloth. 'Very likely. Best Manchester this, by the way.'

Rachel watched the shining scissors flash above the scarlet cloth. Tom would not approve the colour. He would say it was frivolous. But Tom wasn't here, and presented with a *fait accompli* and a length of scarlet flannelette there would be nothing her brother could do about it. Mr Simpson always let them have the cloth at a reduced price because it was for the Ragged School, and to return it would be out of the question.

Another thought struck her. 'Mr Simpson, you don't happen to know of a family named Casey, do you?'

'Casey?' Mr Simpson paused and set down his scissors. He eyed his visitor thoughtfully. Pretty girl, Miss Grey, and tied to a real dry old stick of a brother. Pity. Wasting her time on those ragged kids when she ought to be married with her own. 'Casey,' he repeated. 'Ah, that'll be Jed Casey as was took up before the magistrates last week, drunk in the gutter and cursing the government. A bad lot, thorough bad all through. Steer clear, Miss Grey, that's my advice.'

'Unfortunately I can't.' Rachel tapped her fingers on the mahogany counter-top. 'Joey Casey and his cousin Sally are both on the roll of the Ragged school. Sally is forever coming to school barefoot, although I've twice given her boots, and Joey has been absent for almost a week without any explanation. I shall have to go to the house and enquire.'

'Not you!' exclaimed Mr Simpson in horror. 'Let your brother go! Better Mr Grey does it. It could get nasty, and being a lady, begging your pardon, wouldn't be any protection—and ah, you could have a—well, a nasty experience, miss. A rough area, that. Women not treated like you'd think fit.'

'Oh, I know well enough how women are treated around there,' said Rachel. Children, too. Both Joey and Sally frequently came to school with visible bruises. 'You don't happen to know if there's any illness in the family?' The draper was a mine of information.

'Very likely,' said Mr Simpson, packing up the flannel neatly in brown paper. 'Rats does it. Rats in all them houses down by the waterfront. One of them Casey kids come begging to the door a week since. The little girl. Very likely the same one as you mention. Give her half a loaf of stale bread, I did.'

'You're very kind, Mr Simpson,' said Rachel gratefully. 'I can only thank you on behalf of all the children.'

'Got no kids of our own, me and the missus,' said the draper regretfully. 'Seems like that's the way of it. Them as has got 'em, don't want 'em. Them as wants 'em, don't get 'em.'

Rachel thanked him and stepped out into the high street, the flannel cloth clasped in her arms. The district alluded to by the draper, and where the Casey tribe lived, was a rough one. Disease was rife among its malodorous and ill-lit houses. Rubbish of all kinds was thrown out into the street, and the rats, dogs and children all foraged eagerly for anything that could be found which was edible. Not that there was ever very much. Nothing which could be used or eaten was ever thrown away. A piece of rag, no matter how tattered, could be used to wrap a new-born baby. A nauseous soup could be brewed up from cabbage stalks, bones and half-rotten potatoes. It would not be unusual for a child to fall sick in these slum dwellings. The wonder of it was that any child survived there at all. The daily appearance at school of Sally, and the more erratic appearance of Joey, was in itself something of a minor miracle.

Before she had gone many steps, mulling over all this, her eye was taken by a familiar form, and Rachel was surprised to catch a glimpse of one subject of her thoughts, Joey Casey himself, on the other side of the street. Her first impulse was to call out to him, and beckon him across to enquire about his absence from school, but, even as she opened her mouth and raised her hand, she stopped and frowned, alerted by some instinct. Rachel let her hand drop to her side, drew back a little into the shelter of a shop-front, and watched.

The child was behaving very oddly. He was loitering in a most curious manner, not simply hanging about with his hands in his pockets or kicking a stone along. Joey was skulking in a doorway in a way which was quite furtive, and watching passers-by with a sharp, cunning expression on his pinched little face. Whatever else he was doing, Joey was not watching out for horses to be held. To do that, he would have been jumping about on the pavement, trying to catch the eye of drivers. What he was doing now was quite the reverse. Rachel continued to watch, waiting to see what would happen, and trying to suppress a feeling of unease.

After letting several gentlemen walk by him, and giving them no more than a quick, appraising glance, Joey's eye fell on a man approaching slowly, and apparently lost in his own thoughts. The absent-minded stroller was of striking appearance, not least because he wore a beard. It was not the biblical set of whiskers that some elderly gentlemen of academic distinction sported. It grew out of black side-whiskers, was neatly trimmed, outlining his chin and complemented by a small moustache. It looked so strange, even though it gave the wearer a rather dashing appearance, because beards as such were not fashionable among young men, unless they were of bohemian life-style— and consequently were considered rather suspect. Apart from the beard, he was above average height, but inclined to stoop his head, as if he had spent much time ducking under low ceilings, and was a strongly built man, on whom his coat sat uneasily. This was not because it didn't fit, but possibly because it was obviously brand-new. He also had a peculiar manner of walking along, with his eyes fixed on the horizon, and taking not the slightest notice of people who crossed his path. Other pedestrians were forced to leap nimbly out of his way. The pavement might as well have been his private walkway, and his right to precedence on it unquestionable.

It was almost certainly this air of being oblivious to others which had taken Joey's eye. The man's hands were clasped behind his back, so that the skirts of his frock coat were pushed back and gathered together in a bunch, leaving the large coat pockets prominently displayed out of his sight. Joey slid out of his doorway and set off behind him, like a small, elusive shadow. As Rachel watched, horrified, the child quickened his pace and stretched out a hand...

'Dear lord, he is picking pockets!' breathed Rachel. Without a moment's further thought, she darted across the road, beneath the noses of a pair of lumbering brewer's dray horses, and shouted, 'Joseph! Stop that!'

Startled at hearing his name called, Joey spun round. His intended victim was also alerted. He started, as if recalled to his situation, looked round and caught sight of Joey with his hand still reached out. He then moved with a rapidity and determination which neither Joey nor Rachel had anticipated. He lunged forward, grasped the miscreant by his shirt-collar and began to shake him like a mastiff which had caught a rat.

'Why, you little brat! Got you, by Harry! Think to make off with my pocketbook, do you? I'll teach you different!'

'Oh, no, no!' Horrified, Rachel dashed forward, the parcel of cloth falling to the cobbles, and grasped Joey's arm. For a moment she and the bearded stranger wrestled for possession of young Joseph, pulling this way and that, till the luckless prisoner howled for mercy.

'You're pulling me arms out, Miss Grey! Leggo!'
In an attempt to make the gentleman let go, Joey
neatly hacked him in the shins.

'Ow!' yelled the man, his fury increasing. He
hopped back on one foot, released Joey's shirt, and
then lunged forward and fetched the child a resounding box on the ears.

'Don't you dare!' shrieked Rachel furiously,
wrapping both arms round young Joey, pressing him
against her voluminous petticoats and half strangling
him. 'How dare you strike a child? You—you bully!'

'Bully?' roared the man. 'That child, madam, is a
thief, and vicious besides! I intend to turn him over
to the constabulary, and let them take care of him!'

'Oh, no, you can't!' she gasped, appalled. 'They'll
send him to prison. He's only ten years old.'

'Don't they know right from wrong at ten years of
age these days? Why, when I was little older than that
young rascal, only twelve years of age, madam, I was
sent aboard a man-o'-war, and expected to conduct
myself like a British officer!'

That accounted for the beard. He was a naval man,
and they sometimes affected this fashion, as being
safer than trying to achieve a close shave with a cut-
throat razor on the heaving deck of a warship. But
Rachel had more immediate concerns.

'How is a child to know right from wrong if he's
never been taught it?' she retaliated, squeezing harder
on Joey's neck so that he coughed and spluttered.
'This child comes from a family where he has been
set nothing but bad example.'

'I'm surprised,' said the other sarcastically, 'that
you don't just tell him to go and pick pockets as much
as he likes. Misfortunes of upbringing are no excuse

for breaking the law. Thieving is thieving, and of course the child knows it! Is he an idiot?'

'No!' she declared indignantly. 'As it happens, he is a very intelligent child!'

'There you are, then!' he said triumphantly. 'You condemn yourself and him, ma'am, out of your own mouth. And besides, if you didn't want me to catch him at it, why did you call out and attract my attention?'

'I wasn't meaning to attract your attention, only to stop Joey doing wrong. Please allow me to explain!'

They both fell silent and glared at one another over the top of the purple-faced Joseph.

Rachel, taking lack of active protest as permission to go on, plunged into an explanation. 'My name is Rachel Grey and I run the Ragged School, together with my brother Tom who teaches the boys—I teach the girls—and Joey here—oh, I am so sorry, Joey, I've near choked you, are you all right?—well, Joey here is one of our pupils, only he has been playing truant lately——'

A snort of derision greeted this piece of information.

'And we have been so worried, because he is a very intelligent child, as I told you, and I do believe, and so does Tom, my brother, that he can be educated and taught a proper trade. If you don't care to take my word, please come with me and I'll introduce you to my brother and he will tell you the same.'

All this came out much on one breath, so that Miss Grey was almost as purple as Joey by the time she had finished. But a note of pleading touched her voice. The man had right on his side. If he cared to call for a constable, she could hardly prevent him.

He was staring at her flushed, breathless face and her black curls which had escaped from her bonnet brim and hung in fetching confusion about her face. Her paisley shawl trailed on the ground, and her bosom heaved with emotion so that the row of little buttons on the tightly fitting bodice rose and fell in eye-catching agitation. He made what appeared to be some effort to concentrate his mind.

'And your brother permits you, ma'am, to teach these brats?'

'Yes.' She was slightly startled by this approach. 'Should he not?'

'Most certainly he should not. I consider it entirely unsuitable work for a woman—a woman of decent family, that is.'

Her eyes snapped at him warningly. 'Am I to take it, sir, that you do not consider me to be of decent family?'

'Don't talk rubbish. Of course you are. Anyone can see it. That's why it isn't suitable. That child is spawn of the gutter, probably contagious...' He glared at Joey fiercely. 'He doesn't look as if he's had a bath in his life. If we had lads on board like that, we dropped 'em over the side and let the sea wash 'em off before we hauled them back up again.'

'I hope they could swim,' said Rachel stiffly.

'Tied a rope to 'em, if they couldn't. Never had one drown.' He paused thoughtfully. 'We had to tip a few head down to drain out the water, but they coughed it up all right. What that boy needs,' he jabbed a finger aggressively towards Joey, 'is a damn good thrashing!'

'I see,' retorted Rachel coldly. 'And is that what a naval upbringing teaches? Beating children and half drowning them? Not to mention intemperate language in front of ladies?'

He glowered at her alarmingly. 'You have a sanctimonious way with you, Miss Grey, which goes down very badly with me.'

Joey's sharp eyes flickered from one to the other of them during this exchange. Rightly judging that, by now, the two protagonists were more engrossed in their own argument than in him, the boy suddenly slipped out of Rachel's grasp like an eel, and darted away down the road.

'No, you don't, by thunder!' yelled the bearded man.

He raced off in hot pursuit. Rachel picked up her skirts and, heedless of scandalised glances all about her, ran after them as fast as she could.

Joey was an old hand at evading pursuit. He ducked and weaved, dodging around other pedestrians, darting across roads and through narrow, malodorous alleys, leading them deeper into the ill-favoured slums which he knew so well, and where he could hope to lose them. But his pursuer was fitter than most, and not easily thrown off. Joey took to casting anxious glances over his shoulders, failed to observe that his flight had brought him to the very edge of an open sewer running across the entrance to another alley, missed his footing, tripped and fell headlong with a splash into the evil-smelling stream of refuse, where he struggled, choking, and in real danger of drowning in its ten inches of foul water.

When Rachel at last panted up, gasping for breath, and with her hand clasped to a painful stitch in her side, Joey had been hauled out and stood, bedraggled, crestfallen and foul-smelling, under the satisfied eye of his captor.

'Wh—what are you going to do?' gasped Rachel. The breeze brought a whiff of odour from Joey. 'Oh, goodness...' she whispered, and clapped a hand to her nose.

'Follow me,' said the bearded man. 'What did you say this brat is called?'

'Joey...'

'Walk ahead of us, Joseph!' ordered his captor. 'And don't try running off again!'

They set off in a curious little procession, through a maze of alleys. Like Joey, the bearded man seemed to know his way about. 'Plenty of taverns round here,' he confided to Rachel, as if this were an acceptable explanation.

'And you are well acquainted with them all, I suppose?'

'Lord, yes. When I was a midshipman, I had to accompany the shore party, to go and round up missing hands before we sailed. Hauled them out of every low dive in the district. We're near the waterfront here.'

Sure enough, they emerged from a narrow opening and found themselves at the water's edge, near a wooden jetty. The bearded man took off his coat and hat and handed both to Rachel, who took them, somewhat bemused.

'I'd be obliged, ma'am, if you would look the other way. I wouldn't wish to distress you.'

Rachel retreated and sat down on a stone bollard with her back to the sea, and listened to Joey's protesting squawks as he was unceremoniously dunked in the sea off the jetty. After a moment, curiosity overcame her, and she twisted round in time to see the bearded man kneeling on the wooden planks and hauling a waterlogged Joey back to terra firma, where he sat coughing and spitting out sea-water until he was dragged to his feet to hang from his captor's muscular arm like a bundle of wet tow.

'He can't go home soaked through,' she protested as Joey was propelled forward and both reached her. 'The child will take pneumonia!'

'Couldn't go home stinking like a sewer rat, either.' The bearded man released Joey to take his coat from her, and pulled it on, looking about him thoughtfully. 'The Vigo tavern over there is a respectable enough establishment, as respectable goes hereabouts. We can dry out our drowned rat there. Joseph!'

'Yessir . . .' said Joey obediently, and set off behind his mentor, who had begun to stride quickly towards the doorway of a nearby ale-house.

'What about me?' called Rachel after them, glancing about her apprehensively.

'Oh, you had better come too,' he returned carelessly, over his shoulder. 'It don't do for respectable women to stand about in this part of town.'

It didn't do, thought Rachel, for respectable women to accompany unknown men into low taverns, and goodness knew what Tom would make of it if he knew—which, blessedly, he didn't. But, given the choice, she preferred this to being abandoned to fend for herself on the waterfront.

She was relieved to find that the interior of the Vigo tavern was rather cheerful and jolly. A huge fire crackled merrily on the hearth. Two sailors in the round, tar-hardened hats which earned them their Jack Tar nickname sat peaceably quaffing ale in one corner, and a rotund man with a wooden leg sat before the fire, his good leg nearest to it, and the wooden one prudently away from it. The wooden one had a brownish, singed look, which suggested he had not always been so careful and had occasionally dozed by his hearth, while his wooden stump smouldered. On the walls, paper posters advertised for sturdy lads who wished to serve Queen and Country to come forward and sail in Her Majesty's Navy. One poster, even older, yellowing and tattered, promised a share in French prizes, suggesting it had been tacked up there since the Napoleonic Wars.

Seeing Rachel, the bearded man and Joey enter, the one-legged man jumped up and hobbled enthusiastically towards them. 'Why, dang my britches, 'tis Cap'n Harland, come aboard! Look lively, there!' This was bawled over his shoulder towards regions unseen. 'Cap'n's been piped aboard! Stow what you're doing and show a leg!'

Rachel gathered from this nautical welcome that mine host was a retired seaman. She wondered if he had lost his leg in action. He must have noticed her staring at it, because he pegged forward a little further, lowered his voice, and added hoarsely, 'Powder-monkey, I was, aboard the *Temeraire*. Gun recoiled and took off my leg, only eleven year old I were, like this whipper-snapper here...' He indicated Joey. 'Been without it ever since, and never missed it in thirty year as a ship's cook. This 'ere wooden one is better than a real one. Don't get no broken bones, don't get no chilblains and don't need no footwear!' He chortled happily. 'What will it be, Cap'n?'

'To begin with, Abel,' said the bearded man, 'I need to dry out this piece of flotsam here.'

Joey was summarily whisked away and stripped of his clothes which were hung on a wooden clothes-horse before the fire, hissing and steaming. Joey himself was returned, wrapped in a patchwork quilt, and sat down in the hearth, perilously near the flames. Mine host drew out the poker which was wedged in the coals and appeared glowing red-hot, and thrust it into a half-pint pot of porter, sending up a cloud of steam. The porter was then presented to Joey with instructions to get it down.

'I don't think,' said Rachel, who had been watching all these arrangements take place with bewildering rapidity, 'that porter is a drink for a child.'

'Nonsense,' said Captain Harland truculently. 'I drank it, gallons of it; did me no harm. Spirits, now, I wouldn't recommend, but porter never harmed a soul.'

Abel pegged his way forward to confirm this, adding hoarsely that, begging the lady's pardon, he knew it for a fact that porter was in great demand among wet-nurses as it improved the milk and sent the babies to sleep straight off.

Captain Harland interrupted at this point, before Abel warmed too much to his theme, and taking Rachel by the elbow steered her towards a trestle-table in one corner. There, he observed that they were obliged to wait for Joey to dry out, so they might as well take sustenance. He himself wouldn't mind a tot of rum, and he suggested his lady companion take something as well, seeing that she had run so far, and was still out of breath.

'Wants to let her corsets out,' suggested the ever-helpful Abel, who hovered waiting for orders. 'Her's lashed up in there tight as a stowed hammock. Beats me how women splices themselves up in whalebone contraptions. Finest figure of a woman I ever seen was the female who ran a gin-shop in Port o' Spain. Weighed sixteen stone and never wore—' He caught Captain Harland's eye on him, broke off these interesting revelations, and asked, 'Do I splice the mainbrace, then, Cap'n?'

'No, thank you,' said Rachel firmly, interpreting this as an intention to ply both of the visitors with Jamaica rum. 'Not as far as I'm concerned.' She seated herself on the other side of the table. 'Unless Mr Abel has any tea.'

'I doubt it,' said Harland bluntly, and Abel shook his grizzled head and gave his opinion that tea rotted the guts.

'Then I will have nothing at all,' she told him. 'And I feel we shouldn't linger here. It's not a place for a child, especially if he is to be given strong drink and obliged to watch others drinking.'

She became aware that her own appearance was probably much dishevelled, and tried rather ineffectually to tuck her black ringlets back into her bonnet, and straighten up her shawl.

She caught her companion's eye on her, looking at her a little curiously, it seemed, and stared back at him defiantly.

'You mustn't mind Abel,' he said suddenly in his forthright way. 'He's a good fellow, but not accustomed to ladies in his hostelry, so he's inclined to be free-spoken. The women who come in here don't generally mind it. Harland is my name,' he added. 'As you'll have heard. Daniel Harland, lately captain of Her Majesty's frigate, *Amaryllis*.'

'And when do you sail again, Captain Harland?'

He heaved a sigh. 'I don't. Sorry if that disappoints you, Miss Grey. But I've bought out of the Navy, and now I'm ashore for good. That's why you see me dressed like this, and not like a decent human being, in uniform.' He scowled. 'Life ashore don't equal life afloat. I never met so many rogues and scoundrels passing themselves off as honest men. There's no nonsense like that before the mast. If a man can't do his job and prove himself, he's soon found out.'

'Oh, good grief!' exclaimed Rachel in an unlady-like explosion of frustration. 'Do you think that life ashore can be run like a ship of the line? You have a great deal to learn, Captain Harland.'

'So have you, Miss Grey,' he retorted. 'And if you go on teaching those brats, you will probably learn some things which will surprise you. If you don't catch a low fever off 'em first.'

Rachel pressed her lips together. When she felt able to control her voice, she asked, as mildly as she could, 'What do you intend to do about Joey? Will you report the matter?'

'Not if you don't wish it. It's all the same to me.'

Relief flooded her and showed in her eyes, and a wry look entered his. 'I am very grateful to you,' she said earnestly. 'We do try so hard to keep them out of trouble, and help them.' Consternation suddenly crossed her face and he raised his eyebrows, wondering what was coming now. 'I lost my parcel,' she said. 'I'd quite forgot it. I dropped it as I ran to stop Joey picking your pocket, and it will be no use going back for it. Someone will have found it and made off with it. It was flannel, to make petticoats for the girls at the school.'

'Good God,' he said in disbelief. 'Is it a regular thing that you have to clothe them, too? Don't the poor do anything to look after their own children?'

Rachel drew a deep breath and made a superhuman effort for a level tone. 'I can only conclude, sir, that you have spent a great deal of time at sea, and are quite unaware of daily life ashore. Most poor families try very hard to feed and clothe their children. But how they are to do it, when the father may only have casual work, and a new baby arrives every year, defies answer.'

'Fewer babies,' he said sapiently.

'They can't help having babies!' she said energetically.

'The stork doesn't bring 'em, you know,' he said with a return to his sarcastic tone.

Rachel felt her cheeks burn. 'I am aware——' She broke off and pressed her lips tightly together.

'Are you, indeed? Well, that's something. Most young women of your type seem blissfully ignorant of the matter. Anyhow, that's neither here nor there. I don't approve of your activities, ma'am.'

'Oh, don't you?' Rachel pushed out her chin belligerently. Every day of her life she had to listen to Tom's strictures, Tom's ideas on what she should and should not do. She could certainly do without this man's notions on the subject as well. 'And who are you, pray, to give your unasked opinions on how I spend my time?'

'Someone who has, for all you doubt it, a great deal more experience of life, ashore or otherwise, than you do.'

Abel pegged his way towards them. 'Permission to come alongside, Cap'n? Here's that lad, dried out and smoked like a kipper, and his clothes and all.' He produced Joey, dry and dressed, as if by some sleight of hand.

It was with relief that Rachel saw Captain Harland pay for his rum, thank Abel, and lead the way out of the tavern. As they left, Abel sidled up to Harland, and Rachel heard him whisper in his hoarse voice, 'That's a trim craft, Cap'n. If a man was looking to drop anchor, he needn't look further for good harbour.'

Rachel had no idea what was meant by this cryptic observation, but supposed Harland knew what it meant, because she saw his black eyebrows crease in a displeased frown, and he gestured the tavern-keeper away impatiently.

'Now, you may be off!' he said to Joey, outside on the cobbled pavement. 'And if I catch you up to any such devilment again, it will be the worse for you, and running to hide behind the lady's petticoats won't save you!'

'No, sir!' promised Joey, and darted away before anyone could suffer a change of heart.

'Joey!' called Rachel after him. 'You are to be in school tomorrow!'

'School!' muttered Harland, beside her. 'Waste of time. Might just as well try and educate the ship's cat.'

Rachel chose to ignore this. 'I am obliged to you for being reasonable about the boy. I will make sure Joey gets into no further trouble.'

'Don't promise what you can't deliver. The child has gaolbird written all over him. Send him to sea, that will make a man of him.'

'Did it of you?' demanded Rachel, before she could stop herself.

'Yes, Miss Grey, it did. You'll allow me to escort you back to the high street; this is not a district for unescorted ladies.'

She could not deny this and they walked back slowly towards the high street. Though still afternoon, other taverns were already full and doing a roaring trade. Snatches of bawdy songs floated out from open windows, with shrill laughter from women, and fragments of language unintelligible to Rachel. Her companion kept a bland expression through all of this, and, indeed, almost seemed to have forgotten her. She wondered what he was thinking about.

'I have caused you to go out of your way,' she said awkwardly, when they at last reached more respectable streets.

He roused himself from his reverie and murmured, 'No, no, not much, anyway.' Perhaps forgetful that he no longer wore his naval headgear, but a humdrum civilian top hat, he sketched a salute. 'Good day to you, and good luck.'

'Good luck to you, Captain Harland,' said Rachel sweetly, 'since you are about to embark on a new career on land.'

He peered up into the sky. His skin was very weather-beaten, and his eyes, screwed up now to judge the clouds, were surrounded by a myriad of tiny criss-crossing lines. Beard, sideburns and moustache were touched with an early grizzling among the natural dark brown. Exposure to howling gales, extreme climates and indifferent food, together with the general wear and tear of life at sea, might have made him look a good deal older than he was, but she supposed him a little short of forty. Sent to sea as a midshipman of twelve—a practice blessedly less common now than twenty years earlier—he must have been all of eight-and-twenty years a seafarer. How such a man could ever adapt to life on shore, she couldn't imagine.

He dragged his eyes away from the scudding clouds above, gave her a brief nod and set off down the street. Rachel turned and made her way slowly homewards. And the first thing you will find, Captain, she thought to herself, is that not everyone ashore will jump to your orders as did the crew of the good ship *Amaryllis*!

Tom Grey was a solidly built young man. A habitual tenseness in his manner and voice and a lack of humour in his expression often contrived to make him seem more irritable than he was. Tom's anger was often on a very short fuse—but to his credit he was aware of this and tried hard to overcome it. Unfortunately this stifling of an instinctive emotion fed the very fires he tried to extinguish. He was waiting impatiently for his sister now.

'What took you so long?' He glared at her beneath his untidy mop of curly black hair, so like hers, and which in Tom's case drew attention to the fact that, but for his serious manner and sober dress, he would have been a very good-looking young man and turned quite a few female heads. It was as well no one ever told Tom this—it would not have been well-received.

Rachel disposed her shawl neatly on the back of a chair and unpinned her bonnet. 'You won't care for this, Tom, and I beg you won't lose your temper.' He most certainly would. Briefly, she recounted her adventure and the sad lapse of Joseph Casey. She omitted most of her conversation with Captain Harland, only concluding, 'Fortunately, Harland was disposed to make an exception—much against his will. If it ever happens again, whether it's Joey or another child, he'll drag him straight off to the nearest constable.'

She saw the conflict in Tom's face. On the one hand, he was relieved that Joey was not even now locked up in the local gaol. On the other, his own strong principles inclined him to support Harland's ideas of justice. Matters were complicated by a third issue, of equal importance in Tom's eyes.

'But as for his taking you into a low tavern, Rachel, I can't excuse it. He had no business to do such a thing, even though I understand the problem regarding the child's wet clothing. However, I shall write to Harland and express our gratitude for his not laying the matter before the law. It will not be difficult to discover his address.' Tom hissed in annoyance. 'This is just the sort of thing which does the reputation of the Ragged School no good and is a gift to our critics! I only hope Harland won't put the story about. I shall apologise to him with every possible expression of regret for a pupil behaving in such a——'

To Tom's amazement and alarm, his sister, normally so acquiescent to his wishes, spun round in a flurry of petticoats and darted towards him with reddened face and angrily flashing eyes. 'Apologise? You shall do no such thing, Tom! I absolutely forbid it!'

'But surely, Rachel, you agree that Harland has every reason to feel aggrieved?'

'No, I don't agree. The man is an ignorant, self-opinionated fool. A clever fool, which is the worst kind. He went to sea in the reign of George IV and has come back now, twelve years into the reign of the present Queen, and thinks nothing has changed! He is for sending all small boys to sea, as was done to him, so that they can die of bad food and despair. Those few lucky ones who don't and who are probably the brawniest and least sensitive, are then declared to be "men"! He thinks poor people ought to be forbidden to have babies—'

'He said that to you?' exclaimed Tom, startled. He had been showing increasing signs of concern as his sister pursued this vehement speech, and now he jumped to his feet.

'Oh, Captain Harland will make free with his opinions on any subject! Well, if he knows so much, he ought to know better than to wander along the busy street with his hands clasped, taking no care—and I wish I had thought to tell him so at the time. It's . . . it's most vexing!'

'I see . . .' said Tom doubtfully, eyeing his sister, who threw herself down and propped her elbows on the table and her chin in her hands, thinking of all the things she could have said to Captain Harland and hadn't.

Tom sat down again opposite her, disposing the tails of his somewhat threadbare and shiny frock-coat neatly to either side of the chair, and set himself to composing exercises for the next day's school. The solitary candle on the table shone dully and fitfully on his paper as his pen scratched across it.

He could do with an extra candle, thought Rachel, instead of ruining his eyesight. To say nothing of a new nib in his penholder. But pennies counted. The Ragged Schools Union supported more than a hundred schools for the children of the poor, up and down the country. But it was a charitable organisation, largely funded by donation and hardly wealthy. Even adding both their modest salaries together, it was barely enough for them to live respectably.

She and Tom shared a tiny house near Portsmouth's old high street. They lived there frugally, cared for by an aged housekeeper, Hannah, who was really getting quite past it but, like Rachel herself, had nowhere else to go, so lived on with them, burning the dinners and squabbling with the washerwoman who came in on a Monday to tub the linen. Rachel was twenty-five and Tom ten years her senior. Both of them enjoyed good health, and there was no reason to suppose that, barring accident, they would not both reach the Biblical quota of three-score years and ten.

Rachel's expression grew gloomier. The prospect of another fifty or so years spent with Tom was a grim one, love him dearly though she did. The rest of her life spent in that cramped little house? When Hannah died, or became too feeble and confused even to do the little work she now did, the burden of running it would fall entirely on Rachel. Tom, as he grew older, would become increasingly intolerant and fault-finding. He was a good man, serious and dedicated to his work, but so easily provoked that the children he taught were frankly terrified of him, which was a sad irony, for Tom sincerely had nothing but their welfare at heart.

As for herself, what of her future? She saw herself gradually becoming faded and bitter, a figure of fun. It would not be an unusual thing. There were young women like herself all over the country. They came of respectable families and had some education and were to be classed as 'ladies'. Clinging to this precarious gentility, but without sufficient fortune to live as a gentlewoman should, much less hope to marry, they made shift as best they could with such occupations as were considered suitable for women like themselves. These were few enough, but teaching was one which was allowable. She was lucky to have that.

But not according to Captain Harland. As her train of thought brought her round to the day's events again, her mouth set more obstinately, her chin tilted and a frown marred her smooth brow. Wretched man. It was not just the criticism, unfounded though it was. It was the attempt on his part—unwitting, perhaps—to take away from her the one meaningful thing she had in her life. Her work.

'You are pulling faces, Rachel,' said Tom mildly, without looking up.

Tom's ability to see across a room without apparently removing his attention from what he was doing arose from many years teaching small boys. He had, he was wont to tell his pupils, 'Eyes in the back of my head, and don't you forget it!'

'I am tired,' said Rachel with dignity. 'I am going to bed.'

'Good night and God bless,' said Tom, turning the sheet and beginning a new page.

She stopped by his chair and dropped a light kiss on the top of his head. He looked up in surprise and she said, 'You must not sit too late, Tom dear.'

He took out his watch from his waistcoat pocket and set it on the table. 'No need to make a fuss, Rachel. Until half-past. No longer.'

He would sit there until the candle burned out, and she knew it very well. 'You are a better man than he is!' she burst out with sudden energy.

'Why, who?' He blinked up at her perplexed.

'Captain Harland, of course!'

'Oh,' said Tom, 'are you still thinking about him? I shouldn't let it worry you. You are unlikely to see the man ever again.'

CHAPTER TWO

JOEY appeared at school the following morning, which called for some courage on his part. He sidled in with an apologetic glance at Rachel, and a more apprehensive look at Tom.

'Yes, Joseph Casey,' said Tom to him, in tones which boded ill, 'you and I have something to discuss after school.'

Rachel would have liked to intercede on Joey's behalf, but to do so would have been useless. Nobody questioned the principle of corporal punishment for misdoings, and Tom had a muscular right arm. Now Tom was bent on his correction, inspired by duty, and wouldn't be swayed. The despairing appeal which the child mutely addressed to her with his eyes as she quitted the empty schoolroom at the end of the day, leaving him to retribution, lingered, however, all the way home.

But as soon as she arrived there, a new problem put Joey straight out of her mind. A strong smell of burning met her as she opened the front door, and a hallway full of black smoke. Rachel ran into the kitchen and found a pot of potatoes boiled dry, much steam and smoke, and no sign of Hannah. She grabbed the nearest thick cloth, carefully lifted the nearly red-hot pot from the heat and bore it out into the back yard. There it sat, smouldering malignantly, on the yard paving-stones. Dinner tonight, it seemed, would be cold mutton and bread. Tom, already out of sorts, convinced he had done his duty, but miserable because he hated inflicting pain on a child, would be put into an even worse frame of mind by this unsatisfactory fare.

A creak of the back gate caught Rachel's ear, and she looked up in time to see old Hannah come hobbling in, carrying a jug of milk which she had just fetched from the dairy.

'Oh, home already, Miss Rachel?' Her eye fell on the burnt pot and dismay crossed her face. 'Don't you tell me those danged potatoes have gone and burned themselves again? I did only step out for a minute.'

'Yes, burned again,' said Rachel, with slight emphasis on the last word, but it was no use grumbling. Hannah was simply too old and slow. What was needed was a younger and fitter housekeeper—whom they couldn't afford. Even if they could, what would become of Hannah? They certainly could not afford to pay her any kind of pension, and the little money Hannah had earned over long years in their employ would not have allowed the old woman to have any real savings. The alternative, help in the form of another servant, a skivvy of some sort, who could at least watch boiling pots while Hannah was out of the room, or run to the dairy for a pint of milk, would likewise cost money. But quite a young girl could manage it, someone eleven or twelve years of age, and willing to work for a pittance. She would have to talk to Tom about it, but tonight would not be a good time.

Tom seemed to regard the burnt dinner as a further tribulation sent to try him by Providence. 'We must not, however, be ungrateful for what we have,' he pronounced over the few wafers of cold mutton adorning his plate. He set about cutting slices of bread with great enthusiasm, either to prove some point, or work off some frustration.

They were just finishing this unappetising mess when a thunderous knocking sounded at the front door. They stared at one another in surprise. Tom threw down his napkin.

'I'll go. Hannah is, I believe, washing dishes, and it will take her ten minutes to get there!'

Rachel heard him walk down the narrow hallway and open the door. There followed an energetic exchange of voices, one Tom's, the other unknown, rough and aggressive.

Suddenly, there came the sound of a scuffle, and without warning the door to the dining-room burst open, and Tom appeared, struggling to restrain a huge, shambling, unwashed and ill-clad figure. As Rachel jumped to her feet, this unknown thrust Tom aside with a hefty shove, sending the schoolmaster stumbling backwards, and turned a red-eyed glare on Rachel.

'If'n he won't tell me, then mebbe you will!'

'Tell you what? Who are you?' demanded Rachel, wondering whether it would be prudent to arm herself with a table knife, or whether this might just encourage their visitor to further violence and give him ideas.

'Jed Casey is my name!' He glowered at her. 'Got our Joey in that school of your'n. I never had no truck with the idea. 'Twas the missus had the idea to send the kid to learn his letters. Lot of nonsense and a waste of time. I never learned my letters and it never done me no harm!'

Rachel could have argued this point, but it would have been unwise. Tom had meantime regained his balance and his breath.

'Look here, Casey——'

'You look'ee here to *me*!' growled Jed, clenching hamlike fists. 'I send the kid to school, and now I find he done wrong and bin in trouble. What I wants to know is, what sort of trouble? If my kids is doing wrong, I can take a belt to 'em meself and don't need no one else putting an oar in. You just tell me what our Joey done, and I'll wallop the little towrag!'

'Mr Casey,' said Tom with commendable restraint, 'the...ah...matter between Joseph and myself is settled. Joseph is a very good scholar—even if his attendance record could be better, and I wouldn't wish him in trouble with...ah...any further trouble. The boy has been rather foolish and playing truant. But he promises to do better in future.'

'And is that all?' demanded Casey suspiciously.

For Tom to tell a lie was impossible. But his sense of justice was against Joey being punished twice for the same misdemeanour, and besides, punishment inflicted by Jed Casey was likely to go far beyond anything considered civilised even in often harsh times. Torn between a desire to protect the child, and a compulsive honesty, Tom struggled visibly with his conscience, and then temporised heroically. 'More or less.'

'If I do find,' threatened Jed Casey, taking a step forward, 'that there's more to it, and you bin holding out on me, you'll see me again, schoolmeester!'

With that, he turned and crashed his way out of the house.

Tom sank into a chair, drew out his handkerchief and wiped his sweating brow with a shaking hand.

'Oh, Tom,' said Rachel, putting both arms round his neck and hugging him. 'Sometimes you make me so cross, and sometimes I am so proud of you. You were very brave to stand up to that brute and not tell him about Joey picking pockets.'

Tom thrust his handkerchief away and removed his sister's arms firmly from his neck. 'I'm not so sure I'm proud of myself, Rachel. The man is the boy's father and has a right to know. In fact, the correct thing to do would be to inform the parents that the child is in danger of slipping into crime.'

'You couldn't possibly tell that dreadful man! He would half kill poor Joey, as you well know—and that is why you refused.'

Tom, however, was not to be comforted. Now that danger was past, he was prey to his conscience again, and spent the rest of the evening muttering that sparing the rod meant spoiling the child, and, if Joseph Casey went to the bad, he, Tom, would feel he had only himself to blame.

'Which is all nonsense,' said Rachel sternly. 'You are doing your best to help Joey. Letting Jed Casey beat the child black and blue would hardly help, or be better.'

But it wasn't any use talking to Tom, who was taken with what Rachel privately called one of his fits of morality, and determined to wrestle with conflicting duty and instinct, probably spending a sleepless night over it.

The next day was Saturday, and there was no school, but that did not mean Rachel had a free day. Far from it; it was the third Saturday in the month, which meant it was one she particularly dreaded, when she visited

supporters of the school and collected their donations, or promises of donations, and also any items
of clothing to add to her little stock of cast-offs in
the school cupboard.

Rachel set off with a large basket on one arm. The
list—most of the names on it were married ladies of
charitable disposition—was not nearly as long as she
would have liked. There was nothing for it, she'd have
to knock on a few strange doors, explain her purpose
and hope to add another name to her notebook of
benefactors. She hated doing this, not because she
doubted her cause was just—but because there was
no telling what kind of reception she would get. Some
people believed that educating the poor was to encourage a revolution alongside which the French
Revolution would look like a minor upset. Others were
very anxious that only the deserving poor should
benefit from their charity, and not the shiftless, un-
deserving populace. Sometimes she was directed round
to the back door, as if she were some kind of leper.

The afternoon was warm, her clothing hot and
sticky, and she became footsore. The basket, as it filled
with donated clothing, became very heavy, so that her
arms ached. Rachel stood before the gate of a large,
white-painted villa in Southsea, and wondered if it
might house a possible new benefactor. It was large
enough to be a family house, and it was much easier
to describe the needs of poor children to people who
had children of their own. On the other hand, people
with large families to feed and clothe had little spare
income. Elderly, philanthropic widows were usually
well-disposed, or retired clerics. The smell of the sea
was in the air, for they were near the shore here, and
from time to time a seagull wheeled above the roof

in a lazy swoop of great white wings. Rachel pushed open the garden gate and walked up the path.

The seagulls were the only living creatures to be seen. The house might have been deserted, for all the sign of life. She rang the doorbell and waited patiently, wondering if the family might have gone away. But the door was opened almost at once by a woman in a starched apron and a mobcap who looked disapprovingly at the basket and announced, 'Round the back, if you're selling!'

'I'm not,' said Rachel vigorously. 'I'm collecting on behalf of the Ragged School. I haven't called before, and I wonder if I might see the lady of the house.'

'There's no lady in this house,' said the woman curtly, 'nor has there been, this nine year. And we don't give to charity.'

'Who is "we"?' asked Rachel doggedly.

'He don't—the master. There's no point in me telling him you're here.' She relented slightly. 'If you was to come back, in a day or two, I can look out some bits and pieces of dress material, come in handy for making pinafores and the like.'

'That's kind of you,' said Rachel. 'I'll do that, anyway. But I would like to see the master of the house, if he is at home.'

The housekeeper opened her mouth to refuse again, but then a door opened to the left of the hallway, and a man's voice called, 'Show the lady in, Mrs Brereton.'

'Well!' said Mrs Brereton, obviously very surprised and a little put out. 'Well, then, this way, miss.'

Rachel followed her a little cautiously. She was naturally shy at finding herself in a strange house, but she was also experiencing a curious tingle at the nape of her neck, because somehow the voice had not been altogether unknown. Only, she couldn't quite identify it ... She took a quick look around the hall as she crossed it behind Mrs Brereton. It was well-appointed and in a good state of decoration, and there was a large sandalwood chest of oriental design standing in one corner. A blue-glazed pottery mythical animal, something like a cross between a lion and a spaniel, rolled protuberant eyes at her from a table. The owner was comfortably situated and ought to be able to spare a little money for a good cause. She had no time to observe any more, or to draw any further conclusions, before Mrs Brereton had opened the door of a study, and stood aside to allow her to enter.

Rachel was inside, and the door had shut behind her, before she fully realised that Captain Harland stood in the middle of the carpet, ready to welcome her.

'Good afternoon, Miss Grey.'

'Oh,' Rachel mumbled, and wished she hadn't the large, plebian basket on her arm. She would like to set it down, but hesitated to do so here. The floor was highly polished, the carpet oriental, and to put down a wicker basket full of old clothes seemed quite the wrong thing to do.

He saw her predicament and came forward to take the basket from her and set it down. 'That's very heavy,' he said, with a tinge of disapproval. 'Did you carry it far? Sit down, please...'

He waved a hand, indicating she might sit wherever she fancied, and Rachel sat down on the nearest chair, stiff as a ramrod, with her hands folded in her lap.

'To what do I owe the pleasure of this visit?' He leaned against the empty fireplace and twitched an eyebrow at her. It occurred to her that he looked younger today, in the casual surroundings of his own home, relaxing in shirt-sleeves and waistcoat. There was the scent of good cigar-smoke in the air, the whole room had the aspect of a gentleman's private retreat, and she could not avoid the feeling that she ought not to be here. At the very best, he obviously had not been expecting visitors, and was not prepared to receive any. Perhaps few called here, in any case. After such a long time at sea, his shore acquaintance must be limited. Now she could see that his hair, though scattered through with traces of grey, was still thick and predominantly dark brown, almost black, with a tendency to curl. She deducted a few years from the original forty she had given him, and now judged him to be still in his thirties. She could not, she reflected ruefully, have chosen a less promising door at which to beg charity for the school. He had already expressed his opinion of their efforts, and was not likely to open his pocketbook on its behalf. Rachel debated whether to apologise and withdraw with as much dignity as she could summon in the circumstances, or whether to press on and ask anyway.

Some of her indecision must have shown in her face, because he said gruffly, 'You must excuse my appearing before you without a coat. It's upstairs. There seems little point in sending poor Mrs Brereton climbing up there for it. I can deal with whatever brings you as well in shirt-sleeves as in my jacket. Well, now, I don't suppose this is a social call. I trust I'm not about to be told that the wretched Joseph has resumed his criminal activities?'

Nervously Rachel admitted, 'I didn't come specifically to call on you. That is, I didn't know you lived here.' She hoped her voice did not betray the unspoken qualification—And if I had known, I shouldn't have come! Hastily she continued, 'I'm collecting for the school. We're sadly in need of funds.'

'I see,' he said discouragingly. 'So, not only am I to turn a blind eye to the attempts of that young ragamuffin to steal my pocketbook, I'm to pay for his education as well?'

'If you pay for his education,' said Rachel, gathering courage. 'He will be less likely to grow up a thief.'

'There are plenty of educated thieves in the world,' he said drily. 'And not all of them pick pockets. What's to say he won't one day embezzle his employer's cash? I put it to you, ma'am, that you are simply giving a born criminal the added ability to juggle the entries in an accounts book.'

'No one is born a criminal!' Rachel almost shouted. Her face flushed scarlet and she felt her cheeks burning with embarrassment. More quietly but just as doggedly she added, 'I'm sorry, but I don't believe what you say is true. I know that Joseph isn't our best-behaved pupil. But I do believe he can be helped. Anyway, the others are better.'

'I'm encouraged to hear it. What's that?' He pointed at the basket on the floor.

'It's the used clothing. I'm collecting that, too. I know it's warm now, but when winter comes many of our children will suffer dreadfully from the cold—'

'Oh, yes, the petticoats,' he muttered. 'Miss Grey, does it not occur to you that if you give these children decent clothing, the parents will very likely sell it in some street market for the money to buy gin?'

'If I listened to you,' said Rachel, losing all patience, 'I'd never try to do anything! I'd just give up! Well, I don't give up, Captain Harland. And I do know more about the poor than you do! Not all goes for gin. Why, one of my girls, Sally Casey, came to school barefoot the other day because the boots I had given her had been passed in turn to her elder sister, Jenny. Jenny needed them because she had got work down at the docks, what is called "humping coal". Have you seen the women labourers, Captain? Perhaps you don't recognise them as women. They are mostly dressed as men and their faces are quite blackened with grime and sweat. Their language is frankly foul. Jenny is fifteen years old.'

'I've seen them!' he said briefly.

'But I don't hear you say that it is not suitable work for women!' Rachel declared triumphantly.

'I dare say it isn't, but it is the difference between working and starving. I doubt you would starve, Miss Grey, if you gave up your schoolteaching. Besides, they are a different sort of woman.'

'Not ladies, you mean?' asked his visitor sweetly.

A warning gleam in his eyes told her she jousted with him at her peril. 'Yes, that's what I do mean, Miss Grey.' He moved towards the bell-pull and stretched out his hand. 'Will you take tea?'

Rachel was momentarily thrown off course, but shook her head and, although she thanked him kindly, explained that she had quite a few calls to make yet and must refuse.

'You are not thirsty on such a warm day?'

'I was—but I stopped by the drinking fountain at the end of the street.'

He drew a deep breath and clapped the clenched fist of one hand against the palm of the other. 'This is getting ridiculous! This is a very hot day and you have been reduced to drinking from a public fountain—which I don't consider——'

He broke off and seemed to search for some alternative to the word he had been about to use.

'Suitable?' suggested his visitor innocently.

'Yes, damn it, suitable!' he roared suddenly. 'That basket weighs several pounds. I wonder you can pick it up. You are clearly tired, and you've done more than enough. I'll send out for a cab to take you home.'

'I can walk!' she said sharply.

Harland threw himself down in a chair opposite her, and rubbed a hand across his chin. 'Mmm,' he said discouragingly. 'This brother of yours, does he realise that you tramp about the streets with a basket, like a pedlarwoman, begging pennies and rags?'

It was not the nicest way to describe what she did, but it was apt, as she had to admit. Loyally, she plunged into a defence of Tom's actions.

'Tom is devoted to the school. He works very hard. He really cares about the children, and there is so much he could do, if only we had a little more money. Our books are old and falling to pieces, and I spend hours gluing pages back in. We hoard up broken pieces of chalk because we don't want to open a new box, and when it gets cold, the poor children can hardly hold the little bits of broken chalk they are given, because we cannot afford to light the stove.'

'I don't know what kind of impression you think you are making,' her listener said unsympathetically. 'But every word you say convinces me even more that it's not suitable work for you. This paragon of a brother—how did he take the news of one of his pupils playing truant to practise being a "dip"? You did tell him, I suppose?'

Rachel started to give him a brief résumé of Tom's reaction, but then it occurred to her that, if he knew how well Tom had stood up to Jed Casey, the low opinion he seemed to entertain of Tom might be improved. She told him the whole tale with relish, and he listened in silence until she finished, and sat looking at him expectantly.

'What do you expect me to say?' he asked quietly.

'Why,' annoyance entered her voice, 'that Tom behaved very well. You see, Tom is devoted to the children. Only his manner is a little stiff, and he worries so about doing the right thing—and he loses his temper easily, and is inclined to moralise away at the class, which bores them. Children dislike long homilies, you know.' She broke off in horror, and realised that all this was not what she meant to say at all, and was giving a very unfavourable picture of poor Tom altogether. 'He is really very kind-hearted. But he takes everything so seriously. I try to wheedle him out of it, but one can't be affectionate with Tom, he bristles like a hedgehog. I wish I knew why.'

Harland opened his mouth as if he would answer, thought better of it, and turned his gaze away from her towards the window. He thought he understood very well what was the matter with Tom Grey. The fellow had imposed upon himself from his earliest days a monastic austerity and discipline which was at variance with every natural instinct in his body. He set himself impossible standards, and blamed himself for failing to achieve them. A healthy young man with normal, if suppressed, appetites, Tom not only had never sown the wild oats most young men did, but he had taught himself to regard all manner of pleasure as degenerate and unworthy. What Tom Grey needed was a woman in his bed, but it was extremely unlikely that there had ever been one—or ever would be. It might not worry some men, but it most surely worried Grey, though he would never admit it, least of all to himself. Harland had seen sexual frustrations build up in men after long weeks at sea away from female companionship. Tom Grey lived in a world surrounded by women of one sort or another, and had probably never kissed a girl in his life.

There was no way, thought Captain Harland, that he could explain this to the fellow's sister. She had indignantly denied believing storks brought babies, but it was doubtful she had any real idea exactly how the human species reproduced itself, even less the urge for physical fulfilment in most men. Tactfully, he murmured, 'Perhaps, your brother ought to marry.'

'Oh, yes!' she said enthusiastically, surprising him considerably. She leaned forward, her face quite shining. 'That is just what I've always thought. A wife would cheer Tom up no end.'

'Yes,' he said woodenly.

'It is because of me, you know,' she went on. 'Our parents died within six weeks of one another of the cholera. I was only thirteen, and Tom twenty-three. He had come down from Oxford and was thinking of entering the Church. Only then he found that he had to look after me, and there was little money, and no question of his continuing his studies. So he took to schoolmastering. He undertook to educate me as well, of course—so it was natural that I took to teaching school, as well. But if Tom had not had so many worries and responsibilities, he might have spent more time making friends.'

It annoyed him to hear her take the blame for Tom's misfortunes. He asked, rather crossly, 'What about you? Don't you fancy marrying and having a home of your own? Or do you intend to teach those brats for the rest of your life?'

She coloured. 'It is very worthwhile work!'

'So it might be. There are others who can do it, other women, not so young and not so pretty.'

She jumped up as if she were impelled by a spring. 'I think that it's high time I left, Captain Harland.'

'Oh, don't take fright,' he said. 'I'm a plain man, a simple sailor, and accustomed to speak my mind. Here, you shall have something for your wretched school—on the condition that you allow me to send someone out for a cab to take you home immediately.'

It was late, and she was footsore and weary. Rachel battled briefly with her inclinations, and surrendered. 'Very well, thank you.'

He rang the bell for the servant and sent out for the cab straight away. Perhaps he thought she might change her mind. She was rather afraid he might change his about giving some donation to the school, but he went to a desk and returned with a sealed packet which he handed to her. 'Take this, and don't open it until you are home.'

'Thank you,' she said awkwardly, and gave him a shy smile.

He stared at her for a moment, then picked up the basket and carried it out into the hall. Rachel followed him and, not knowing quite what to say, glanced round and observed, 'You have brought these things from your travels?'

'What?' He frowned. 'Oh, the box, and the lion-dog.'

Rachel laughed. 'What is a lion-dog?'

'That's what the Chinese call them. Funny little dogs with long hair, yapping all the time. The Chinese believe them very brave, and put statues of them before their temples.'

'I should like to travel,' said Rachel wistfully. 'We have a globe in the school, and sometimes I sit and spin it, close my eyes, and stop it, saying, "That's where I'll go!"' She caught the expression on his face, blushed and added hurriedly, 'Take no notice, it's only my nonsense!'

He said nothing, and as they stood there, staring at one another, there came the sound of a door closing upstairs, and a faint sound of a treble voice.

Rachel looked at him startled. 'Why, there is a child in the house!'

'You imagine it!' he said brusquely. He pulled open the front door.

So plainly was this an invitation for her to leave the house that Rachel could do nothing but step outside. She stood uncertainly on the doorstep, until trotting hoofs and the rumble of wheels announced the arrival of the cab.

Harland handed her in, and reached up the basket. 'Goodbye, Miss Grey.'

'Goodbye,' she said uncertainly.

The cab rolled away. Rachel tried to look up at the front of the house before it was out of sight, but its upper windows reflected the late afternoon sun, and were so many oblongs of shining light, betraying nothing behind them.

*   *   *

'I heard a child, Tom,' Rachel said obstinately. 'I'm quite sure about it.'

The last of the mutton had arrived, served up as rissoles. Even Tom was hard put to express their good fortune in this meal. He pushed a lump of gristle aside, after seriously contemplating whether he ought to eat it on principle.

'I dare say you were mistaken, Rachel. Or even if you did hear a child, you say he has a housekeeper. Possibly she is a widow with a child.'

'Then why didn't he say so? Why deny it? I heard that child, *he* heard the child, and he knew I had heard it, too. I am not deaf, Tom, and not stupid. I don't fancy things. He positively hustled me out of the front door, yet only a little earlier he was offering me tea. Once I heard that voice, his manner changed completely. There was a child in that house and he didn't wish me to know it.'

'Hmm.' Tom set down his knife and fork with a sigh of relief. Hannah hobbled in with a shapeless, colourless lump on a plate, which turned out to be a boiled pudding. They vied with one another to see how little they could take, Tom virtuously declaiming that gluttony was bad for health and soul, Rachel observing more practically, 'What an awful pudding. Hannah has used too much flour, and she must have let the pot boil dry again. My portion is dried out and leathery.'

'Mine's—all right, most of it,' said Tom determinedly.

'You know, Tom,' Rachel put down her spoon, 'we must get Hannah some help. It's too much for her, caring for the two of us.'

'It would cost too much, Rachel.'

'It would more than pay for itself, if it led to less waste of good food, through burnt potatoes and meat, and soup boiled away.'

Tom considered this thrifty view of it, and then grunted, which generally meant that he was thinking it over, and would give his opinion, when—and not before—he had formed one.

Rachel let the matter rest there for the time being. 'Oh, Tom, I quite forgot!' she exclaimed. 'He gave me a donation for the school. I'll fetch it!' She jumped up from the table and returned holding out the small packet.

'You have not opened it,' observed Tom.

'Well, no...' Rachel stared down at it doubtfully. 'Perhaps you had better do so.'

Tom pursed his lips and said a little brusquely, 'No, he gave it to you. Open it up, Rachel. I hope he's seen fit to be generous.'

Rachel sat down and opened up the packet with nervous fingers. She peered inside, and then turned a white face towards Tom. 'Oh, Tom...it is a great deal of money! I had no idea... I shouldn't have accepted.'

Tom's self-restraint gave way at last. He removed the packet neatly from her fingers and shook the contents out on to the tablecloth. 'Fifty pounds!' he said. 'You pleaded our cause very well, Rachel.' His eyes rested on her with an expression in them she had not seen before.

'But—I didn't... I only told him the school needed money. Perhaps it's because of Joey Casey?' She seized at this possible explanation. Then she shook her head. 'No, I don't think he feels very kindly towards Joey.'

'Possibly,' Tom said in a voice which seemed almost jagged with suppressed emotion, 'he feels kindly towards you.'

'What nonsense!' she exclaimed angrily. 'And I wouldn't have expected such an idea to come from you, Tom.'

Tom chose not to answer this straight away. He got up and locked the money away in the metal strong-box which housed donations for the school. Then he turned towards her, tucking the key into his waistcoat pocket. 'I think you should not call at that house again, Rachel.'

Tom had made a tactical error, but hadn't the intelligence to see it. The last thing Rachel would ever have wanted to do, or intended to do, was call again at the Harland house. But having Tom forbid her to do so, obviously because he considered that in some way she had taken Captain Harland's fancy, caused a tide of scarlet to spread up her throat and into her cheeks.

'May I ask why not, Tom?'

Tom's face set obstinately. 'Because I say so. I don't consider it proper. The man appears to have no wife. It could be misconstrued.'

'Mis— By whom?' she gasped.

'By anyone who learned of it. I don't intend to argue the matter out, Rachel. That is my decision. You are not to call at the house again, nor communicate with Captain Harland. I will write and thank him for his generous support.'

Rachel rose trembling to her feet. 'I have always deferred to your judgement, Tom. Many a time, I've had a contrary opinion and I've kept it to myself in the cause of peace. I see now I was wrong to do so.

I've encouraged you to consider yourself entitled to say whatever you like, even if it is to insult me. What are you suggesting? That I made eyes at Captain Harland, like a love-struck maidservant?'

Tom's face grew puce with fury. 'I will not have you talk in that way, and I will not have my wishes ignored! I am the head of this house, and of this family. I'm your elder brother, and you'll do as I say—both in this, and in any other matter!'

'You mistake me for one of your pupils!' she threw back at him. 'I am twenty-five years old and of age! I earn my keep and am no burden on your purse. I think I'm old enough to decide for myself what's right for me to do!'

'It's very late,' her brother said harshly. 'I shall see you in the morning, Rachel, when, I trust, you will have had time to reconsider your rash words, and see fit to apologise!'

He stormed out of the room, slamming the door, leaving his sister prey to conflicting feelings. Fury abounded, but also a genuine unhappiness that she and Tom should have quarrelled. Rachel's eyes fell on the empty packet which had contained Daniel Harland's fifty pounds, and it seemed to her as if that, and its donor, must be the cause of all this upset. She was filled by an illogical but deeply felt resentment directed towards Harland and, try as she might, she could not overcome it. She went to bed, but slept very badly.

Rachel could not know it, as she tossed and turned on her crumpled pillows, but in the villa at Southsea Dan Harland was also awake.

He had not, in fact, gone to bed at all, but turned up and down the study floor, scowling to himself. After a while he paused to light a Havana cigar. He was not a great smoker, but he felt restless and wanted something to occupy himself. If he didn't smoke, then he might be tempted to take a drink. One drink often led to another. The aroma of the cigar entered his nostrils. Tradition had it that these cigars were rolled in the making on the thighs of voluptuous Cuban maidens. The only female cigarette workers Dan had ever seen had been built like stevedores and had either brown teeth from smoking their wares, or no teeth from chewing on the raw sugar cane, and hands and forearms stained yellow from their work. Legend was understandably more fanciful.

The notion, however, brought his thoughts to women in general and Rachel in particular. She had spoken to him of her brother a great deal more freely than she had intended. To him, that suggested that she had no one else to talk to, to whom she could confide her problems. He permitted himself a bitter smile. He could understand Tom Grey, without ever having set eyes on the man. But he himself was in danger of going much the same way.

His wife had been dead these nine years. Dan never thought of her without sadness, mixed with rage. Originally, there had been only rage. He had been the most unforgiving of men. Now, older and wiser, he had more understanding for the loneliness she must have experienced, young, beautiful and lively, left behind when he went on long sea voyages. Naturally enough, when temptation had come her way, she had succumbed to it. It had been a silly little piece of nonsense, and she had confessed it to him, like a guilty child. To this day he did not know whether she had expected him to forgive her. Perhaps she feared that he would find out anyway, and wanted to put her version of the story first.

Whatever the truth of it, he had not forgiven. He had driven her away and she had gone, her reputation in ruins, rejected by her friends, unwanted by her lover. She had died quite soon after, in a filthy lodging house, and alone. He had paid for the funeral, but had not attended. Her grave, in the little country churchyard high on the chalk hills behind Portsmouth, grew steadily more overgrown with the years. Occasionally the churchwarden wrote and asked him to do something about maintaining it. Generally, he didn't answer. He had destroyed her portrait, and every sign of her about the house.

Every sign but one. She had left him one thing which could not be destroyed. Dan ground out the cigar. He picked up a candlestick and left the room, climbing the staircase, the shadows leaping about wildly as the candle flame guttered in the draught. He moved quietly along the corridor, and gently turned the knob of the door at the far end.

Moonlight fell into the room, and across the bed. Harland stood, looking down at it for a while. As he turned away, a floorboard creaked beneath his foot. There was a movement from the bed, and a child's voice asked fearfully, 'Papa?'

'Yes, yes.' Dan turned back. 'It's only I. You aren't afraid, not dreaming again?'

'No...' The voice sounded uncertain.

Dan went back to the bedside, set down the candle and sat down on the edge of the bed. 'Houses creak at night; it doesn't mean monsters.'

'I see them,' the child said simply.

'The old wooden ships, when I first went to sea as a little boy, they creaked and groaned enough to keep you awake and stop you sleeping at all,' he told him. 'Not like the new metal hulls they are starting to build nowadays. Steam clanks and chugs, but in the old days, when the wind howled in the rigging, it sounded like a sea-monster, though it was only the storm. Sometimes it sighed and sounded like singing, and the sailors told all manner of tales about mermaids and such. But there is always a practical explanation for these things, and nothing to fear.'

The child propped his chin on thin arms. 'I should have liked very much to go to sea and have adventures, as you did, Papa.'

Dan shook his head. 'No, Pip, no, you would not.'

'I could do it, if I were strong enough,' Pip said wistfully.

'Not even if you were strong enough.'

'Did you sleep in a hammock?' asked Pip. He had asked the question a hundred times. He wanted to keep his father there, sitting on the bed. He was afraid of the dark, afraid of being alone.

'Sometimes, not always. Sometimes a berth.'

But the child was determined to follow a set pattern of questions and responses, already rehearsed a dozen times. 'Tell me how the sailors sewed themselves in the hammocks to keep away the rats.'

'I've told you before, Pip. And it makes you dream about the rats, and there are none in this house. Mrs Brereton sets traps, and we hardly ever catch a mouse.'

'Tell me again,' wheedled Pip. 'I shan't dream, truly.'

Harland sighed. 'Well, on a ship you have rats without number. They live down in the hold, and at nights come out and go scampering about the living areas looking for scraps of food. So what the sailor does is, he takes a sailmaker's bodkin and thread, and a small, sharp knife into the hammock. Then, beginning at his feet, he sews the two sides of the hammock together, so that it is like a peapod, with the Jack Tar safe inside. When he gets to the top he leaves the tiniest opening for air, and sews on right up. Then the rats can come and jump all over him, but can't reach him. In the morning, when the cry goes up, "Show a leg!" why, the sailor takes his knife and cuts open the stitches and out he jumps.'

'Why does the man call "Show a leg!"?' demanded Pip. 'Why doesn't he say, it's time to get up?'

Dan scratched at his beard. 'Because—because in Lord Nelson's day, sailors sometimes smuggled their women aboard.'

'Why?'

'Oh,' said his father vaguely, 'to do their mending and such, you know. So the bos'un would go down to the crew's quarters and cry out, "Show a leg!" and he knew, by the leg, if it was a man or a woman.'

'Why, are women's legs different to men's legs?' Pip looked puzzled.

'They aren't different, just a bit thinner and—well, it's like the difference between a table-leg and a chair-leg. A chair-leg is altogether more elegant.'

Lord knew, thought Dan to himself, what idea of women the child was getting from all of this. Chair-legs, indeed . . .

He leaned forward and pulled the covers up round the child's thin body. 'Now you must go to sleep. I can't sit here all night, chatting about such nonsense.'

The child lay back on the pillow. 'Will you leave the candle, Papa?'

Dan put the candle down carefully where it could not fall, or touch against anything. He put out his hand and briefly stroked the child's fair hair. It was like fine silk. 'Now you will go to sleep, eh?'

'Who was the lady?' asked Pip unexpectedly.

Dan was startled enough to exclaim roughly, 'What, spying on me now?'

'I didn't spy. I only looked down through the banister, and then Mrs Brereton called me away. She was a very pretty lady.'

'Yes, a very pretty lady,' Harland said gruffly. 'Forget about her, Pip.'

CHAPTER THREE

When school reassembled on Monday morning
Rachel was feeling listless and irritable, and it was
difficult to concentrate. Tom was likewise in a bad
mood, probably because she had not apologised. The
ill humour of each of them was fed by that of the
other. Tom looked severe, Rachel grew obstinate, Tom
became truculent, Rachel mutinous . . . and so it went
on. Tom had not actually mentioned an apology
again. But only because he was hardly talking at all.
He probably regretted some of what he had said, but
it was not his way to admit himself at fault. They
spoke to one another in monosyllables over the
breakfast-table and were icily polite over such matters
as passing the milk jug and pouring tea.

The school's appearance and atmosphere were not
likely to cheer anyone up. The one room which housed
it was dark and unpainted. There was a damp mark
on the walls. Fortunately, thought Rachel with a sigh
as she opened her register for the day, the weather
remained warm. When winter came it was icily cold
in here, but they could not afford to light the pot-
bellied iron stove in the corner until Jack Frost
whitened the ground and children and teachers had
fingers too blue to turn the pages of their tattered exercise books. But even now enough dampness lingered
in the store cupboard to have got into a box of chalks
and ruin the entire two dozen it held. What was more,

two writing slates were discovered to be broken and, to top it all, Sally Casey did not appear for roll-call.

'First one Casey, then another. That family is stony ground!' said Tom fiercely, hurling fragments of slate into the waste-paper basket, and breaking into his longest speech since their dispute.

'Sally loves to come to school,' said Rachel, worried. 'I do hope she isn't ill.'

Tom grunted and stalked over to his side of the room, where he taught the assembled boys. One look at the schoolmaster's face told them that today Mr Grey was not to be trifled with. They fell into an apprehensive silence.

'Right!' said Tom grimly, seizing a piece of chalk and advancing on the blackboard. 'The main trading ports of Britain...'

The main trading ports of Britain. How dull and tedious it sounded, thought Rachel. Why not talk about the exciting harbours of the world? What about Macao and Shanghai, Naples and Genoa? What about all the places Captain Harland had sailed to and knew?

They struggled on somehow, however, until shortly before lunch, when a thunderous knock at the door caused all work to cease and everyone to jump and look round. In tense silence they watched it creak open and reveal a burly figure in knee-breeches, cape and three-cornered hat. At the sight of him the children froze into immobility, fixing him with awestruck and apprehensive eyes. They all knew the beadle, and knew, too, that his appearance boded ill for someone.

'Morning, sir and ma'am,' said the newcomer. 'I begs your pardon for intruding.' He sniffed, drew a large, non-too-clean handkerchief from a side-pocket and blew his nose noisily. Rachel thought that, if he looked rather red about the nose, it wasn't because of cold. His eyes were bloodshot, the lower lids sagged like an aged spaniel's and his cheeks were mottled with purplish veins. Snuff spotted the front of his uniform.

'I come,' he said, returning the handkerchief to his pocket, and casting a prejudiced eye towards the assembled children, 'on an errand, sent by Mr Grantham, the magistrate. 'Ee's got one of your kids down at the court. Brought up this morning on a charge of vagrancy.'

'One of ours?' Rachel gasped. 'Not Sally—Sally Casey!'

'Sarah Casey,' confirmed the beadle. 'Nine-year-old. Done for vagrancy at midnight last night. Wandering in the streets without means of support and in a suspicious manner. Mr Grantham, when he heard that the kid was a pupil of the Ragged School, said someone should be sent for, and speak for the kid, or against her, as it turns out. Character witness, like.'

Rachel whirled round and seized her shawl and bonnet. 'I'll go, Tom. You must manage the whole class somehow.' Tom opened his mouth to protest, but she gave him no time. 'It's best I go, Sally trusts me. Lead on, Beadle, please.'

As they hurried through the streets, Rachel tried to find out more from the officer of the court, but he either had little more information to give, or declined to give it. His own view of the matter was summed up with, 'Them kids is nothing but trouble. Little sluts them girls, most of 'em, young as they is. You wouldn't credit it, ma'am, but I seen it all. Ought to be sent to the treadmill, the lot of them.'

The magistrates' court was a gloomy place at the best of times, and it was not the first time Rachel had seen it. The background of many of their children was such that from time to time a child would find its way before the magistrates, usually on a charge of theft or damage. The items stolen were generally food of some kind, or washing from clothes-lines. The value never amounted to much, but the law was unrelenting and the age of the offender no protection. Rachel's heart sank at the thought of Sally in this miserable place.

In the entrance, a young woman slouched on a wooden bench. Her hair was lank and uncombed, and her features, which might once have been pretty, drink-sodden and ruined. She wore a cheap, garish gown, a dirty woollen tartan shawl, and a crushed bonnet, bedecked with a battered bunch of cherries. As they came in, she hurriedly thrust away a gin bottle into a pocket.

'Mrs Casey!' exclaimed Rachel, recognising this slattern as Sally's mother. 'I've come to see if I can help Sally.'

'Little brat,' said Mrs Casey in slurred tones. 'I done me best, and my man in gaol—how's a woman ter manage? Little brat . . .' Her voice ranged between aggressive and sullen, and she stared defiantly up at them. 'I ain't taking the blame. Ain't nothing to do with me. I didn't know the kid was out. I thought she was asleep with the others. What am I supposed to do? Count 'em? And you needn't give me that high and mighty look, neither, Miss Schoolmarm. You wants to have a few kids of your own, and then you'd know something about it!'

'This way, ma'am,' said the beadle, taking Rachel's arm and tugging her towards a further door. 'You don't want to stand here talking with that doxy.'

''Oo are you calling names?' demanded Mrs Casey, lurching to her feet and swaying unsteadily. 'I'm a decent woman. If my man ain't no good, it's no fault of mine. Breaking rocks, he is . . . and getting fed by the government for doing it. Who feeds me and my kids? I got eight of them living, and they're always hungry. I sold me wedding ring, only bit of jewellery I had!'

'Aye,' observed the beadle heavily, 'and bought gin with it.'

'Pot calling the kettle black!' retorted Mrs Casey snappishly, arms akimbo. 'You ain't got a crooked elbow yourself, by any chance, I suppose?'

'Sit down and keep quiet, or you'll be run in yourself for disturbing the peace!' he growled. 'You come with me, ma'am. Mr Grantham is waiting.'

Rachel had met the magistrate before. Grantham was a capable and intelligent man, a widower of five and forty who had been left with a young family on his hands. Fortunately, an unmarried sister had been available to run his house and raise his children, so Mr Grantham had not troubled to remarry and lived comfortably on a private income, devoting himself to public works of one kind and another. He was a sincere and honest fellow, large and bluff in appearance, who always tried to do his best for the younger offenders who appeared before the bench, and he was much respected in the community. Rachel was at least heartened to think Sally's fate lay in this man's hands, and not in those of some more elderly, crusty or incompetent member of the bench.

Grantham came forward to meet her now, enveloping her hand in his broad palm, and shaking his head ruefully. 'Do sit down, Miss Grey, and thank you for coming. Now, here's a sorry business. I thought you would want to know of it. The little girl is only nine years of age, and makes a good impression. But she has been taken up for vagrancy before, you know, and the law is very strict.'

'But I can't understand what she was doing out on the streets so late!' Rachel exclaimed, taking the chair he offered her and looking up at him worriedly.

He stooped over her confidentially. He was in some ways rather like a large bear, deliberate of movement and as solid as a rock. The children who came before him were often overawed by him, but never in fear of him, and the parents respected him. It said much for Mr Grantham's integrity that he enjoyed this reputation. The magistrature, as a body, did not stand high in most people's estimation.

'The way these people live leaves much to be desired, Miss Grey. Now in this case, it seems that the father is serving a prison sentence and the uncle, one Jed Casey, is keeping an eye on his brother's family during his absence. In keeping an eye, I fear he's quite exceeded what you or I would think his duty. In short, he has quite ignored the biblical strictures against lusting after his brother's wife.' Grantham twitched a bushy eyebrow at her. 'It seems he divides his time and his—ah, attentions, between his own wife and his brother's. Last night, he appeared drunk at his sister-in-law's lodgings, bringing with him gin or other spirits. Both he and the woman sat late drinking. Both were no doubt quite drunk and unable to know what they were about. At least, that is the kindest interpretation I can put on it. The children were in the room—the family lives in one room—and somehow the little girl fell foul of him. He struck her several times until she managed to escape his grip. She then ran out and was afraid to go back for fear of further beating. She remained roaming the streets until well after midnight, when a constable on patrol came across her in a doorway. I am loath to send the child to a house of correction where she will be in the company of many who are quite hardened in crime. To return her home will also be quite useless. She will simply reappear here. The workhouse cannot take her... since in theory she is supported by her mother. So what's to be done?'

Rachel thought feverishly, and then had a brainwave. 'Supposing, Mr Grantham, my brother and I were to offer a home to Sally and give assurances regarding her good behaviour? As it happens, we've been thinking of engaging a girl to help our housekeeper. We could lodge, feed and clothe Sally, see that she continues to get some education, and pay a little, say, a shilling a week in wages. How would that do?'

He considered. 'As far as I am concerned, Miss Grey, it'll do very well. But we shall need the mother's consent. Beadle!' He raised his voice and the red-nosed beadle reappeared so quickly, it was obvious he had been listening outside the door.

Mrs Casey was called in and the arrangement explained to her. She immediately lay claim to her daughter's wage of a shilling a week. 'Either it's paid to me, or she don't go. Kid don't need no money. I do.'

Rachel was obliged to agree to this, though it went against the grain. A tear-stained, frightened Sally was brought from the local cells where she had been locked up in the company of two prostitutes, a drunken fish-seller and a lunatic tinkerwoman, and released into Rachel's custody. At first she did not understand that she was to go home with Miss Grey, but when it was explained at last the child's joy was overwhelming. She certainly showed no wish to go home with her mother. Mrs Casey's farewell of her daughter consisted of grabbing a hank of Sally's hair, tugging it fiercely and snarling, 'Mind yer manners—and the shilling is mine, don't you ferget!'

Later that same evening, as Sally settled into her new home, she became the subject of some conversation elsewhere in the city.

'An excellent dinner, Dan,' said Mr Grantham appreciatively.

Captain Harland offered his guest a cigar. 'Glad to see you. I don't have much company and get heartily sick of my own.'

Mr Grantham watched him sit down and lean back in his chair. He had sympathy with Harland's situation, being himself a widower. Harland, however, had not the good fortune to have an unnattached female relative on whom to call in his hour of need. It must be extremely difficult for him, with a sickly child on his hands, and little or no companionship. Grantham drew on his cigar and cleared his throat. 'Yes, I dare say you find it a little lonely. But now you're ashore for good, old chap, you'll be wanting to make some alterations in your household, I expect, to take care of that.'

His host stirred. 'In what way?'

'Well.' His old friend hesitated. 'The child, for example. Fine little fellow, but there's his education...'

'Pip can't be sent away to school!' Harland said fiercely. 'His health won't permit it. You know he cannot walk very far. He spends more time than ever in that damned chair, and it's one reason why I bought out. Every time I came home, the child had faded more. Every time I went away, I feared——'

He broke off, leaving unspoken his fear, because Grantham already knew it. It was enough to have buried the mother, without having to bury the child, also.

'Quite, quite,' Grantham murmured consolingly. 'But I wasn't thinking of school. I agree, wouldn't do at all. A private tutor, however...'

'No!' came the vehement reply. 'I never met a tutor who wasn't a bully and a drunkard—if not worse.'

'Now, look here,' protested the other. 'You can't let the child grow up as ignorant as a little savage!'

'He can read, and write, and reckon up his numbers. He doesn't need anything more.'

'Rubbish,' said Mr Grantham mildly. 'Have you— ah, considered a lady? A governess? A woman, naturally, of some refinement.'

'Some damn bluestocking who would make the child print pages of hooks all day? Some pious old prism, who would put muslin drawers on the piano legs?'

'Not all are like that. Why, only today I had dealings with a lady teacher quite unlike that, a Miss Grey, who teaches the Ragged School.' The magistrate was startled to see Harland lean forward, quite a fierce expression on his face.

'Miss Grey? I've met the woman. She teaches slum brats and pesters decent householders for money to pay for it. When she isn't doing that, she's sewing clothes for them.' He frowned. 'What business, if you don't mind my asking, had you with her?'

Mr Grantham explained, relating Sally's story. Dan snorted. 'It follows. Miss Grey, in my opinion, rushes in where angels fear to tread. Oh, she means well, but it will end badly, see if it don't.'

Mr Grantham reflected that education did not seem to be a topic which could easily be discussed with his host. He watched Harland's handsome, slightly truculent figure, as he got to his feet and went to the brandy decanter.

'Well, Harland, I wasn't only thinking of the child.'

Dan paused in the act of pouring out a glass of brandy for his guest, and shot him a very direct look. 'Go on.'

'Good lord,' said the magistrate, 'if I didn't know you, I'd be quite alarmed. You look very much as if you want to set about me.'

Dan chuckled unexpectedly, and returned with the brandy. 'Here, this I brought over myself from France. Give me your opinion. As regards my manner, you know me. Speak your mind. You know I prefer it.'

'I'm thinking of you, dear fellow. You're what? Seven and thirty? Why, you're a young man. You can't mean to shut yourself up here with Pip. Not good for you and not good for the boy. Now, I know that your marriage didn't end well, and I'm sorry for it . . .'

Harland turned away so that Grantham could only see his back. The magistrate went on determinedly, not to be put off, 'But it's my opinion, you should think of marrying again. You've been a widower nine years. The boy needs a mother. Don't take offence, now.'

Dan turned back towards him. 'I've taken no offence. As a matter of fact, I've been giving the matter some thought.' He saw that the magistrate looked surprised, and smiled drily. 'I am human, you know. You don't remember Ellis? He was captain of the *Carthagena*. He took a fever in the West Indies and died there. I was many years his friend, and I've always kept an eye on his widow. She's a—a very excellent woman, and handsome. I have some reason to think that she—well—she's not indifferent to me. Frankly, I've been thinking about it.'

'She's met Pip?' Mr Grantham asked shrewdly.

'No, not yet. She has no children of her own, but I'm sure she'd take to Pip.'

Which was not to say, thought Mr Grantham, burying his face in the brandy glass, that Pip would take to her. 'Ellis? Ah, yes. I recall the lady. Well, she's handsome, certainly.'

'You think, then, that I could do worse?' Harland came back and pulled up his chair nearer to his friend's. 'I mean, if I decided to pay my addresses to Mrs Ellis?'

'You could do worse, certainly.' Mr Grantham fidgeted. 'I would advise, however, that she meet the child. After all, it's only fair—on the lady.'

'Well, yes, I could ask her to come and take tea or something. Would that be in order? Socially, I mean. I'm not well-acquainted with these niceties. I can ask her to come and take tea? I've known her a long time, and her husband was midshipman with me when we were boys of thirteen.'

Mr Grantham eyed his anxious face. 'Oh, yes, I'm sure it's in order.'

Harland's features gained a darker flush. 'The fact of it is, she being a widow and much of an age as myself, I'd find it easier to speak to her about marriage. I mean, if I was to go setting my cap at some young girl, at my time of life, I'd more than likely make a confounded fool of myself. I can't start and re-learn how to go courting now. I can't be doing with writing love letters and so on. Now, Charlotte Ellis won't expect all that.'

'Oh?' murmured Mr Grantham. 'Won't she?'

'Look here, Bob,' the Captain said firmly. 'I can see what you're thinking, but it's as well to be honest about the matter. It's because I made such a poor fist of my first marriage that I'm looking towards a woman like Charlotte Ellis now that I'm considering taking the plunge again. The plain fact is, I was sent to sea as a boy of twelve, as you know, so my experience of family life was summarily cut short, and confined to my early years. I won't tire you with an account of my early life at sea. Two or three times I nearly died from the fever or from bad water, and I saw plenty of my young friends sewn up in canvas sheets and committed to Davy Jones' locker. Young Pip thinks I had a life of high adventure at his age, but I wouldn't send any youngster through it!

'However, I survived it all and was a lieutenant at twenty with every hope of preferment, and thought myself a fine fellow who had travelled the world and could hold his liquor, and catch the eye of any pretty girl who took his! I married at the age of twenty-four, and I was as confident I should succeed in that as well as I'd done in other things. But the simple truth was, and I admit it frankly now, that I hadn't the slightest idea how to be a half-decent husband or father, or take responsibility for a family of my own at all. When I married, I vaguely supposed these things arranged themselves. I took Bella on a honeymoon trip to Paris, and made myself obliging visiting the sights and trailing along behind when she went shopping, and flattered myself I'd done my duty. But I found it a deadly dull, land-lubbing sort of a business, and I couldn't wait to get back to sea. At the first opportunity away I sailed, leaving Bella at home, quite alone, in a brand-new house, full of brand-new furniture and brand-new servants who were set to cheat and deceive her at every turn. I never gave it a second thought. It never crossed my mind that a twenty-year old bride might be bored, or unable to cope and driven to despair, needing my presence or support. Letters from me arriving six weeks late from the four corners of the globe, and an Indian shawl or two as a present when I did come home, were poor substitutes for a flesh and blood husband who was there. Bella was an orphan and had no one but an elderly aunt. My parents were dead. She was quite alone.

'I was at home when Pip was born, and I might have taken more interest. But at every turn I tripped over a nursemaid or a wet-nurse or the doctor, or some female come to visit and view the baby. I felt completely superfluous, so as soon as I knew Bella safe and churched, and the baby christened, away I sailed again.'

Dan paused and stared into the flames dancing in the hearth. More quietly, he went on, 'That another stepped forward and took my place when I was away appeared to me then as a treachery never to be forgiven. God knows, it was only a foolish mistake on poor Bella's part, and perhaps He has seen fit to be more merciful about it than I was. Well, I got my punishment, and poor Bella was sacrificed as well. As for Pip, poor little scrap, there was no one to take any interest in him, and little wonder the child didn't thrive and has always been ailing.'

He made an effort to pull himself together, turned his gaze back to the silent magistrate, and continued more briskly, 'There's little point in crying over spilt milk. But I mean to try and make less of a mess of the second half of my life than of the first. But you will understand that I'm not tempted to consider marriage to another young, impressionable girl, with whom I should have little or no understanding and who couldn't supply the want of domestic knowledge I so obviously lack! Now, Charlotte is a widow. She knows how marriage goes. She has experience in running a household and managing servants. She has no romantic expectations, which is not to say we can't be friends. It would be a practical and sensible arrangement, and I don't see why she and I shouldn't come to terms very well.'

There was something more than a little defiant about the way he spoke these last words, and there was an aggressive set to his bearded jaw. He leaned forward with his shoulders hunched and his bronzed hands clasped on his knees, as if he anticipated some contrary argument, and Grantham thought, with momentary amusement, that his friend looked very like a carved figurehead from one of the old wooden walls in which he had begun his seafaring career.

The magistrate swirled the remaining brandy round the glass, watching its tawny depths turn from brown to gold and back again. Then he shifted his burly frame awkwardly and murmured, 'As you say, Dan. A very sensible way of looking at it.'

'You don't sound as though you mean that,' Harland observed, eyeing his companion with a sudden flicker of amusement in his own eyes.

'No, confound it, I don't!' Grantham burst out energetically. He struggled with his feelings for a moment, then muttered, 'Dash it, it's not my business, and what I think is neither here nor there! Mrs Ellis is a fine woman, and all you say makes sense. It makes too much sense for my liking, if you must know. No one was ever able to plan his future so neatly!'

'Tell me the flaw in it,' Harland challenged him obstinately, 'and I'll be glad to hear it.'

The magistrate fairly leapt out of his chair. 'You're a young man, confound it, not an old one! Give me all the same reasons when you're sixty, and I might be impressed! Now it just sounds dashed cold-blooded. Now then, I don't intend to speak my mind any further on the subject, and have probably said too much already. You may ask me my opinion of this brandy, which I think is a very fine one.'

The loss of the parcel of flannelette was a severe one, but Rachel could hardly go back and tell Mr Simpson and ask him for a second length. She knew very well the draper would not refuse, but it would be to presume on his kindness, and was out of the question. So instead Rachel rummaged about in boxes and trunks at home, and finally managed to find a pair of old curtains out of which she might hope to cut two skirts for the little girls. Tom was out for the evening and would not return until later, so she had the sitting-room to herself, and spread out the curtain-cloth on the table, carefully chalking round a paper template and preparing to set about it with a pair of sharp scissors. It was a job requiring a considerable amount of concentration. Faintly, in the background, she heard the door-knocker, and thought, there's Tom, returned early and forgotten his key. But she paid no more attention and continued to cut carefully along her chalked lines, the tip of her tongue protruding from between her teeth and her brow furrowed in concentration.

'There's a gentleman come, Miss Rachel,' said Hannah, appearing in the doorway, and making her mistress start and almost cut too far.

Rachel looked up, scissors in hand, and was seized for a brief moment with a fear that Jed Casey might have returned. Even as this thought crossed her mind, she realised that the old housekeeper would not have called Casey a gentleman, and at the same moment she saw herself looking full at Captain Harland.

She was so taken aback that for a moment she simply stared at him, and then she managed to pull herself together and stammer, 'My goodness, Captain Harland, I am so sorry...' She became aware of the scissors in her hand and dropped them with an unseemly clatter. 'Do—do come in.'

She had no idea what could have brought him, and thought how tiresome and typical it was of him to come tonight, when Tom was out of the house. Harland accepted her invitation and stood with his hands clasped behind his back, looking curiously around the sitting-room. It was lit only by the oil-lamp on the table where Rachel had been working. The evenings were getting cooler now, but there was no question yet of a fire, and the hearth was empty and cold. Rachel felt a pang of embarrassment, and for the first time was ashamed of their modest home. The furniture was all very old and shabby, and truth to tell it was not all that well-dusted. Hannah was apt to overlook nooks and crannies. The pattern was almost worn clean off the carpet, and the whole room presented a very poor appearance, especially when compared to Harland's own comfortable dwelling.

'I'm afraid,' she explained, 'that my brother is out. He'll be back shortly.'

'No matter,' he said. 'I came to see you. May I sit down?'

They sat either side of the empty hearth, and Rachel wondered if she should call for Hannah to bring a pair of candles to help out the inadequate oil-lamp. But, before she could do so, her visitor spoke again.

'I'm disturbing you, perhaps?' His thick black eyebrows rose in question.

'No, not at all. I'm only sewing, for the school, you know.'

'Oh, yes, the school...' he muttered disapprovingly. He glanced around the room again. 'You live here alone with your brother? Just the two of you?'

'Yes,' she said cautiously.

'And you keep house for him?'

'Not exactly, Hannah does that...and now we have some help—well, of a sort.'

'Yes, I know,' he interrupted unexpectedly. 'My friend Bob Grantham came to dine with me yesterday evening. You're acquainted with him as a magistrate, I understand. He—told me about the little girl.'

'Oh, yes, Sally,' Rachel said, more and more at a loss to know what could possibly have brought him here. 'She's a cousin of young Joey, whom you met. Quite a disreputable family, I'm afraid, but the children are all very bright.'

'So you tell me.' He sounded as if he did not altogether believe her. 'However, your brother doesn't depend on you to keep house—I mean, he could manage here without you?'

'Here, possibly, but not at the school!' she said a little sharply. 'And if I may say so, that's a strange sort of question. What brings you, Captain Harland?'

Quite without warning, he smiled at her. 'Well, Grantham was impressed at your taking in the child, and spoke very warmly of you. I thought I might call and say, I also think it very good of you to take care of the little girl.'

Rachel tried hard not to be put off by the smile, and surveyed him. 'Captain Harland, I find it very hard to believe you care twopence what happens to Sally or any of our pupils.'

He leaned forward slightly. 'You misunderstand me, Miss Grey. I'm by no means a man who hates children.'

Rachel wished the room were not so gloomy, and fidgeted in her chair. If Tom were to return now, and find them sitting here in semi-darkness, he would think it very odd.

She stood up. 'I'll tell Hannah to bring a candle. The lamp did well enough when I was working at the table, but it hardly does to receive visitors by.'

She hurried down to the kitchen, and with some difficulty a whole candle was found—it wouldn't do to return with a half-used stub—and crammed into a respectable candlestick and Rachel returned with it herself.

'It is somewhat quicker,' she explained, 'to do things oneself than to ask Hannah.' He probably thought their domestic arrangements sadly lacking, but it could not be helped. She had not asked the man to call. It struck her that Harland seemed more ill at ease than she did, as if he turned over something in his mind and did not know how to broach it.

Her instinct had not misled her. He had come here with a definite purpose, but how to explain it was proving dashed difficult. He heaved a mental groan and glanced at her surreptitiously. She was a remarkably pretty girl for all her plain gown and dreary surroundings. It did not make his errand easier. But as he looked about the room he gained some resolve. Anything had to be better than this, even what he had to suggest. The threadbare respectability of the house stirred an inexplicable annoyance in him. But the school must be a hundred times worse! He had not seen it, but he could imagine it. Grantham had told him where it was located, and Dan knew it for a rough area, risky by day and violent by night. That a decent girl like this one was daily exposed to scenes of filth and misery and the real possibility of violence appalled him. As he thought of it, Dan's features set in an uncompromising scowl. The brother must be quite out of his mind. But although the pair of them, brother and sister, lacked all common sense—in Dan's view—he had to admit that neither lacked courage. Especially the girl.

'You are never afraid?' he asked suddenly, genuinely curious to hear her view of it.

'Of what should I be afraid?' She stared at him in surprise.

He was both nonplussed and angered by what seemed to him to be less innocence than a serene obstinacy. With a vehemence which startled her, he retorted, 'Because what you do is fraught with danger! You can't ignore it, surely? The families of those children include quite a few rascals and some out-and-out criminals! You told me so yourself. Did not one of them appear here only recently, threatening violence? Even the children themselves have it in them to make serious trouble. Do you never get your windows broken? Dead cats left on the doorstep? Attempts to burn down the school? Bob Grantham tells me that kindly souls who attempt to work among the poor are frequently repaid with black eyes and chipped teeth!' His attention focused again on her pretty, intelligent face with its frame of black ringlets, listening to him with ill-concealed impatience. 'I should not like to think that might happen to you...' he added more quietly.

'These things happen,' Rachel admitted, 'but I told you how well Tom handled Casey, and he's more than capable of handling any other problem... even if he is a schoolmaster, which I don't suppose you think much of as an employment for a man!'

'Grey may do whatever he chooses, because he is a man——' Dan began, and was swiftly interrupted.

'And what am I? An incompetent idiot?'

He wanted to shout, No, you are a pretty girl with the strength of a fly and not the slightest idea what dangers you run! But it was hardly his business to explain the nature of those dangers to her. But how she bridled when she fancied the brother was criticised and rushed to his defence. He wondered if that was due to devotion on her part and an over-developed sense of admiration for the fellow, or whether she hid some deep-seated feeling of dissatisfaction by her unwillingness to admit any criticism. Dan was more than curious to meet Tom Grey, and his wish was about to be granted. There came the sound of the front door slamming and Tom's voice in the hall, as he handed his hat to Hannah.

'There he is now!' Rachel exclaimed.

She jumped to her feet with such evident relief in her voice and manner that Dan was forced to admit that his visit so far had been far from successful, the more so because he still had not found any way to come to the matter which really brought him. He grimaced ruefully, but then reflected that perhaps first tackling the muscular paragon the brother appeared to be might be best, after all. Talking to men was considerably easier than talking to women. He was no great hand at talking to women. Tom Grey, unless he was completely mutton-headed, ought to be more amenable to reason. If he could persuade Grey, persuading the girl would not be difficult. Especially since she valued the brother's opinions so highly. Dan got to his feet and took up a resolute stance as Tom entered.

'The housekeeper told me you were here,' Tom said, holding out his hand. 'I'm pleased to make your acquaintance, sir, and to be able to thank you in person for your generous subscription to the school.'

Dan took the outstretched hand, and apologised for calling when Tom was out. 'I hope you don't mind,' he said.

Tom looked rather as if he did mind. He glanced at Rachel and said, 'Perhaps you could ask Hannah to bring the tea-tray? We are a little old-fashioned in our ways here, Captain Harland. I dare say the tea-tray is not brought in much of an evening now in many homes, but my sister and I like to observe a routine.'

You might, thought Dan drily. I doubt she does. The girl is working away like a bottle of ginger-beer with the fizz all stoppered down. One of these days, there will be an almighty explosion. He only murmured aloud that he had no wish to disturb their evening routine, and watched Rachel go out.

Hannah had already put the tea-tray in the kitchen. But Rachel, looking at it in some despair, realised it wouldn't do at all, as it was. She hunted through a drawer for a clean cloth, and sorted through the cups and saucers for three which matched and were not cracked. She wondered if she should send Sally running down to the little grocery at the corner for twopennyworth of best tea, because they only bought in drawing-room tea when a guest was expected, and generally drank the cheaper kitchen variety. But it was getting very late, too late to send out a child.

'He will have to make do with kitchen tea!' she said rebelliously. She left Hannah to bring the tray, and set off back to the sitting-room.

But, as she reached the door, she became aware that some heated argument was taking place on the other side of it. Tom was protesting about something, but his voice sounded unusually unsure. Harland, on the other hand, sounded his usual obstinate and assured self. She could not make out many words, but she could hardly press her ear to the door panel, so the only thing to do was knock and then walk in briskly.

Both men looked up. Harland was standing by the table on which her sewing lay, with his hands clasped behind his back, which seemed to be his favourite stance, while Tom turned up and down the room by the fireplace looking extremely agitated and waving one hand to support his speech in a way which was quite unlike him. But at the sight of his sister he made a visible effort to pull himself together, and neither did Harland seem to want to continue the argument in front of Rachel.

'Forgive me,' he said hurriedly. 'I'm not much of a tea-drinker, and I really should . . . I've taken up too much of your time. Grey—Miss Grey,' he bowed towards her, 'your servant.'

He walked out rapidly, almost upsetting Hannah and the arriving tea-tray in the hall, and a slam of the door announced that he had let himself out.

'Whatever was all that about?' demanded Rachel, bewildered.

'Nothing at all!' said Tom shortly. But he did not look as if he thought it nothing.

Tom remained very quiet that evening, after Harland's departure. The next morning at breakfast, and during their walk to school, he still stayed sunk in thought. Even at school itself he seemed to have his mind on other matters, and the boys, observing it, took the unexpected opportunity to pinch one another and throw scraps of chalk at the girls, and try to reach across and pull their apron strings. Tom seemed more aware of the fabric of the schoolroom than its inmates. Rachel saw him glare round it irritably several times. He scraped at peeling paintwork with his fingernail, muttering that the trustees must be made to pay for redecoration and that there was no excuse for the window-panes being unwashed. Tom normally never took notice of these things, and Rachel did not know whether to be exasperated or amused.

It was one of those pleasant, mild early autumn days. The high street, as they walked homewards along it, was bustling with a cheerful crowd. A ship must be newly arrived, because sailors in their white bell-bottomed trousers, monkey jackets and round, hard hats were everywhere with wives and sweethearts hanging on their arms. Shopkeepers were doing a roaring trade, children ran along the pavements, in and out of the knots of pedestrians, vehicles of all kinds rumbled along the thoroughfare and the London Mail had arrived and decanted exhausted travellers, together with their bags and boxes.

Tom seemed to cheer up slightly, and Rachel took his arm. 'I hope you're over your fit of the sulks, Tom. Whatever did Captain Harland say which upset you so much?'

Tom flushed, but for once did not detach his arm from hers. Brother and sister made a handsome couple, and several of the young women whom arrival of the ship had brought into town cast speculative glances at Tom. Rachel wished, as she had done many times, that Tom would meet some nice, respectable, cheerful girl and fall in love. She sighed.

Tom, misinterpreting the sign of distress, bent his head anxiously and exclaimed, 'I didn't mean to upset you, but it's true Harland did leave me with much to think about.' He paused, appearing to search for words, then went on awkwardly, 'I always tried to do my best for you, Rachel.'

She squeezed his arm. 'Why, yes, Tom dear. I know you have.'

'But I haven't!' he burst out. He stopped in the middle of the pavement and took his arm from hers as he turned to face her. 'You see, I truly never thought that there was anything wrong in your teaching at the school.'

'Nor is there,' she said simply.

'But there is!' he insisted, growing agitated. 'It's no place for you—such miserable, poor sort of surroundings, and the children so very grubby and ill-behaved, some from the very worst families——'

'Tom!' Rachel interrupted, a tense note entering her voice. 'It's not, by any chance, Captain Harland who has put all these qualms into your mind? Because if so, he is the very last person to judge, and it's no business of his!'

'Yes, it is Harland,' Tom admitted. 'I didn't like his saying it, but he's right. The school is no place for you.'

'That man,' cried Rachel, bursting into anger and stamping her foot on the pavement in a way which greatly amused a couple of passing midshipmen, 'is a perfect wretch! Who is he to say what's right or wrong?'

'Perhaps it's not quite his business,' replied Tom obstinately, 'but I still have to admit he is right, and so I've made a decision. Don't argue, Rachel, because my mind is made up and I shan't change it. You shall not teach at the school any more.'

'What?' she gasped, colour draining from her face. 'I can't just . . . just abandon the children! And what should I do instead?'

'Stay at home. Other girls do. As for the children, I shall teach boys and girls together until another lady teacher can be found; someone older—a widow, perhaps.'

'Tom!' she cried in dismay. Her horror had good grounds. To begin with, she enjoyed teaching, and the idea of being summarily torn from her young charges was genuinely painful. But as for Tom's blithe assumption that she should be content to stay at home...at home? With Hannah and Sally and absolutely nothing to do all day?

'There's my salary,' she argued. 'We need it.'

'I dare say we do, but we shall manage without it perfectly well. We shall just have to make economies.'

'What economies, for goodness' sake?' she almost shouted. 'Our housekeeping is already pared to the bone!'

She was sorry for these words the moment she had spoken them, because to Tom they obviously seemed further criticism of the way he had looked after his sister.

'I'm sorry, Rachel,' he said stiffly. 'But that's my decision, and we might as well start straight away. From now on, you'll stay at home.'

'This is all Harland's fault!' Rachel cried. She looked around her wildly, as though some help might present itself, and saw, clip-clopping towards them, an empty cab. 'And I mean to go and tell him so!' she stormed. She flung up a hand to hail the cab.

'Now, wait a moment, Rachel!' Tom grabbed her arm.

But she shook him off furiously and scrambled into the cab, calling out Harland's address to the driver.

'Rachel, get down from that cab instantly!' yelled Tom, red in the face and sprinting alongside as the vehicle rolled forward and the cabbie whipped up his mare to a trot.

'Get off the road, Tom. You will be run down! And don't follow me!' she shouted back.

Even as she spoke, Tom was obliged to leap for his life, and the cab bore her rapidly away from him.

'I want to see Captain Harland.'

Mrs Brereton gazed astonished at the dishevelled apparition on the doorstep. She recognised the young lady well enough as having called a few days earlier, but not looking like this, with blazing eyes, tumbled curls and bonnet askew.

'Well, miss, I'll tell him,' she began doubtfully.

'Thank you, I'll tell him myself. Where is he? In his study?'

The young lady marched in, brushed past the housekeeper and flung open the door to the study.

He was sitting at a writing-desk, apparently composing some letter which was giving him trouble, because he was scratching the pen energetically through a word. He looked up, startled, tossed down the pen, sending great blobs of black ink across his page, and scrambled to his feet. 'Miss Grey?'

'Captain Harland!' returned Miss Grey determinedly. She shut the door firmly in the distraught Mrs Brereton's face. 'You look surprised to see me, but I don't see why you should. Not if you have any conscience, but I dare say you don't. How dare you persuade my brother that teaching the Ragged School is not suitable work for me?'

'Because it isn't!' he said sharply, recovering his aplomb. 'The surroundings are squalid, the children unwashed, their language uncouth, and I dare say they have lice and fleas as well,' he concluded.

'It's no concern of yours, even if they do!' she retorted furiously. 'You had no business to speak to Tom.'

'I'm entitled to express my opinion,' he retaliated.

'Not about *me*!'

A silence fell. He scratched his beard and muttered, 'Well, perhaps I could have managed it better.'

'There is no "perhaps" about it! Now Tom has forbidden me to teach at the school, and what am I to do all day? Sit home and twiddle my thumbs? To say nothing of the loss of my salary. I dare say it wouldn't occur to you, but it's meant a great deal to me these last years that I haven't been a drain on Tom's purse. I've always paid my way. Perhaps a woman's not supposed to worry about things like that—but I do! Now I'm thrown on Tom's charity!'

'You are not thrown on his charity—he's your brother, for pity's sake!' Dan burst out, beginning to lose his temper. 'It's his duty to look after you!'

For a moment he almost thought she was going to attack him physically. She darted forward in a flurry of petticoats and shawl, the bonnet finally slipping off her head completely to hang around her white throat by its taffeta ribbons, and her black ringlets falling about her flushed face.

'I can look after myself!' she flung up at him, both fists clenched.

She was not much above five feet two, and he stood six feet in his stockings, so she did rather seem to bounce up at him like an infuriated terrier. It struck him, quite irrelevantly, that she had no need to augment her own hair with false curls, as did so many.

But she had grown alarmingly red in the face and, as had been Abel, he was concerned that her tight corset combined with her emotion might present him with a swooning female on his hands. He saw that he had unleashed a tempest when he had only anticipated a squall, and sought to pour oil on these troubled waters.

'I'm sorry——' he began, but was not allowed to finish.

'You are not!' she snapped. 'It amuses you to meddle, Captain Harland, and you don't care a straw how it upsets me or ruins my life, or disturbs the school or anything!'

Harland's jaw set grimly. He strode past her to the door and pulled it open. She wondered whether he was about to throw her down the front steps, but instead he said abruptly, 'There's someone I should like you to meet. Please come with me.'

Rachel tugged resentfully at the taffeta strings which constricted her throat, and holding the bonnet in one hand, and her skirts in the other, followed him up the main staircase and along the corridor at the top of it. He pushed open a door and stood aside for her to enter. Frankly curious, she squeezed past him and went in.

It was a nursery. Despite the fact that a fire was not really necessary and none had been lit downstairs, one blazed merrily on the hearth here, heating the room uncomfortably. On a rug before the flames lay a small boy on his stomach, engrossed in a large tome.

He looked up and, seeing them, got awkwardly to his feet and stood hesitantly staring at them, rubbing the sole of one foot against the other leg.

'Now, Pip,' said Dan to him, 'here is Miss Grey come to meet you, so you must be a gentleman, you know.'

Pip edged forward, eyeing Rachel with a mixture of curiosity and shyness. She supposed the child about twelve years of age, but rather slight and small for his years. His skin had the translucent quality of illness, but his eyes were bright and clear. It struck her that this was an intelligent child, but one whose life lacked variety or challenge. The way he watched her indicated that he certainly rarely saw strangers. She held out her hand, smiled, and said, 'How do you do, Pip? I hope we don't disturb you.'

He took her hand gravely and replied, 'No, ma'am, I was only reading.'

'Well, I like a book very much,' she told him. 'What is it you're reading?'

Pip fetched his book, a venerable tome which turned out to be a gazetteer. 'I read about the places where Papa has been,' he confided to her. Rachel, forgetting that she was not alone, knelt down in a welter of skirts and spread the book on her lap. Pip squatted down beside her and turned the pages, taking them from the West Indies to Cape Horn and informing her how to take readings at sea with a sextant, about which he seemed to be very knowledgeable, and pointing out the straits through which it was difficult to take a ship above seven hundred and fifty tons burthen. He was a quaint child, his head full of nautical lore, and she began to suspect that his father had been his principal instructor.

Perhaps guessing what was in her mind, Harland, standing over them both, stirred. 'As you will gather, Miss Grey, this is my son, Philip. He reads very well, even if mostly atlases, and writes a fair hand, and reckons up his numbers accurately provided he can see the point in it, and his geography is better than mine. But I'm afraid he has no Latin nor French, nor is he at all acquainted with good literature, and his history is so scarce that I doubt he knows Cromwell from Canute.'

'Perhaps he has not been well-taught?' she suggested, and blushed, because she did not know whether Harland himself really had been the teacher.

But he was nodding. 'Yes, you are right. He has not been well-taught, but there is no question of his going away to school.'

The child cast a quick, intelligent but unhappy glance at his father.

They have made him feel he is an invalid, thought Rachel sympathetically, and the child is made unhappy by it. He'd like to be like other boys. He seems fit enough, just a little weak and pale. There is open seashore not five minutes walk from here, and he ought to be there, throwing stones in the water, not shut up alone. Why, this room is like a hothouse. I fancy his father is over-protective.

'In fact,' Harland said, 'when you arrived just now, I was trying to write to you, and ask you to call and discuss just that matter.'

'I see.' Rachel froze. 'Perhaps we should continue this conversation downstairs, Captain? Goodbye, Pip, I'm very glad to have met you, and I hope we shall meet again.'

They returned to the study and she put her bonnet down on a chair, draped her shawl over the back of it, and turned composedly to face Harland, who eyed her uneasily.

'I begin to think it possible, Captain Harland, that you have been extremely devious, not only with regard to me, but in your dealings with my brother.'

'Now, look,' he burst out, 'I know how it must seem, but it's not quite like that. It is my opinion that you should not teach in that school. But I don't say you shouldn't teach. Philip needs someone who has experience and is well-qualified—and don't say I should get a tutor, because the last person I need is some sadistic, half-educated oaf with a penchant for the bottle and beating small boys!'

'There are many excellent tutors, Captain Harland. But you are going to suggest I come here and teach Philip, aren't you? I suppose you think I shall feel sufficiently sorry for the child to overlook how badly you have behaved. Well, I don't overlook it, and what's more, I don't feel sorry for Pip. He has a comfortable home, a father who is clearly devoted, and his future is secure. The children of the Ragged School have nothing, except what Tom and I can offer. They need me. Pip doesn't.'

'And you think,' he said quietly, 'that the children of the wealthy cannot be in need?'

Rachel took a deep breath. 'I think you should look for someone else.'

'So,' he said, his voice growing sharper, 'because you're angry with me, you'll take it out on Pip?'

'Oh, nonsense!' she burst out. 'I'm doing no such thing. Besides, there's Tom. I can't believe you mentioned this scheme to him, because I know he wouldn't approve.'

'Of your being a governess? It's a perfectly respectable calling.'

'No, of my being a governess here!' she retorted.

There was a long silence. 'I see,' he said at last. He suddenly sounded despondent, and Rachel's heart experienced a pang of remorse. Whatever his faults, the man was devoted to his child and had clearly hoped she would agree. It must be difficult for him to raise the child without help. 'You won't reconsider it, then? I can offer you comfortable quarters here, your own sitting-room, and any salary you care to name.'

'That is not the point...' she began, but the memory of that pale, lonely child with the bright, intelligent gaze came to her, and she knew that, whatever the rights and wrongs of it, she would accept. In a last, desperate attempt, she protested, 'I have no Latin, and my French is no more than adequate.'

Harland stepped forward and seized her hand before she could prevent it. 'Then you will come?' he asked her eagerly.

'Well,' she floundered, 'I'll come for a trial period and we'll see how it goes.'

'Good!' he said, and sounded so satisfied that she was seized with a suspicion that she had made a great mistake and given in far too easily. 'It was Grantham who suggested you—in a roundabout way. He called Pip a little savage, and so he is—but I particularly want him to make a good impression on——'

'On whom, Captain Harland?' asked Rachel, her suspicion growing by the minute. She took her hand firmly from his.

'On the lady I hope to marry,' he said frankly. 'I mean, I want Charlotte to think well of Pip, and I rely on you, Miss Grey, to—well, polish him up, as it were.'

There was a silence. 'I see,' Rachel said eventually. It was an added dimension to the situation, and not one she was altogether sure that she liked.

Although, she thought to herself, her brain leaping furiously from one half-perceived possibility to another, it is not my business what Harland intends to do with his own life. If the man plans to remarry, it's hardly odd. I don't suppose he's yet forty. It will also be good for the child to have a mother. But for some reason she was disturbed by the notion and disliked it. But that, in turn, was probably because it had been sprung upon her.

'Captain Harland——' she began loudly.

'Yes, Miss Grey?' A slightly quizzical expression entered his eyes.

Rachel flushed, partly because her voice had come out sounding much more loud and aggressive than she had intended, and partly because she had suddenly noticed that his eyes were a fascinating hazel in colour. In a certain light they tended to take on a golden-brown hue, and yet in another the irises assumed shades of grey-green. 'Captain Harland,' she repeated, less belligerently but still firmly, 'is there anything else about your household that I should know?'

He shrugged. 'No. It's a simple and straightforward household, as you have seen for yourself. Largely a bachelor establishment, for all that there's a child about the place.'

Rachel's misgivings increased. 'Then I suggest that at first I come and teach Philip on a daily basis. I can travel to and from my home quite easily.'

He frowned. 'Surely you will find such a daily trip back and forth very tiring? I had meant that you should live in, as most governesses do.'

'Yes, but you see, there is Tom——' she returned hurriedly.

'What of him?'

'Well, he—he's used to my being at home. What should he do without me?'

'As I have done these past nine years. Manage without a woman in the house.' Harland paused. 'Other than Mrs Brereton, of course. But you have a housekeeper, don't you? And the child, Sally, to run and fetch?'

'Ye-es . . .' agreed Rachel doubtfully.

'Then I cannot see,' said Captain Harland, 'that Mr Thomas Grey need present us with any problem.'

Oh, but he will, thought Rachel in gloomy prognostication of storms ahead.

CHAPTER FOUR

TOM listened in silence as his sister explained Harland's offer. Silent, but not impassive. His face grew paler, the set of his mouth tighter and a muscle began to twitch in his jaw, so that by the time she eventually came to the end of her speech he fairly seethed with suppressed reaction.

'Well, Tom?' she asked apprehensively. 'What do you think?'

'Think?' He stared at her. 'I think the fellow is confounded impudent, and I'm at a loss to understand how you could encourage him! You will refuse.'

She was prepared for argument, but the bluntness of his speech, the way in which he simply disregarded the possibility that she might have her own ideas on the subject, lit a fire of rebellion.

'It's a most civil offer, Tom. We have arranged that I can live at home and travel to Southsea daily, so there's no reason for you to object.'

'No reason for me——' Tom spluttered, and his complexion grew purple. 'Of course I object! See here, Rachel——' he was beginning to breathe heavily, and pearls of sweat appeared on his temples and forehead '—Harland came here and set out his reasons why you shouldn't teach at the school. At the time I admitted he was right. But my intention in telling you that you should not continue at school any longer was that you should stay at home.'

'And do what?' Rachel shouted, losing her temper. 'Die of boredom? Whom should I talk to? To Hannah and Sally? What should I do? Read every novel the circulating library has to offer? What kind of life is that? What's more, Tom, you are making this decision for me not only without considering either the alternative or my views, but without seeing for yourself what the situation in Harland's household is. The little boy is plainly intelligent, and to teach him will be a real challenge. Is he to be left like—like an untended plant, just to grow wild or wither? If you saw him, Tom, I know you'd understand.'

'Harland can find someone else!' Tom answered in a stifled voice.

'But he has asked me. It's a compliment. What's more, I mean to take up his offer. And the salary is more than generous.'

The reference to her salary was a mistake. Tom's eyes glinted and his mouth set obstinately. 'We can manage on mine.'

'No, we can't. Don't talk so foolishly, Tom.'

'Very well, then,' said her brother. 'It seems you are set on it and anything I say is foolishness. We shall see what comes of it. The arrangement will not work.'

Nor did it, as Rachel had to admit with heavy heart after the first fortnight. It would have done, she told herself with mounting fury, if Tom had only been willing to lend his support. But that he steadfastly refused to do. When she returned home at the end of the day, it was to find Tom sitting dark-faced and monosyllabic. She would ask him how his day had gone, but he never asked after hers. This was doubly annoying, because there were several points on which she would have liked to ask Tom's advice. At first she tried to do this, thinking that an attempt to involve him might bring him around. But she was soon disabused of the hope.

'I can't think why you're consulting me, Rachel,' said Tom stiffly. 'You seem so able to make decisions for yourself. I'm sure anything I have to say can only be superfluous.'

Rachel eventually lost her temper and accused him of being mentally blinkered, of sulking and of idiotic stubbornness. Needless to say, these accusations did not improve the climate. Tom received them with the air of a martyr who knew that in the end clouds of witness would prove him right, and the lions wouldn't find him so easy to chew up, either.

When at the end of the month she proudly brought home her first salary, matters became worse. Regretfully she had to acknowledge the reason. She was not only paid as much as Tom, but slightly more. She should have realised, when she first accepted Harland's offer, that to agree to so high a salary would be unwise. To Tom, his sister's success began increasingly to appear as his failure. He could not support her, he could not offer her a home in which she wished to pass her days, and if the situation remained as it was he would become increasingly dependent on her. To Tom, who so clearly saw himself as the head of their little household, such a state of things was intolerable.

Dan had made a private resolution not to interfere. He had expected that there would be some hiccups in the arrangement at first. He might disagree with her ideas for Pip, but he would let her get on with it unless things looked liked getting too much out of hand. In the same way, he would let her sort out matters with her brother. But when increasingly she arrived in the morning with a doleful expression and left at night to go home looking as if she was about to face the Inquisition, he could no longer keep silent. One evening, a little before she was due to leave, he sent a message asking that she would come down to the study.

Rachel found him pacing restlessly up and down. He said, 'Sit down, sit down, Miss Grey...' and indicated a chair with a brusque movement of his hand. When she had done so, he came to an abrupt halt before her and said baldly, 'You have a face as long a fiddle. I have put up with it for over a month, but I can't put up with it much longer. I might as well have engaged a professional mourner. I suppose it is Grey. Well?'

'Captain Harland!' Rachel leaned forward and clasped her hands. She had been seeking some way of broaching the subject, and was relieved that he had taken the initiative. 'I know you will find this excessively odd, but do you think you could pay me less?'

'What?' He stared down at her as if she had gone mad.

'Well, you see...' She began an incoherent account of Tom's reactions and the reason for them. As she spoke, growing increasingly agitated, her ringlets quivering and her eyes fixed imploringly on his face, Dan found it more and more difficult to concentrate on what she was saying rather than on the picture she presented.

She had a heart-shaped little face and rather full, pouting lips. Her eyes were dark blue, almost violet in hue, and when she became emotional they seemed to glow like amethysts. Yet, for all its prettiness, it was no china doll's face. The features were vibrant with life. The long black eyelashes fluttered over the violet eyes like the wings of exotic butterflies, the full lips pressed together and then parted abruptly over straight, small white teeth and, sometimes, when she had been talking for several minutes and her mouth grew dry, the tip of a pink tongue appeared and curled upward to moisten her upper lip in a way which he thought must be the most erotic thing he had seen in his life—and he'd seen quite a few in sailing the world. She did this now; the tip of the tongue flickered into view and then she bit the bottom lip as well with her top two teeth and sat back, the violet eyes fixed on him.

'Damn it!' he exclaimed unintentionally. She looked taken aback, so he went on hurriedly, 'Now, look here, this has to be settled once and for all. I thought I would let matters sort themselves out, but that was a wrong decision on my part. Should I go and talk to Grey?'

'Oh, no!' she exclaimed quickly. 'It wouldn't help at all.'

'Hmm. Well, I hardly know what I can suggest, Miss Grey. I understand your argument about the salary—and I'm frankly astonished your brother is paid so little. I'm sure his responsibilities at the Ragged School—well, that's not my province. But what is my province is how much I pay you. I consider my son's education important. The salary I pay you reflects that. I've not the slightest intention of paying you less. After all, it's not my fault the trustees of the Ragged School are so miserly with regard to

Grey's salary. What I can see, quite clearly, is that you are unhappy. You bring your unhappiness here. That was not what I had in mind. The last thing Pip needs is a governess with a long face. As I see it, you must make up your mind. Either you close your ears and eyes to Grey's prolonged sulks, or you come here permanently and remove yourself from Grey's miseries. Live in. It's the usual thing anyway, and what I originally had in mind. You could do so much more with Philip. He would like it, I'm sure. I agreed to your suggestion that you come on a daily basis at first because I wanted to see how you got on with the boy. Now I have no hesitation in suggesting you come here full-time. When winter comes, in any case, you can hardly be travelling back and forth in bad weather and in the dark. Even Grey cannot be blind to that!'

'I dare say he's hoping it will make me give up altogether,' she blurted out. 'But I don't want to give up, truly.'

Dan hardened his heart. 'Then the choice is yours.'

She rose to her feet, her fingers plucking nervously at her skirts. 'I may have a week to think it over?'

'Yes, of course.' He turned away. 'Let me know.'

Truth to tell, Dan had found himself in a situation not dissimilar to Rachel's in some respects. In making all these arrangements, he had overlooked the possible reaction of Charlotte Ellis to the news that he had engaged a governess for Philip, and so broke it to her with some apprehension. Women could be very awkward. They took all manner of notions into their heads. Quite illogical. But to his relief Charlotte had not objected, and she was sympathetic to the present problem when he took it to her drawing-room and explained it.

Dan had sat for some minutes balancing a delicate bone china cup and saucer of weak tea before finally setting it down on a nearby table already laden with bric-à-brac. The room was as feminine as his own home was resolutely masculine. It abounded with embroidered firescreens and crocheted antimacassars. Its windows were draped with lace curtains—a pair even framed the mirror, tied back with pink velvet ribbons. Dresden figurines and vases of flowers filled every available table or shelf space. Charlotte presided over it all, including the tea-table, with charm and dignity, as if one of the Dresden figurines had taken life. She picked up a silver teapot now and raised an enquiring arched eyebrow.

He said, 'No, no, thank you...' and saw her put it down again with some relief. He had never drunk so much tea in his life.

'I am so sorry,' said Mrs Ellis, 'to hear you have run into some little problem with the governess.'

'Not with her—with her brother,' said Dan bluntly. 'He's a difficult fellow. Very possessive.'

'I dare say,' said Charlotte kindly, 'that he wishes to do his best by his sister.'

'Oh, I suppose so,' muttered her visitor.

'My dear,' said Mrs Ellis, laying one slender white hand on his sleeve, 'you must not let this worry you. I'm sure everything will sort itself out splendidly.'

And, thought Mrs Ellis to herself, the girl will give up the post. And good riddance. Governess, indeed! The brother sounds a man of perfect good sense to me! Let us hope he also has the courage to stick to his guns. Poor dear Daniel has no notion of what's best for that child. He needs a woman to take him in hand.

'I'm sure,' coaxed Mrs Ellis, leaning forward again in a rustle of taffeta, 'that what you would really like is a glass of wine. I'll have Maria bring the sherry.'

'You are a first-rate woman, Charlotte,' said Dan. 'You won't mind my speaking bluntly. But you're understanding.'

'Oh, I should hope so!' said the lady. 'I was six years married to poor Harry.' She patted her hair, and the sunlight glinted dully on the gold wedding band on her finger. 'We shared every problem. A trouble shared is a trouble halved, you know!'

'Oh, yes, old Harry,' murmured Dan. 'He was a good chap.' He looked again about the comfortable, feminine room, and leaned back in his chair, relaxing. 'Yes, I shouldn't mind a glass of sherry at all.'

In the end it was Pip, the centre of it all, who resolved the matter. They were packing up at the end of the day when, without warning, the child took hold of Rachel's hand and asked anxiously, 'You won't go away, will you, Miss Grey?'

'Why—no!' she exclaimed immediately, wondering how he had guessed what was afoot, as he obviously had. Then her heart sank. 'Although there are other ladies, Pip, who could teach you.'

'I don't want any other lady. I want you.' Pip swung his feet from the chair. They did not quite reach the floor. Though twelve years of age, he was very small. 'My mama went away. She went away when I was very small and I don't remember her. I wish she hadn't.'

Rachel put her arm round him. 'I shan't go away, Pip. I promise.'

She had not expected Tom to agree to her departure to live in as governess at Southsea, nor did he. He turned pale when she told him of it and sat for a few minutes in silence, which was far worse than if he had straight away flown into a rage.

At last he said in a strangled voice, 'So you will leave me altogether, Rachel?'

'I am not leaving you, Tom...' She looked at him in exasperation. 'But living in will be so much more practical.'

Tom's gaze was wandering about the room. To him it looked shabbier and gloomier than ever, and he thought with real pain in his heart that he was not surprised that she should prefer the comforts of Harland's home. But, without Rachel in it, this house which they had shared for so many years would be worse than a tomb. He wanted to tell her so, but the words eluded him. Instead, the sullen fires of resentment, which had lain half-subdued in his heart since she had first come home and told him of Harland's offer, were rekindled and flared up with renewed vigour.

Seeing him hesitate, she took his hand and begged, 'Do please, say you agree, Tom.'

He looked up sharply and snatched away his hand from hers. 'Agree?' he whispered incredulously, as if unable to credit his ears. 'Agree?' he burst out in a roar which made her jump back in alarm. 'Are you out of your mind?'

Rachel was appalled at the expression on her brother's face and the ferocity of his tone. Her heart seemed to wither inside her at the prospect of yet another first-rate quarrel on the subject of Harland. But she had made up her mind, and even now did not altogether abandon hope of persuading Tom, even at such a late stage. 'If you could have heard the child, Tom. You would understand——'

'I understand,' interrupted Tom, breathing heavily, 'that you propose—you, an unmarried girl—to take up residence in the household of a widower who is himself not yet forty! Good lord, have you thought of the possible gossip? No, I dare say not, because you have no knowledge of the way of the world. To me, Harland has every hallmark of a—of a man who knows his way about women.' Tom leapt up from his chair and began to stride about the room in agitation, striking the palm of his hand against the furniture as he passed by to emphasise the points of his argument. 'You don't understand these things, Rachel. I can hardly explain the—the details to you. But the fact is, you are too young—he is too young! You are—you are, frankly, too pretty.'

'Tom!' she exclaimed, surprised.

He flushed. 'I dare say I've never said so before, but there has been no cause to say it. You are—well, a most attractive girl. I've always thought it. I've always been very proud of you, Rachel. I don't suppose Harland is as blind as a bat. I doubt he hasn't noticed it as well!'

'This is all nonsense, Tom!' cried Rachel energetically. 'To begin with, he is hoping to marry a lady named Mrs Ellis. He told me so. She's the widow of another sea captain and he's quite set on it. That's why he wanted me to begin at once and "polish the child up", as he put it. As if the poor little boy were an occasional table! Nor should I be alone with him in the house. There is the housekeeper, Mrs Brereton, a most respectable woman. And a kitchen-maid...both of them sleep in. And there's a gardener too, comes in every day.'

'I don't suppose,' said Tom fiercely, 'that Mrs Brereton is twenty-five, or that the kitchen-maid is anything but a plain Jane with lank hair and bad teeth.'

'I haven't seen the kitchen-maid. Mrs Brereton is about five and fifty, I suppose. Does it matter?'

Tom fairly leapt in the air like a cossack dancer. 'Of course it matters! I forbid it, Rachel. I forbid it absolutely!'

Rachel stood up and smoothed down her skirts with a trembling hand. 'Tom, you must make up your mind. Either I return to teach at the Ragged School, or I take up a post as governess to Philip Harland.'

'I've told you,' Tom snapped, 'I don't wish you to return to the school.'

'Very well, then,' she said with as much composure as she could. It was obvious Tom could not be brought to agree, and the decision must be taken in the teeth of his opposition. 'I shall go to the Harland house as governess.'

Tom swung round on his heel and walked away. After a while, during which he stood with his hands behind his back, clasped beneath the skirts of his frock-coat, his voice came taut and bleak. 'If you leave this house to go to Harland's, then you shall never return here, Rachel, come what may of it.'

'W-what?' she stammered. 'Tom?'

He turned back to face her. 'I mean it, Rachel. If you persist in this extraordinary and foolhardy notion,

you will not set foot in this house again. I shall consider you to have forfeited the title of decent woman!'

The blood surged to her face. 'This is intolerable!
Why, you talk as if I were going to the dogs. I'm going
to teach his child, not share his bed!'

'There!' shouted Tom, lunging forward and shaking
his fist under her nose. 'You see? Already you're using
coarse expressions and talking of things no decent girl
should mention!'

'Oh, fiddlesticks!' cried Rachel. 'Why, there are respectable girls taking up situations as governess in
households all over the country.'

'None of them is my sister!' yelled Tom.

'I am going, anyway,' she told him with a shaking
voice. 'And I hope you come to your senses, Tom.
Because I think you've gone clean out of them!'

And there the matter rested. To quit the home she
had shared with Tom in such circumstances was heart-
breaking, but the rupture was clearly final. She knew
Tom well enough to realise he would not change his
views.

To enter on a life of independence, having burnt
her boats behind her, was also daunting. Supposing
Harland decided after all that she was not suitable?
Supposing Pip, despite his plea that she remain, should
suddenly take a dislike to her? Supposing Mrs Ellis,
when she became Mrs Harland, had some different
view of how her stepson should be educated? And,
even if all worked out well, the day would come when
Pip was too old to need a governess and she would
have to seek another post.

Governess. It was an unenviable career. She was
left entirely to her own devices. She must support

herself or finish destitute. For the first time, Rachel realised how much she had depended on Tom. Not financially, perhaps, but in every other way. Tom had always been there, ready with advice, well able to cope with any emergency, rock-like in his support if not always in sympathy.

No more. She was alone, an independent woman. She had dreamed of such a thing, but reality was in truth quite frightening. Under their modest roof she had been mistress. Now she was in that limbo world between paid companion and upper servant. Not quite a lady. Genteel rather than a gentlewoman.

However, the die was cast. Rachel removed herself and her worldly goods to the house in Southsea in a hansom cab, and began a new life.

Pip at least seemed delighted to see her, and skipped about the house until he grew breathless and had to sit down. He clearly tired quickly, but that, Rachel suspected, was because he had led too sheltered a life, not because he was constitutionally unable to cope with day-to-day hurly-burly.

With the ghost of Tom invisible but ever-present at her elbow, Rachel explained firmly to Captain Harland that she could not dine with him of an evening. She would dine earlier in the nursery with her young charge. Of course, if he wished her to come down later and sit with him of an evening, she had no objection. He might like a hand of cribbage.

'Cribbage?' said Dan, staring at her aghast. 'What on earth makes you think I play cribbage? And I fail to see why you must eat every meal with Pip.'

'Because once you are married I am sure your new wife will not want me at table every night. And until then—well, it might cause gossip.'

'Among whom? Who should know of it?'

Rachel floundered, but carried on determinedly, 'People always know. Mrs Brereton very likely would not think it fitting.'

'I do not,' said Captain Harland vehemently, 'make my arrangements solely on the grounds of Mrs Brereton's approval!'

'No, but she has been your housekeeper for many years, and it would be foolish to upset her.'

He looked nonplussed but gave in. In fact, after a few minor problems had been sorted out, the arrangement worked very well. She dined with Pip early in the evening and, once he was in bed, went downstairs armed with her embroidery or a book and sat in the drawing-room. Sometimes Harland joined her there, sometimes he didn't. Sometimes he shut himself in his study and smoked his cigars. She could smell them all over the house. Occasionally Mr Grantham came and dined with him, and then Rachel would retire to her own sitting-room upstairs, but otherwise there were few visitors to the house.

But more often than not, as time went by, Dan would arrive in the drawing-room of an evening and there they sat for an hour, sometimes talking—he described the foreign ports he had visited—and sometimes in silence as he read the newspaper or a book. If something in the newspaper amused him, he would read it out to her. But one evening he arrived with a box and board and declared, 'Now then, this is a game I'm sure you will do well at! Though women generally don't. No logic. Chess. Do you play?'

'No,' she confessed.

'Aha!' said Captain Harland, setting out the pieces. 'Then let's see that educated female brain get to grips with this! You shall take the white pieces and I shall take the black—your life having been, I'm sure, entirely virtuous—and mine—well, never mind!'

After a few games she mastered the idea of it fairly well, and his cheerful tolerance of her moves changed to a grim scowl as he hunched over the board and muttered into his beard.

'Are you sure you haven't played before, Miss Grey?'

'Quite sure. But I'm quite used to board games. Tom and I...' She fell silent at the thought of Tom, then resumed, 'Tom and I used to play at draughts.'

Harland glanced at her. He knew her quarrel with her brother still grieved her and he felt responsible for it. But there was nothing he could do. Tom Grey might come around in time, or he might not. If the fellow is anything like me, thought Dan with some regret, he won't.

Rachel also spent a good deal of time playing at simple card and board games with Pip. She had decided, wisely, that it would be best to make a friend of the child before beginning formal lessons. It was not difficult to make a friend of Pip because the child pined for companionship. As they walked along the stony beach, he prattled on endlessly until Rachel's ears fairly ached. The sea breezes and the new dimension to his life had already worked wonders on Pip. His father, noticing it, thought wryly that he should have done something like this before, found someone to take the child in hand. But there were not too many Miss Greys about in this world.

It was inevitable, however, that sooner or later some squall must disrupt the amicable alliance. When it came, its violence shook Rachel to the core.

She and Pip had been turning out a cupboard in the corner of the nursery. It appeared to have been used as a store for any items not wanted in the house, not only old toys and books, but weird and wonderful curios brought back by Harland from his voyages. Some of them Rachel set aside as useful illustrations to a future geography lesson. Some were so peculiar their use could not be guessed at all. There were even one or two oriental bronzes which were quite indecent.

'Goodness!' said Rachel, putting the prancing temple houris back in their cardboard box. 'I'm not surprised these were hidden away!'

Pip was quite convinced that the cupboard contained an elephant's tusk. He had seen it once, when searching for something else. But hunt in every box and bag though they did, no tusk appeared.

'I suppose,' said Rachel thoughtfully, staring up at the high top of the cupboard. 'It might have been put up there.'

She dragged up a chair and clambered up. The top of the cupboard was thick with dust, and obviously nothing had been moved up here for years. But there was a strangely shaped canvas container. Coughing and sneezing as clouds of dust flew up into her face, Rachel dragged it towards her and lifted it down.

'What is it?' asked Pip. 'It looks like a frying pan. It's got a handle.'

'I think,' she said slowly, 'it's a musical instrument. Just a moment.' The leather buckles which fastened the bag were stiff and dry, but at last she got it open.

'Why,' she exclaimed in delight and surprise, 'it's a guitar!'

'Can you play it, Miss Grey?' asked Pip hopefully.

'Just a little. But we shall have to buy new strings. They can only cost a few pence.' She touched the instrument gently. The shiny wooden case was painted with flowers, and she knew that a woman must once have played this.

Once it acquired its new strings, the guitar proved to be in very good condition. On top of the cupboard it had neither suffered damp nor warped in too much heat. With a little practice, Rachel found she could pick out a few tunes. Pip tried, but his hands were too small, though he struggled manfully until his fingers were quite sore.

But their joint efforts came to an abrupt end one rainy afternoon when they were seated on the window-seat in the schoolroom. Rachel was picking out 'What shall we do with the drunken sailor?' and Pip, who could only be brought to sing sea shanties, was singing along lustily, when their merry little musical party was summarily interrupted.

Rachel became aware that they had an observer. She stopped playing and looked up. Daniel Harland stood by the schoolroom door. She thought she had never seen anyone look so angry.

He said tersely, 'Run along, Pip!'

Pip bit his lip to see his father look so grim, and slid off the window-seat obediently. When they were alone, Dan walked across to where Rachel still sat with the guitar on her knee and ordered, 'Give me that.'

She held out the instrument towards him and asked, puzzled, 'What is wrong? Did you think it the wrong sort of song for Pip?'

He ignored her question. 'Where did you find this?'

'On top of a cupboard. I bought new strings...' Her voice trailed away.

'You had no business to do any such thing. If you want a musical instrument, I'll buy you a piano. You will not play this.'

It all seemed so illogical and stupid, and he did not see fit to offer any explanation. Rachel became annoyed. 'Why buy a piano I can't play? I can play the guitar. Only a little, I admit, but with prac——'

'I said you will not play it!' he shouted. Suddenly he whirled round, holding the instrument by the neck, and struck the body of it against the wall. It tore the wallpaper, knocked a dent in the plaster and the neck of the guitar snapped immediately, so that the instrument hung mangled from his hand. He dropped the smashed remains on to the floor. 'No one shall play it!' he said harshly. He turned and strode out, slamming the door behind him.

'Oh, dear,' said Rachel, and then, in crosser tones, 'What a nuisance! Such a lovely guitar, and broken beyond repair. And what a fit of temper!' She picked up the poor guitar and surveyed it gloomily. 'Well, this is ruined. It had best be thrown away.'

She took the guitar downstairs and gave it to Mrs Brereton. 'This is broken and had better go on the gardener's bonfire.'

'Why, bless us!' exclaimed Mrs Brereton, wiping her hands in her pinafore and taking the broken instrument gently from Rachel's hands. ''Tis Mrs Harland's guitar! I remember it well. He brought it back—the master—from Spain, it was. 'Twas the first thing he ever brought back for her from one of his sea voyages. She used to play it and sing so pretty.

He liked to listen to her. I thought it was gone with all the rest of her things. There, now—to think it was here all along.'

'I never thought,' said Rachel, dismayed. 'I never thought it might be Pip's mama's. Of course Captain Harland was distressed to see me playing it.'

Mrs Brereton pursed her lips. She set down the broken guitar and appeared to make up her mind to some difficult task.

'It's not my place to gossip, Miss Grey. But there's things you should know. The master and his wife, they fell out... It was a sad business. She was a pretty little thing, but had a mind just like a butterfly. It flitted here and there, and couldn't seem to stay on one thing for more than a minute. He was away a lot, the Captain. Had to be, being a seafaring man. She was bored, and the devil finds work for idle hands, as they say. There was—there was this one gentleman used to come a-calling. I was employed here as cook then. It was a much grander household than it is now. I tried to warn her how people would talk. She never would listen. "Oh, don't be so silly!" she'd say to me, and laugh. She was young and there—human nature being what it is...' Mrs Brereton shrugged and spread out her hands. 'The master found out when he came home, of course. I fancy she told him because she was frightened that someone else would. She believed she could wheedle him around, I do believe. Poor child. She had no more sense and no understanding of the man she was married to!' The housekeeper sighed. 'He's a powerful unforgiving man! He turned her out, there and then. Never would allow her back. He'd made up his mind to it, you see.'

'Like Tom,' said Rachel softly. 'Yes, I understand.'

Mrs Brereton lowered her voice and adopted a conspiratorial demeanour. 'Just between you and me, miss—don't you ever breathe a word of this, now—when he wasn't at home, she would come secretly every so often to see her baby. Because he wouldn't allow her near the child, you know. Wouldn't have her name spoken. She'd come quiet-like to the kitchen door and I'd smuggle her up the back stairs, because I hadn't the heart to close the door in her face, her wanting to see her own child. So I did let her stay a few minutes. He never knew of it. He'd have turned me away too, had he discovered it!'

'Poor soul,' said Rachel sadly. 'What became of her?'

'She died, miss. I saw her change. She got so thin and so poorly dressed. My heart fair bled to see her. But it would have been no use begging the master to help her. One time she did give me a letter for him. I fancy her money was quite gone, and the parish wouldn't help her because she was a married woman with a husband. But he tore it up unread in front of me when I handed it over, and ordered me never to accept another. The parish officers came when she died to say he must pay for the burying of her, since he was her lawful husband and the parish wouldn't bear the cost. She's buried up on the hill behind the city, at Purbrook. She lived there as a little girl. I like to think she's back there now among people who knew her as a little lass.'

This sad little tale—by no means an uncommon one—haunted Rachel for the rest of the day. Though Harland had only behaved as anyone would have expected him to, she found it churlish in him to deny his estranged wife any financial support, no matter how badly she might have behaved. A married woman had no right to her own property. Married women who had run away from their homes found scant sympathy from the parish. The law required that any aid given them was recovered from the husband. Since husbands in these circumstances were singularly loath to comply and seldom paid up, the parish officers usually took the more prudent line, and refused all aid in the first place. Surely Harland had not expected his wife to find work and support herself? What on earth could the poor creature have done? Young, probably very little educated, surrounded all her life by servants, she was helpless.

That evening it grew chilly. Rain still fell outside and a fire was lit in the drawing-room. She had not seen Dan for the rest of the day and, when she went downstairs that evening, she supposed, in the absence of cigar-smoke odour, that he might have gone to dine with Mr Grantham. Rachel sat by the fire and opened her book, but her eyes stared unseeingly at the print. She kept imagining that poor woman, creeping up the back stairs with the aid of a sympathetic servant, to peep at the baby from whom she had so ruthlessly been parted.

It was there that Dan came upon her later when he returned. She had not sent for candles, and sat in the firelight with the unread book open on her lap. The flames danced on her face and gown, and made the brass fender and fire-irons glisten. He was not a man who found it easy to admit his faults, but he knew himself at fault now and knew he must say so. But he hesitated, not only because he sought the words, but because he was strangely fascinated by the blue-black sheen of her abundant raven ringlets in the fire's glow.

Bella had been fair-haired and skinned, the sort of wishy-washy beauty fashionable at the time. He had been much taken when he first met her by her fairy-like daintiness and child-like humours. Too late he had discovered that these were not qualities altogether desirable in a wife. He and Bella had never sat and talked of an evening as he and Rachel had already done several times. What could they have talked about? Poor Bella's head had been as empty as a baby's rattle, with just enough lodged in it to make a musical tinkle when agitated.

Dan pulled himself together and walked across to her. At first she did not look up. He said, 'You think I behaved unreasonably today, and you are right. I am sorry.'

She looked up then. 'I am sorry, too, because I had no idea the guitar had belonged to Mrs Harland.'

'Mrs Brereton told you, I suppose?' he asked, and she knew he did more than ask if the housekeeper had told her the provenance of the guitar. He wanted to know if she knew the whole story.

Rachel said quietly, 'Yes, she did.'

'Well, there you have it . . .' Dan sat down opposite her and rested one foot on the fender, staring down into the flames. 'If you really want a guitar, I shall buy you another, of course. But to be frank, I'd rather you played some other instrument. I meant it when I said I'd buy a piano. I believe no respectable home is without one nowadays.'

'I couldn't play it,' she said honestly. 'It would take too long to learn. Pip and I shall sing unaccompanied. That will put the seagulls which roost on the roof to flight, if nothing else!'

He smiled faintly. 'I might buy the piano anyway. I believe Charlotte plays.'

Mrs Ellis. No doubt she had all the accomplishments.

'I have been calling on Mrs Ellis,' Dan went on. 'She promises she will return the visit one day soon. You had best tell Pip.'

Rachel raised her eyebrows. 'What shall I tell him? That she's coming to tea—or that you hope to marry her and she will be his new mama? Because if it's the latter, I think you should be the one to tell him.'

'Very well. When the time comes. Not yet.'

When the time comes. Grantham was right, thought Dan wearily, the whole idea was nonsense! One couldn't pick out a wife as one would pick out a new coat. Charlotte was an excellent woman, but perhaps it wouldn't work out, after all.

He did not know why he suddenly lacked courage at the thought of what had previously seemed an excellent plan. Dan gave himself a mental shake and told himself to show a bit of gumption. The only problem was that this courtship of Charlotte Ellis was taking longer than he had anticipated. Charlotte had an unexpected liking for sitting and chattering—that was, she expected him to chatter and he was rapidly running out of subjects of conversation. She also seemed to expect things like flowers. Not that he minded or was mean, but he tended simply to forget them, and had to dash to the florist at the last moment. A grown man of his age, arriving on a lady's doorstep clasping a wilting bunch of whatever flowers were left in the shop by the tardy time he got there, looked a perfect fool, in Dan's opinion. If he meant to marry Charlotte, then he had better close the deal as soon as possible, and then all this flower-buying and social chatter could stop!

'Yes,' he said aloud, suddenly and with such resolve that Rachel looked up at him in surprise. 'Pip does need a new mama—so I had better look lively and do something about it!' He leaned forward with his hands on his knees and added seriously, 'Look'ee, Miss Grey, I've been two months dancing attendance on Mrs Ellis, and she must have got my meaning by now. You can give me a woman's opinion. Do you think I should ask her? Straight off, I mean.'

'To marry you?' exclaimed Rachel. 'Goodness, I don't know! She had better meet Pip first.'

'Yes, yes, you are right.' He snapped his fingers. 'I'll arrange it.'

Rachel looked at him with some exasperation. He probably managed excellently afloat, but he hadn't the slightest notion how to go about anything on land. She had been harbouring unkind thoughts about him, after learning of his treatment of his late wife. But now she realised that what he had done had been in anger and without thinking through to the inevitable results of his actions. He probably regretted it, and it was his punishment that he must live with it. But it isn't Pip who needs taking in hand and polishing up! thought Rachel. It is his father, I do believe!

But something Harland had said had lodged in her head. He had spoken of Pip needing 'a new mama'. But Pip already had a mother, even though, sadly, she was dead. The point is, thought Rachel obstinately, that the child has not a single memory of his mama—who obviously loved him and risked coming here to see him. It's as if she never existed. Harland has no right to do that to the child. He might have quarrelled with his wife. The child had not.

The more she thought along these lines, the more she resolved to do something about it. She could not talk to Pip about his mother, because she knew nothing of her. Mrs Brereton did, but it would be unfair to ask the housekeeper to do something her employer would be so against. Because Dan would be furious if he found out. So much was clear.

'I know,' said Rachel. 'The first fine day we get, Pip and I shall go into the country.'

As luck would have it, two days later saw the sun beam down and the roads and hedgerows dry out.

'Now, then,' said Rachel to Pip, as she buttoned up his jacket. 'We are going to take a cab, Pip, and go out of the city and up on to the hills behind. They are made of chalk and very interesting. We shall go to a place called Purbrook, which I'm told is very pretty.' She wedged Pip's cap firmly on his head and took his hand. 'Come along!'

High upon Portsdown Hill the breeze blew straight in off the sea. Rachel and Pip tramped along the country lanes. Only a few weeks ago the notion of taking Pip on such a jaunt would have seemed unthinkable. But although they stopped at regular intervals for Pip to get his breath—and Rachel, too, if truth be told, since ladies' fashions were not designed for walking—Pip was clearly in his element away from the confines of the house in which he had been so long imprisoned. He filled his pockets with pieces of chalky rock from the subsoil to see if it really wrote like chalk when he got home, and sat at the top of steep slopes to slither down them in a way which did his pantaloons no good at all. They had brought apples with them, and sat on the dry, springy turf and ate them, looking out towards the sea. Here Pip was able to contribute his own grain of knowledge.

'Those buildings are forts, ma'am, built to keep Boney at bay!'

'Napoleon? Goodness. They must truly have feared to see him land here!'

'Yes, ma'am, but he never came,' said Pip, sounding disappointed. 'So we had to fight him at Waterloo instead. But you know, Miss Grey, it was Trafalgar that really counted.'

'Indeed, Pip?' No doubt the senior service had its own view of history.

'Yes, ma'am. Because you see, although he had a jolly good army, Boney always had a rotten navy. Not like ours. Ours is the best!' said Pip with sturdy patriotism.

'I understood Admiral Villeneuve to have been a most gallant gentleman and sailor,' she offered mildly.

'But he kept losing,' said Pip. 'And killed himself because he was dishonoured!'

'People sometimes make too much of honour!' said Rachel firmly. 'Don't throw that apple core away. It's untidy. Go and feed it to that horse over there in that field.'

The churchyard was small and the more remote corners overgrown. Directions from the sexton took them to the furthest corner of all and a mossy headstone on which the lichen had entered the carved lettering and made it almost illegible.

Rachel eyed the long grass with disapproval, and Pip leaned forward and traced the half-obscured lettering with his finger.

'Isa-bell-a Har-land.' Pip paused. 'Is it my mama, Miss Grey?'

'Yes, Pip.'

'I know her name was Isabella because Mrs Brereton told me so once, when I asked her. Should we have brought flowers, Miss Grey?'

Rachel looked about her and spied some wild flowers growing nearby. The sexton, when applied to, managed to produce an empty jam-jar from a shed.

'If we come again,' said Rachel, 'we'll bring proper flowers and a vase.'

'But she will like these flowers, won't she?' asked Pip anxiously, getting up from the jam-jar and dusting his knees.

'I'm sure she's very pleased with them,' Rachel said.

The following Sunday, when they returned in a party from church, Dan said, 'If you have a spare moment, Miss Grey, I'm sure Philip can divest himself of his own coat and wash his hands unsupervised.'

Her employer had been very quiet for the last two days, and Rachel followed him into the drawing-room with some apprehension. Both on the walk to church and on the walk home, he had spoken scarcely a word to her, and she knew the signs from many years of dealing with Tom. Captain Harland was seriously displeased.

Rather to her surprise, he poured two glasses of sherry, one of which he handed to her, saying briefly, 'Here, drink this.'

Presumably he felt she had some need to fortify herself. Rachel's heart, which had sunk to her toes, now leapt up in alarm. Was it possible some dreadful misfortune had befallen Tom and the school, and he was seeking some way of breaking it to her?

Dan sat down and stretched out his long legs, looking up at Rachel who stood before him. His features appeared more weather-beaten than ever, as if they had been carved out of oak. 'I had thought, Miss Grey, when we had our contretemps over the guitar, that you understood my feelings about my late wife, and my wish that there should be no attempt to bring her back to life in front of the child.'

He had discovered the trip to Purbrook. If he had been openly furious, as he had been over the guitar, Rachel could have faced him. But this was a different kind of anger. It ran deep, and it was cold and deliberate. She suddenly thought, he must have run his ship with a rod of iron. From the junior officers of the wardroom down to the Jack Tars before the mast, discipline must have been complete.

'Will you allow me to speak my mind, Captain Harland?' she asked, setting down her sherry glass before her shaking hand spilled the liquid and betrayed her alarm.

He nodded and waited.

'I understand your feelings about your late wife,' Rachel plunged into speech. 'And I do respect them, believe me. But she is still the child's mother! He has a right to his mother. He never had any quarrel with her. This—this complete shutting out of her, as if she never existed, it's unfair, and it's not good for Philip and it's not good for you.'

He drew in a sharp breath. 'Nevertheless, that's how I wish it to be. You deliberately chose to go against what you knew I would wish for my son. It was a deliberate attempt to deceive me, Miss Grey, and I had thought you more reliable than that!'

In a sense, he was right. Rachel said dully, 'Yes, I meant it for the best, but I should have discussed it with you first. I didn't because I knew you'd refuse—so I did deceive you. I dare say you wish me to leave.'

'By no means!' he said brusquely. 'I merely want you to follow my wishes in this very important matter. Now, then, there is to be no more of this putting flowers on the grave of a mother the child cannot remember, and who by her behaviour put herself outside the pale of decent society and forfeited any right to the name of mother!' His voice, until now under icy control, began to rise. She saw his hands tighten on the arms of his chair and the knuckles show white through the sun-bronzed skin.

Unwisely, in the face of these danger signs, Rachel attempted to pursue her argument. 'Whatever Mrs Harland did, and I don't make excuses for it, she still loved her baby——'

He leaned forward, his face contorted with rage, and roared, 'A woman who loves her child does not behave in a way which brings dishonour on the family name that child bears! My wife was an adulteress! Is that what you wish the child to know? Talk to him of his mother, and sooner or later you will be forced to answer questions you have no wish to hear, to tell him the whole story! It is better that Philip simply knows his mother is dead—and that she is never mentioned! Never, do you hear me?'

Shaken, she stammered, 'Y-yes...'

He leaned back in his chair and relaxed very slightly, but still tense in manner and voice continued, 'So it is not to happen again. I am the more determined this shall be so, because I hope Philip will learn to look upon Mrs Ellis as his mother. What you are doing can only confuse the boy. Do you understand me?'

'Yes,' Rachel repeated almost inaudibly.

'Good. Now, then, Mrs Ellis has kindly agreed to come and take tea here today, in order to meet Philip. Please have the boy ready at four.'

Rachel swallowed, her humiliation complete. 'Yes, sir.'

CHAPTER FIVE

By FOUR o'clock Pip was ready in so far as he was washed and dressed in his best and his hair had been brushed. But he was also as mutinous, awkward and generally uncooperative as only a small boy could be once he had set his mind to it. Rachel, who until now had found her charge a most amenable child, found him quite exasperating. But she was not without some sympathy. It was a frightening prospect for anyone to know that he was about to be put on show and accorded marks, as it were, for his behaviour and conversation. For a child it was the worse, because he did not know what dreadful consequences might follow his failing to pass the test, or why he was being obliged to go through it in the first place. Harland, to Rachel's private annoyance, had given Pip no inkling as to why Mrs Ellis had really come. Pip, an intelligent youngster, sensed very well that there was more afoot than had been explained to him. He felt he was being used in some way, and he disliked it.

'I don't want to go down and meet this lady,' he said for the tenth time, with jutting lower lip and ferocious scowl.

'It's to please your papa, Pip. You know you'd want to do that!' she wheedled.

'Why is this lady coming to tea with us? Why can't she have tea in her own house?'

'Now, Philip!' said Rachel, cutting short the increasingly embarrassing line of questioning. 'Let me hear your speech again.'

'I can't remember it.'

'That's untrue. It's only a short speech. I know you haven't had time to memorise very much. But I also know you have a very good memory, so let me hear you.'

Pip met Miss Grey's determined eyes and, with very bad grace, recited in a gabble, with no audible punctuation, 'I am very pleased to meet you ma'am it is very good of you to come and take tea with us how fortunate that the weather has remained so fine may I pass you a piece of cake?'

'I hope you are not going to say it all at once like that!' said Rachel sharply. 'And the bit about passing the cake comes once she's replied and everyone has settled down again.'

'She isn't going to kiss me, is she?' asked Pip in ill-disguised horror. 'Or pat my head?'

'I don't know. If she does, you must put up with it and not scowl like that. Now, come along!'

'I shan't recite,' said Pip, as they descended the staircase. 'I shall say, I don't know anything.'

'You know "St Agnes' Eve"—well, most of it.'

'No, I don't. I only know, "Ah, bitter chill it was..." After that, I've forgotten it. What kind of cake is there?' asked Pip, his mind suddenly shooting off at a tangent and a more optimistic note entering his voice.

'Two sorts, I saw the tray in the kitchen. Seed cake and sponge cake.'

'I don't like seed cake.'

'If seed cake is all that is left, then seed cake is what you will eat. Philip!' They paused at the bottom of the stairs. 'I am relying on you,' said Rachel. 'If you behave badly, it will reflect on me. Mrs Ellis will think I've taught you no better.'

She gave his jacket a last twitch and tidied a stray lock of fair hair, then tapped on the door.

The familiar drawing-room seemed somehow quite different. Although nothing about the furnishing was changed and the sun shone in brightly, it had gained a stiff and unwelcoming air and become an intimidating place. All the best china was out on the tea-tray, together with a silver teapot which she had not seen before. Rachel felt Pip shrink beside her and grasp her skirts as he too became aware of the strange new feeling in the air. The first person to meet her eye on entering was Dan, who rose to his feet, declaring, 'Ah, here is Philip!'

Rachel propelled Pip forward and, with her heart beating violently in her breast in a way she could not explain, turned towards the lady seated a little to her right.

Mrs Ellis was not altogether quite as she had visualised her from references to the lady made by Dan Harland. From all Harland had said, Rachel had supposed Mrs Ellis a motherly sort of body with no-nonsense taste in dress and a straightforward manner. But this was no such person! This was a very handsome woman of perhaps three or four and thirty, in a very fashionable gown layered with alternate flounces of daffodil yellow and pale green silk, a bonnet with a ruched silk brim lined within with sprays of artificial mimosa, and a lace shawl. A daffodil-coloured parasol leaned against her chair. Her hair, as much of it as could be glimpsed framing her face under the ruched bonnet, was auburn and she had a sharply tilting nose and large, slightly prominent blue eyes.

Mrs Ellis held out a gloved hand and asked, 'How do you do, Philip?' in tones of exquisite gentility.

Pip hesitated, was pushed again by his governess, sidled across the carpet, took the lady's hand and pronounced, 'How do you do, ma'am, how fortunate the weather is so fine—and why have you come to tea?'

His father looked as though he might explode, and Rachel wished to sink through the floor.

'Have you had a piece of cake?' continued Pip, grimly determined to get through the rest of his rehearsed speech by hook or by crook. 'There's seed cake and sponge cake, and the seed cake is very nice and I'm sure you'd want it. There's an awful lot of it,' he added gloomily, with a sidelong glance at the cake-stand.

Mrs Ellis raised a playful finger. 'Now, I spy a little fellow whose eyes are bigger than his tummy!'

'No, they're not!' said Pip indignantly. 'I'm not a little fellow. I'm twelve. I'm not small for twelve!' Passion entered his voice, and suddenly Rachel realised with dismay that the child was near to tears. 'I'm not small for my age. I'm not!'

'Philip!' said his father sharply. 'If you cannot behave you will have to be taken out again.'

'He's been so excited,' said Rachel hastily, 'about meeting you, ma'am.'

Mrs Ellis, whose expression had frozen during Pip's outburst, thawed marginally and murmured, 'Dear little chap...' but there was much less warmth in her tones.

'Thank you, Miss Grey,' said Dan. 'Perhaps you'd come and fetch Philip again in half an hour?'

Rachel started and realised it was time for her to withdraw. She left the room with considerable foreboding.

For half an hour she sat upstairs wondering how it was all going. At least Pip did not summarily reappear, expelled from the drawing-room in disgrace. But when she redescended at half-past four to collect her charge, she found that the atmosphere in the drawing-room had worsened and was charged and tense. Mrs Ellis was clearly preparing to leave. Pip stood in the middle of the floor looking quite miserable and very tired. As soon as he saw Rachel, he scuttled across the carpet to her and grasped her hand, burying his head in her skirts.

His father, very red in the face, said sharply, 'Come and take proper farewell of Mrs Ellis, Philip.'

'Shan't!' said a muffled and desperate voice from the folds of Rachel's dress.

'Pip!' she whispered. 'Come along.'

Somehow Pip was dragged across the carpet and persuaded to mutter a goodbye. But as soon as it was done he turned and fled the room.

'He is not used to company, ma'am,' said Rachel as calmly as she could, meeting Mrs Ellis' eye. 'And inclined to be excitable by disposition. He's highly strung. It has all been a little too much for him.'

'Indeed?' said Mrs Ellis coldly. 'You have not long been his governess, Miss Grey?'

'No, ma'am, not above six weeks.'

'Miss Grey—has accomplished a great deal in such a short time,' said Dan, a little curtly.

'This is your first post as governess, I believe?' pursued Mrs Ellis, her prominent gaze running over Rachel and noting every detail of her dress. 'Forgive me, my dear. I do think that ringlets are not quite *comme il faut* in a governess. A plainer hair-fashion... You do not mind my mentioning it?'

'No, ma'am,' said Rachel tightly. It made no difference if she did. This would no doubt prove the first of many criticisms if she remained here after Mrs Ellis became Mrs Harland. As a lowly governess she must learn to accept them unflinchingly. Dan had turned aside, and she could not see his face at all. She murmured, 'I must go and find the child...' and left hurriedly.

Pip had shut himself in the schoolroom and refused to come out. Rachel decided to leave him there. The child was thoroughly upset and would have to be given time to calm down. Before this could be achieved, however, his father appeared on the landing before the schoolroom door and tried the handle. Finding it locked, he ordered sharply, 'Philip, open this door at once.'

'Won't!' cried a desperate small voice through the panels.

'Don't disobey me, sir!' shouted Dan furiously, striking the door a resounding blow with the flat of his hand. 'Do as I say, and open up at once.'

'Captain Harland!' called Rachel, hurrying towards him. 'Please—not now.'

'Go back to your sitting-room, Miss Grey,' said Dan brusquely. 'You have nothing to do here!'

'The child is distressed——'

'He is distressed? *I* have been humiliated! I told you to have him ready. Is that the best you could do? Lord knows what Charlotte thought. Philip!' Dan shook the door-handle furiously. 'Open this damn door at once.'

'Don't swear at the child!' stormed Rachel, darting forward and pushing herself between Harland and the door, forcing him to release the handle. 'It's not his fault. The child isn't a fool. He knows something is afoot which is going to affect him, and it concerns Mrs Ellis. You should have told him of your intentions regarding that woman.'

'By "that woman" you refer to Mrs Ellis, I take it?' Dan snarled at her. 'Mrs Ellis is a most refined and well-bred lady. The child behaved like a gutter urchin!'

'Rubbish!' cried Rachel, stamping her foot. 'He's upset. That—lady—doesn't know the first thing about children, that was obvious! Anyone can see the child is sensitive——'

'Sensitive?' shouted Dan, thrusting his bearded face into hers. 'He is confounded impudent!'

'Captain Harland,' said Rachel coldly, drawing herself up, 'kindly go back downstairs until you have your temper under control!'

For a moment she really thought he was going to have some sort of fit. But then he whirled round on his heel and strode away. Rachel leaned back against the still closed door with a sigh of relief.

Pip emerged from the schoolroom at bedtime, white-faced and red-eyed, and said miserably, 'I've been sick.'

'Where, Pip?'

'In the waste-paper bin in the schoolroom. I'm very sorry. I couldn't help it.' His voice trembled.

'Oh, my dear,' said Rachel, dropping on her knees and putting her arms round him. 'Of course you couldn't. Now, hop into bed, Pip, and I'll bring you some milk. Don't fret about the mess; I'll clean it up.'

Daniel Harland, who had been standing in shadow at the bend of the staircase, listening and watching, turned and went quickly and quietly back down again, to avoid meeting her on the stair.

Pip sat up in bed and drank his milk, watched by Rachel who sat on the quilt. When he had finished, he handed the cup to her and said politely, 'Thank you.'

'I hope you're feeling a bit better, Pip.'

'I'm all right,' said Pip. 'I didn't like that lady. And she didn't like me.'

'Oh, Pip, I'm sure——' Rachel began, but he interrupted her, leaning forward in the bedclothes, his little face flushed.

'No, she didn't!'

He showed signs of becoming agitated again, so she soothed him as best she could, tucked him up, kissed his forehead and left him to a good night's sleep, the best thing for him in the circumstances.

Dan Harland stood outside the room. Rachel gave a start when she saw him and, holding up her candle so that the light fell on his face, whispered, 'What do you want?'

'To say goodnight to Philip. Have you any objection?'

'Not if you only mean to say goodnight. But if you mean to grumble, I object very strongly. He's only just settled down. He's been in a terrible state. He was sick. It was just nerves.'

'I don't mean to grumble, as you put it—but if you think it wiser, I'll leave it till tomorrow.'

'Perhaps you should,' Rachel said.

He turned aside, then paused and asked, 'Won't you come downstairs for a little while? It's not so very late. This has been a most difficult day.'

He sounded tired. Disappointed, too, thought Rachel. He had cherished such high hopes of the impression the child would make on his intended. She went downstairs with him, and in the drawing-room he said, 'Perhaps we could have some tea or something. I recollect, when you lived with your brother, you always had the tea-tray in of an evening.'

'Yes, because it was done when we were children. It's old-fashioned now, I suppose. Mrs Brereton has had extra to do today, and I don't like to bother her further.'

'I don't know what happened when I was a child,' Dan said, pushing his hands into his pockets and wandering away towards the fireplace. 'I left home at Pip's age. Don't remember much before that. We had a pond in the garden I used to sail paper boats on. Like Pip, I had a fancy to be in the navy, you see. Unlike Pip, I actually found myself afloat! The difference between dream and reality was quite a shock.' Dan looked up at her. 'I am no great hand at managing domestic affairs, Miss Grey, as you will have seen. No great hand at bringing up the child. No great hand at any damn thing, really, except sea-going matters. Little use they are nowadays.'

The drawing-room seemed quite different now to what it had been that afternoon, and it was not only

because of the subdued light. It was as if some op-
pressive force had been removed. Mrs Ellis was no
longer there. Her absence was as tangible as her
presence had been. Dan's manner, the longer the time
since her departure became, eased and his anger
abated. It occurred to Rachel that not only Pip had
been on trial. His father, too, had felt himself put to
some test. He'd failed it, and from that stemmed his
anger. Although his burly frame looked as im-
movable as ever, Rachel sensed the inner frustration
he could not express in either words or actions, and
his bitter disappointment that this day, of which he
had obviously hoped so much, had gone so badly.
She fancied she could distinguish a note of resignation in his voice, but perhaps it was only her fancy.
And yet, it was as if she had some instinctive
knowledge of this man and his innermost emotions.
Rachel moved towards him impulsively and put out
her hand to touch his sleeve.

'You worry so much and are so conscientious—why,
you are quite like Tom in that way! But things cannot
be perfect. No child ever was! And surely, if Mrs Ellis
is to come here as your wife, it is better she see the
child as he really is, a normal little boy—and not some
totally unnatural creature on his best behaviour!'

'Poor Pip,' said his father suddenly. 'He was so
worried that he would be left nothing but seed cake!
He kept trying to feed it to Charlotte, and telling her
not to eat the sponge cake, there was something
dreadfully wrong with it!'

Without warning, Dan collapsed on to the nearest
chair and put both hands over his face. 'I didn't know
whether to be angry or to laugh. I'm sure, if Charlotte
had not been so affronted, I should have laughed out

Take 4 Medical Romances

Mills & Boon Medical Romances capture the excitement, intrigue and emotion of the busy medical world. A world of love and romance... often interrupted by love and romance...

We will send you 4 BRAND NEW MEDICAL ROMANCES absolutely **FREE** plus a cuddly teddy bear **and** a surprise mystery gift, as your introduction to this superb series.

At the same time we'll reserve a subscription for you to our Reader Service. Every two months you could receive the 6 latest Medical Romances delivered direct to your door **POST AND PACKING FREE**, plus a **free** Newsletter packed with competitions, author news and much, much more.

What's more there's no obligation, you can cancel or suspend your subscription at any time. So you've nothing to lose and a whole world of romance to gain!

FREE

Doctor from the Past

Your Free Gifts!

We'll send you this cute little tan and white teddy bear plus a surprise mystery gift when you return this card. So don't delay.

Fill in the Free books coupon overleaf

FREE BOOKS CERTIFICATE | EXTRA BONUS

YES please send me my 4 FREE Medical Romances together with my Teddy and mystery gift. Please also reserve a special Reader Service subscription for me. If I decide to subscribe, I shall receive 6 new books every two months for just £7.50, post and packing free. If I decide not to subscribe, I shall write to you within 10 days. The free books and gifts will be mine to keep in any case.

I understand that I am under no obligation whatsoever – I can cancel or suspend my subscription at any time simply by writing to you. I am over 18 years of age.

We all love surprises, so as well as the FREE books and Teddy, here's an intriguing mystery gift especially for you. No clues send off today!

7A9D

Name: _____
(BLOCK CAPITALS PLEASE)

Address: _____

_____ Postcode _____

Signature _____

The right is reserved to refuse an application and change the terms of this offer.
You may be mailed with other offers as a result of this application. Offer expires December

NO
STAMP
NEEDED

Reader Service
FREEPOST
PO Box 236
Croydon
Surrey
CR9 9EL

SEND NO MONEY NOW

loud!' He gave a muffled snort. 'He said it was poisoned!'

'What?' exclaimed Rachel incredulously, watching her employer's shoulders begin to shake.

'Yes, yes! I swear! He told Charlotte that Mrs Brereton was quite mad and frequently put poison in the dinner.' Dan let his hands fall and leaned back in his chair, looking up at her startled face. 'Mark me— that child is a monster!'

'He is most certainly not!' she said indignantly. 'He has imagination.'

'Imagination, you call it?' The mirth left Harland's face as suddenly as it had appeared there. 'Lord knows what Charlotte thought. Nothing good.'

Rachel made no reply to this, and after a moment he went on, in an altered tone, 'I am sorry about the— I am sorry Charlotte said what she did about your hair.'

'Oh, that,' said Rachel. 'It's the least awful thing which has happened today. She's right, anyway. I have to learn to be a governess. I'll brush all the ringlets out tomorrow.'

'No!' Dan leaned forward and spoke quite vehemently. 'I like them. I like your hair the way it is. Leave it. I like the curls.'

'Thank you, but you cannot take my part against her, you know.'

He got to his feet. In the shadows she could not see his face clearly. The pair of candles on the chimney-shelf and the fading glow of the fire did little to dispel the room's gloom. Dan stretched out his hands and took hold of hers.

'Do you think me a most confounded fool, Rachel?' His voice was quiet, a little husky.

'Of course not!' she protested. But she was both startled and confused at hearing him call her by her Christian name. No man who was not a relative or in his dotage had ever done so, and she was not sure how she should react. She tried to tell herself that it was no different to hearing her name from Tom. But it *was* different. The sound of it on Dan's tongue seemed to invest it with a meaning it never had before, and the syllables to vibrate in the very pit of her stomach. She opened her mouth to say, You should call me Miss Grey, as is proper; but for some reason she was reluctant to do so, and was almost avid to hear him say it again. Ashamed of her weakness, uncertain and nervous, she began to wish she had let him ring for tea so that Mrs Brereton might come in now and disturb them, obliging him to release her hands. To withdraw them herself from his was what she should do. But with his use of her name a strange paralysis afflicted her so that, though she knew what she must do, she could not do it. Thus she remained standing where she was, close to him in the firelight's glow, both hands fast imprisoned in his broad clasp.

'You are quite cold,' he said in some concern, mistaking the shiver which ran through her and was communicated to him through her fingertips touching his palm. He began to chafe her hands gently, making things a hundred times worse and leaving her feeling so weak at the knees that she thought she must surely subside down on to the carpet at his feet if he didn't stop. 'Are there no fires lit upstairs?'

'Only—only in Pip's room and in the schoolroom,' she faltered. 'I told the girl not to light mine when she brought up the coal-scuttle this morning. It seemed wasteful.'

'What nonsense! I don't intend you to freeze for the want of a few shillings' worth of coal! It's to be lit tomorrow, mind.'

'If you wish.' She gave her hands a little tug, but he still held fast to them.

'I want to say something to you, Rachel. No, don't try and get away. Stay and listen.'

'Yes?' she whispered.

'We have not seen altogether eye to eye these last few days. I'm sorry for it. I meant what I said when I told Charlotte you had accomplished a great deal in a short time with Pip. I thank you for it. What I didn't say to Charlotte was that you have accomplished a great deal with me, too.'

'Captain Harland——' Rachel began anxiously.

'You see, I am awkward ashore,' he hurried on, not allowing her to interrupt. 'And being in charge of a ship of the line does one no good. I have become too accustomed to have people jump to my orders and to give those same orders without explanation. You said I should have explained better to Philip what this afternoon was all about, and so I should. And I should have explained better to you, when you first came— about my marriage. If I had done both those things, all the upsets which have taken place this last week would not have happened. You will stay, won't you, Rachel?'

His grip on her fingers tightened as he stooped over her. 'You will put up with my being so curmudgeonly, and stop here? I dare not ask it for my sake, I ask it for the boy's—but it is for my sake, too.'

'But of course I will stay...' she faltered.

'Bless you,' he said, and, raising her fingers to his lips, kissed them.

'Captain Harland!' she gasped. She jerked her fingers free at last, stumbled backwards and, with a sudden complete loss of composure, grasped her skirts in both hands and fled from the firelit drawing-room.

Mr Grantham, proceeding along the high street, tipping his hat to the occasional acquaintance, stopped short at the sight of the brougham drawn by the smart pair of matched bays. It stood outside Simpson's, the draper's, awaiting its owner. It was familiar to the magistrate. He crossed the road and raised his stick in salutation to the coachman who touched his hat. Mr Grantham waited by the carriage door and was rewarded by the jangle of the shop doorbell and the bowing figure of Mr Simpson as he showed out a valued customer.

'Mrs Ellis?' said Grantham, taking off his top hat. 'Good day to you, ma'am.'

'Why, dear Mr Grantham,' said Mrs Ellis, extending a kid-gloved hand, 'how very nice to see you.'

'I was taking a stroll, dear lady, and noticed your carriage. As a matter of fact, I was intending to come and call on you, but I've been a little busy of late—no shortage of minor lawbreakers, I'm afraid!'

He eyed the lady's obviously brand-new carriage-dress of green velvet skirt and a tightly fitting little bodice which looked like a highly romanticised huntsman's jacket. The weather had grown cooler this week, and light dresses no longer did for out of doors. Her bonnet had a brim lined with shot taffeta pleats and a curled feather, and he thought—that was sent down from a London milliner or I'm a Dutchman! A handsome woman and a very expensive one. Well, no doubt Dan Harland could afford to pay the bills which would arrive on his doorstep once he was married to her. But it would not stop at taffeta bonnets and yards of lace such as were obviously contained in the package held by Simpson, who hovered obsequiously in the background. The lady was used to her own carriage and would want to keep it. She would want to travel up to London and probably to the continent. She would give lavish and excellent dinners to large numbers of guests. If Harland thought he was marrying into a quiet domestic sort of life, he was wrong. And in his new married life there would be little room for the child of his first union.

'I am going your way,' said Mrs Ellis. 'Let me take you and we can talk while we drive along.'

'You are too kind, ma'am.'

He handed her gallantly into her carriage, pulled himself in to join her, and took the package which Simpson, scurrying forward, handed up.

'Much appreciate your custom, madam!' said Mr Simpson. Four shillings and sixpence worth of lace. A good sale, that.

He was rewarded with a gracious nod of the head. The carriage rolled forward.

'Now, then, ma'am,' said Mr Grantham in his bluff way. 'I'm all agog to hear your news. You've called on my friend Harland, I believe, and made the acquaintance of the youngster. How did you find the boy?'

'Thoroughly spoiled!' said Charlotte, disposing her velvet skirts neatly about her. 'That is not his father's fault, of course. I'm sure Daniel has done his best, but he doesn't know how to handle a child. As a result, the imp runs circles round his papa. As for that so-called governess...'

'Ah, Miss Grey…' murmured Mr Grantham. 'I am a little acquainted with her.'

Charlotte Ellis cast him a quick glance and amended in her head the next few sentences she had meant to speak. 'The governess, Grey, is all very well. Quite a genteel sort of girl. But again, not what is needed to bring the child into line.'

'And what do you suggest, ma'am?' asked Mr Grantham blandly.

'Boarding-school, my dear Grantham! Depend upon it, the best and only answer! Some establishment where the discipline is strict, the food plain, the dormitories are not overheated and the children are toughened up. The child Philip is puny. He needs fresh air, plenty of manly sports, cold baths and a plain diet. He has been mollycoddled.'

'You don't feel, dear lady, that being so unused to the company of other boys, especially the sort of older boy who all too frequently plays the bully in establishments of the sort to which you refer——'

'Oh, he'll get used to it!' said Mrs Ellis shortly. 'My youngest brother, William, got used to it when he was sent away to school. He was just such a headstrong child, but school knocked it out of him in no time. He came back as quiet as a mouse. I shall make it my business to seek out a school for Philip Harland. Somewhere a fair distance away, so that he will not be forever travelling back and forth at holiday times. Such a nuisance. Yorkshire might do very well. He shall be packed off at thirteen and reappear at sixteen, that's my intention. And then the navy can have him.'

'You think,' said Mr Grantham mildly, 'that his father will agree to all this?'

She put her hand on his arm and smiled charmingly at him. 'My dear Grantham, Daniel dotes upon the boy, but he can be brought to see how misguided his devotion is. He does the boy no favour. Philip's education is minimal. He hasn't a scrap of Latin. That will have to be made up. Six months at a crammer should do it. It's amazing what the dullest and most obstinate boy can learn in six months if he knows he will be beaten if he doesn't learn it! You shall see, I shall talk Daniel into letting the boy go inside a month. He will see it is all for the best. One must be a little cruel to be kind. Children need discipline, and discipline is what Philip Harland shall have. Only leave it with me.'

'You are a resolute woman, ma'am,' said Mr Grantham.

'Indeed I am!' said Charlotte frankly. 'And I am quite clear in my own mind what I want.'

Sally Casey was a child of the slums. Frail in build, she was nevertheless wiry and active, and her mind was as sharp as a needle. But in the back streets she had early learned that brute force often carried the day. It was ever-present. In the home or in the street, violence, drunkenness and debauchery of every kind were everyday events. To Sally, the quiet, orderly home of Schoolmaster Grey and his sister—afore she upped and left so sudden—was as she had always imagined heaven. There was plenty to eat. No one shouted. No one struck you. No one got drunk and left empty bottles lying about. It was wonderfully clean—no cockroaches and not even a single flea or clothing louse to make your life a misery. There were carpets on the floor and a fire in the kitchen. There were pictures on the walls. Real pictures with paint. Not crudely coloured printed sheets. Sally was the happiest she had ever been in her short life. She never sighed for her old home and her brothers and sisters. Her one fear was that all this could suddenly end, and she would be sent back to her old life.

Even the schoolmaster was not so bad on his own home ground. Sally had always been afraid of him in school, but at home Mr Grey proved less of an ogre. He didn't like Sally to run up and down the stairs and make a noise, or bring in mud on her boots. But he did not mind her playing hop-scotch on the flagged stone yard behind the house and had even, one evening, brought a piece of chalk from school and marked out numbers on the flags for her.

'Now, then, Sally,' said Tom, when he had accomplished this task and tidily returned the chalk to his waistcoat pocket. 'When I call out a number, say, ten—you hop on any number of squares provided the total of the numbers written on them does not exceed ten. Do you understand? For instance, you may hop on three, four and three again.'

Sally, whose arithmetic had always been a weak point, improved immensely under this scheme, and could reckon up in her head with great accuracy and at speed in no time.

This afternoon, a much warmer one than there had been all that week, Sally was in charge of the house. Mr Grey was at school and Hannah had gone to the butcher. Sally had left the back door open so that she could hear if any visitor rang at the front door—which was unlikely—and passed her time hopping about her hop-scotch court, singing to herself. Totally engrossed, she failed to hear the squeak of the back gate.

She did not realise anyone was there until a dark shadow fell across her numbered flagstones. She looked up, expecting Hannah. But it was not Hannah.

''Ello, Sal,' said Jed Casey agreeably, closing the yard door behind him. 'All alone, is you, then?'

'Hello, Uncle Jed,' said Sally nervously, backing away from his shambling, unkempt form. 'He's not here, is schoolmaster, if you wanted him. Hannah will come back soon.'

'Oh, I'm not anxious to see schoolmeester,' said Jed, his eyes moving to the open kitchen door. 'Come over here, Sal.'

'What do you want?' mumbled Sally.

'Nothing, come here, like I said.'

Sally edged towards him. Jed's large, calloused and grimy hand shot out and grasped her thin arm in a vicious grip. 'Don't start caterwauling now! I ain't going to do you no harm. Not if you're a good girl and do like I say. You hear me?'

'Yes,' whispered Sally, tears starting to her eyes from the pain in her arm. 'What you want, Uncle Jed? I wish you'd go away!'

He gave her a shake. 'That's nice, that is! I come ter see you, Sal, and that's what you says to me! Well, let's see what else you got to say. Tell us, now, Sal— schoolmeester, does he keep school's money about the house?'

Sally's pale little face, which had been as white as a sheet, now flushed scarlet, and Jed chuckled. 'I see he does. Know where it is, Sal?'

'No!' she whispered desperately.

Her reward was to be shaken until she cried out in terror and her arm hurt so much, she thought it must

be broken. 'Now,' said Jed, 'we try again. Where's
he keep it, Sal?'

'In a big black box,' she gasped. 'But I dunno where
the key is, honest.'

'Show us the box!' ordered Jed curtly.

Sally burst into tears. 'I daren't! I shall be blamed!
I shall be sent away! I shan't live here no more and
they'll put me in prison!'

'Not if you does like I say. You says, you was sitting
out here in the sun, all alone, and you fell asleep,
leaving back door open. You didn't see nothing, right?
Nothing and no one! Now, you take me to that box,
Sal, or it will be the worse for you! Go on, now, before
the old woman comes back!'

He gave her a hefty shove and sent her stumbling
towards the door. Sally, tears streaming down her face,
led him to the parlour and the school's japanned cash-
box on the sideboard.

'Hmm,' said Jed. 'Don't need no key. Break that
open easy with a penknife or a bit of rock.' He picked
it up and shook it. 'Nice and heavy. Got a few guineas
in there, I warrant!' Watched by the petrified Sally,
he carried the box out into the yard and set it down.
The iron poker used to stir the kitchen stove served
to smash the lock. Jed threw back the lid, stuffed the
contents quickly into his pockets, glanced round and,
picking up the box, threw it behind the pile of stacked
kindling. 'You just tells your story!' he ordered the
frightened child. 'You was asleep, you saw nothing!'

He let himself out of the yard gate and set off
rapidly down the road. He was not worried about the
kid. If she had any sense, she'd tell it just like he'd
told her. Even if she told the truth, there was only her
word. Jed had three or four good friends ready to

swear he had spent the afternoon throwing dice down on the waterfront and had never left them.

'Good day's work,' said Jed to himself cheerfully. He turned into the nearest public house and downed half a pint of neat gin, just to celebrate.

CHAPTER SIX

PIP'S nervous upset led to a return of his nightmares, which he had not suffered for some weeks. Nearly every night, Rachel was awakened by hearing him cry out. She would jump out of bed and hurry along to his room to soothe him and settle him down again. By day Pip was listless and irritable. He would not learn his lessons, and wanted only to copy maps from the gazetteer. Inevitably, her own sleep disturbed and her concentration constantly challenged by day, Rachel became exhausted. It was that particular kind of exhaustion which afflicts anyone who has to deal with a fretful, wakeful child. Much as her eyes itched and her brain grew sluggish from weariness, she could not sleep herself. She lay awake, tossing restlessly on her pillows, half listening for Pip's call and half-prey to her own confused and tormented thoughts.

Charlotte Ellis' pale face, protruding blue eyes and pointed, tilting nose danced before her in the darkness. The prospect of Charlotte entering this house as its mistress before very long seemed to be a little short of a recipe for disaster.

Pip will not take to her, and most decidedly she's taken against Pip! Rachel thought, pushing back damp locks of tangled hair from her burning forehead. She will find some excuse to get the child out of the way. Even if she can't bring that about immediately, she will find some way to be rid of me!

She did not doubt Charlotte's ability to achieve both these objectives. But the thing which worried her more than either was that Dan Harland himself would be sure to be made wretchedly unhappy by his choice of wife. For a while, Rachel wondered how he could even have considered marriage to Charlotte in the first place. But, thinking it over, she decided that the idea must have originated with the lady.

'She has planted the notion in his head and let him think it's his own idea!' muttered Rachel resentfully. 'She wants a husband. To be a widow is inconvenient. It restricts her social life. She wants to shine in mixed company, and it's difficult to do that and keep one's reputation without a husband in the background!'

Rachel would mull all this over in increasing frustration and eventually sit up and thump the pillows, declaring, 'I can't help it! If he's set on it, he'll do it! Why should I care?'

But she did care. Her heart became a lump of lead in her chest every time she thought of Charlotte. She tried to tell herself it was because of her attachment to Pip—which had grown deep and sincere in the short time she had cared for him—that she felt this way. But she knew it was not only because of Pip. It was because of Dan, and it was because of herself.

Wide awake in the midst of yet another restless night, Rachel threw aside the bedclothes and searched with her bare toes on the floor for her slippers. Her head ached abominably and her tongue stuck to the roof of her mouth with thirst. She managed to relight her bedside candle, and threw a light shawl around her shoulders before taking up the candlestick in her left hand and letting herself out of the room and into the dark corridor beyond.

It was well past midnight and the house was blank-
eted in the smothering darkness of dead of night when
everything in it sleeps. Yet it was not completely quiet.
A myriad tiny noises were audible. Wood creaked in
changing night temperatures. A tree rustled its leaves
against the window and tapped on the panes with twig
fingers. Coals apparently long dead on abandoned
fireplaces fell in upon one another unexpectedly with
a dry, husky rattling as the faintly smouldering cinders
were sieved through the grating into the ashpan below.
Rachel put an ear to Pip's door, but he seemed to be
sleeping soundly tonight. She hoped that meant he
was getting over his upset.

Until the next time! she thought gloomily. Until she
comes again!

She continued on her way to the kitchen and the
glass of water she sought, cautiously descending the
main staircase. At the foot of it the longcase clock,
invisible in a dark corner, sent her heart leaping into
her mouth by suddenly striking a single deep note.
As its echo faded in the empty hall, her ear caught a
new sound, a creak—too loud to be settling wood,
and caused by someone moving behind a door of the
room to her right.

Oh, dear heaven, an intruder! thought Rachel, her
heart giving another great painful leap of alarm. She
crept past the door and made her way to the drawing-
room further down the hall. Its door had been left
ajar, and a quick glance round by the feeble, flick-
ering light of her candle revealed nothing amiss in
here. Rachel selected the polished brass poker from
the fire-irons and returned to the hall.

With candle in one hand and poker in the other,
she found herself in something of a fix, but solved it

by putting down the candle on an occasional table. Grasping the poker firmly, Rachel turned the doorknob with her free hand and peered into the room beyond.

The fire in here had been reawakened. It burned sullenly and a dull red glow bathed the room. In it, she saw a shadowy figure standing by a cupboard on the further side of the room. Rachel pushed open the door and demanded loudly, 'Who is that? What are you doing?'

The figure started, swore, swung round and, as it did so, let fall something from its hand. It shattered on the floor with a deafening crash.

'Rachel?' came Dan's voice. 'What the devil are you doing, creeping about at this hour?'

'Oh!' gasped Rachel, both relieved and embarrassed. 'It's only you, after all. I thought it was a burglar!'

She stepped forward a little, but he ordered, 'Wait there—there's broken glass!'

He moved towards a table, and after a moment the bright flame of an oil-lamp lit the room. It revealed Rachel still standing in the doorway in her nightgown and shawl, and still grasping the poker in a business-like fashion.

'You can put that down,' he said briefly.

She muttered, 'Oh, yes...' and looked about her a little helplessly. For the want of a better solution, she leaned the weapon against the wall.

He was fully dressed himself, though in his shirt-sleeves, and had obviously not gone to bed at all. She thought he looked dishevelled but, conscious of her own lightly clad appearance, drew the shawl more tightly about her and offered, 'I was on my way to the kitchen. I thought everyone was in bed.'

He gave a grunt by way of reply.

She asked more curiously, 'What are you doing?'

'Having a quiet drink. Solving my problems with the aid of a drop of the Liffey water, as our Irish friends would have it!'

Then she saw that the broken glass on the carpet was the remains of a cut-glass decanter, and at the same time the smell of the spilled liquor struck her nostrils. The bright light of the oil-lamp also showed that his face had a flushed look, and his voice seemed slightly slurred to her ear.

'I'll fetch a pan and brush!' she said quickly, turning to go on her errand.

'Leave it!' he ordered sharply. 'Let Mrs Brereton see to it in the morning.'

'But I can——'

'I said, leave it be!' he almost shouted. As she stared at him, he gestured towards a chair and added, 'Sit down there. Go on!'

Rachel seated herself cautiously. He seemed so unlike his normal self that she began to wonder if she ought not to have kept the poker by her, after all. He kicked some of the glass aside with his toe and, glancing sideways at her, asked truculently, 'Never seen me drink, have you?'

'No,' she admitted. 'Only the occasional glass of wine.'

'I'm not a drinking man—not on a regular basis. Not any more.'

'Were you once?' The question slipped out before she could stop herself.

'Oh, aye, once...' He scowled moodily into the hearth. 'I'd stay away from it for a while, then shut myself up and drink myself insensible. Not a good way to go on. I've not done it for a long time. This——' he waved his hand dismissively at the broken decanter '—this is nothing.'

An old bad habit, conquered with difficulty, but reappearing under deep emotional stress.

'What troubles you?' she asked quietly.

'You do.'

Dan moved across the carpet towards her and bent over her chair. He put out his hand and caught at a lock of her black hair, tumbling loose over her shoulders. 'You do, damn it, Rachel!' he repeated thickly. 'From the moment you first came to this house, no, before that——'

She could smell the whisky on his breath now, and stammered, 'Don't—you shouldn't, can't——'

'How, can't? I'm flesh and blood, Rachel, and so are you—look at me, dammit, when I'm telling you what——'

Rachel threw up her hand and struck away his, which had clasped her hair and now fumbled clumsily at her shoulder.

'You're telling me nothing! It's not you talking, it's the drink.'

'Oh, the demon drink, is it?' He caught her wrist. 'Don't be alarmed, dear respectable Miss Grey, at finding yourself all alone with this most disreputable, drunken fellow! The governess...' Dan chuckled. 'Charlotte has taken a dislike to you, Rachel. She smells a rival! She calls you "Grey", just that. "Grey is too young and flighty!" she told me. She thinks your being here improper. Flighty, Rachel! What do you think of that?' He began to laugh, and her alarm was replaced by anger.

Rachel pulled her wrist free and exclaimed energetically, 'I don't care what she says! When she comes here, I shall leave—and that will be an end to it.'

'No need for that . . .' Dan put one arm either side of her, imprisoning her in her chair. 'You'll always have a place in this household, Rachel. What it is, now, that's up to you. These things arrange themselves in households all over the country. Arrange themselves for mutual convenience, I mean . . .'

'I'll excuse your speaking in this way, because I believe you drunk!' Rachel said tightly. 'But I won't allow you to go on. Take your arm away and let me leave!'

'Temper, Rachel!' He clicked his tongue reproachfully. 'And I know you do have a temper. What else seethes and bubbles under that prim exterior? Why don't you stop pretending and be yourself?'

Be herself? And what was that? Miss Grey, the teacher of the Ragged School, the governess—or was she that shadowy, elusive creature, that other Rachel Grey who asserted herself at unexpected and unwished moments, who whispered strange and shocking things she had no wish to hear, prevented her from doing what she should, and who filled her sleeping brain with wild and fanciful dreams in the small watches of the night?

She said aloud doggedly, 'I am me. I'm what I want to be.'

'No, you are what Tom Grey has made you!' he retorted vehemently. 'A sermonising and self-righteous old spinster like himself!'

Waves of anger flowed over her both at the unkindness of this description of herself and the insult to Tom. Yet the schoolmistress in her made her retaliate sharply, 'Tom cannot be a spinster but a bachelor, and you are not only wrong but muddled!'

'I said spinster and I mean spinster!' Dan declared. 'A bachelor is a fellow with blood in his veins and fire in his belly. Tom Grey has neither, and is a real old woman if ever I met one. All he lacks is a crocheted shawl and a glass of ratafia! But wait a little—aha!' Dan nodded with the gleeful satisfaction of the inebriated who has caught out the sober. 'I wager Grey don't drink, not even ratafia or elderberry wine. Grey, wager my last guinea, is a luminary of the Temperance Movement! Clashing cymbals and banging drums, handing out tracts and imploring lost sinners like me to turn aside from the demon drink—yes, that's Grey's mark, all right!'

Without warning, he lurched away from her and, flinging both arms in the air, burst into a rousing baritone which made the room shake. 'Join us, join us!' roared Dan, not unmelodiously. 'Join our happy band!' He began to caper about on the carpet, both ungainly and threatening, yet comical, so near did he seem to losing his balance altogether. Yet by some miracle he avoided the furniture and kept on his feet. The dance turned into a sort of hornpipe with extraordinarily complicated steps, until he got carried away by the rhythm and exercise of it and stopped singing to whistle and jig about with his hands in the air.

Not knowing whether to laugh or be afraid, she ordered, 'Stop that!'

Rather to her surprise he did so, and came stumbling back to her chair.

'You are wrong about Tom, and you shan't insult him or make fun of him to me!' she shouted angrily into his face.

'No, I'm not wrong about him. Not wrong about you, either.' His voice dropped to a husky whisper which set the alarm bells ringing in her brain and every kind of demon loose in her body. 'Not wrong about you, Rachel, my dear...' He lifted one hand and stretched it out to touch her face, running his fingers lightly the length of her jaw from the lobe of her ear to her chin. She uttered a kind of stifled moan and turned her head away.

'Don't do that, please!' she gasped.

'Why? Does it frighten you? You, Rachel Grey, always so intrepid and always bold enough to speak her mind to me on every other matter. But not on this, eh, Rachel?'

'I don't know what you mean——' she mumbled.

'Yes, you do know, and what you don't know, you'd like very much to find out, wouldn't you?' Dan chuckled, and her heart began to beat so wildly that it seemed it must jump out of her chest.

'I'll show you, if you like. Why don't you learn that lesson with me, eh?'

He stooped further, obliterating her view of the room, so that she saw only him and he seemed to fill the whole world. She was both trapped and yet mesmerised, like the legendary rabbit before the snake. That other Rachel Grey had taken over again, mocking her and holding her limbs fast and powerless. She saw his face coming closer and thought, he is going to kiss me, but was neither shocked nor afraid, only curious. She felt strangely detached, because all this was happening not to her, Miss Grey the governess, but to that other Rachel who teased her in her dreams and now danced triumphantly in her head. She could smell the sweat on his skin now and feel the glow of the heat from his body. As if in a dream, she turned up her face towards his and her lips parted in a movement both of offering and of surrender.

It was the touch of his mouth pressing against hers and the warm moistness of his tongue encountering hers which awoke her from her strange submission. Rachel gasped. She jerked away and twisted her head aside so that his bearded chin scraped against her jaw. She threw up both hands and, inspired by desperation, thrust them against his chest with all her strength. He caught at her arms, and there was a brief wrestling match which she would certainly have lost, if the chair had not tipped up unexpectedly, causing Dan to lose his balance for a second and, trying to regain it, to release his hold on her.

Rachel scrambled out beneath his arm and, free at last, ran to the door, where she turned and panted, 'Keep your ardour for Mrs Ellis, who will appreciate it!' She grasped the skirts of her voluminous nightgown in both hands and, heedless of the amount of bare leg revealed, darted out of the door and upstairs, to the sanctuary of her own room.

He stumbled to the foot of the stair and shouted after her, 'Rachel!' but mercifully did not attempt pursuit. She was able to lock her door and, breathless, lean her perspiring forehead against the panels. After a while, when her thudding heart had slowed, she twisted round and slid down the door until she sat on the floor with her back against it, and rested her head on her knees.

'Don't play about with your food, Pip! You'll spill the milk. There! Now see what you've done!' Rachel snatched up the napkin and mopped up the spilled milk.

'I don't want any breakfast,' mumbled Pip, contrary, and kicking his feet against the table-leg, which he knew was not allowed.

'Yes, you do. Why, the poor children I taught in the Ragged School would give anything for a good breakfast such as Mrs Brereton cooks for you every day.'

'Then let them have it! I don't want it. Tell me where they live and I'll take it there myself!' retorted Pip defiantly.

'Philip!' she almost shouted, and then sighed and fell silent.

There was no point in scolding the child and parting from him on bad terms. Because she would have to leave this house—today. After last night's encounter she could no longer stay. Harland had been a little drunk, but not so much that he would have forgotten it all this morning. If he apologised, as he should, the situation would still remain unmended. If she accepted his apology and stayed, the suspicion must always lurk in his mind that perhaps her objections had been feigned, after all. If she refused his apology, it was tantamount to a farewell.

Even if neither of them mentioned it ever again, the episode would remain unspoken but unforgotten between them. From time to time she would catch his eye and both would look away, both knowing the other remembered.

As soon as Pip has finished his breakfast, she thought, I shall go down and tell his father I intend to leave today. And go where, Rachel? she asked herself wryly. Not back home—Tom had made that clear. She could not bear, in any case, to hear him say, 'I told you so!' She would find some cheap lodging house and seek another post.

Like poor Bella Harland, I shall count my pennies, thought Rachel, until my money runs out. What then?

'Can I go now?' asked Pip, seeing her attention had wandered, and hoping he might escape without having to finish his egg, after all.

'Yes,' she said absently.

There was a tap at the door.

'Gentleman to see you, Miss Grey,' said Mrs Brereton. 'Says he's sorry to call so early, as well he might be at a respectable house like this! But it's urgent, and will you go down? He's in a great taking-on. 'Tis Mr Thomas Grey, miss, your brother.'

'Tom?' cried Rachel, leaping to her feet. All thought of her own dilemma flew straight out of her head. Only something approaching a disaster could have brought Tom to this house so early in the day and in breach of his expressed resolve. At the same time, there was no one she longed to see more at this moment, and his arrival seemed the answer to a prayer.

Tom showed signs of having dressed in a great hurry. His hair was tousled, his coat unbrushed and his shirt-collar crooked. He was pacing restlessly up and down the hall. As soon as Rachel appeared, he first started forward with an expression of relief, then obviously remembering he had sworn never to acknowledge her again, turned fire-red in the face, brandished his hat which he still held in his hand and finally said in a muffled voice, 'I apologise for it being so early——'

Just at the sight of him, Rachel wanted to burst into tears. As it was, she ran and threw both arms round him, exclaiming, 'Oh, Tom, dear, whatever is wrong?'

'Hah-hum...' mumbled Tom. He patted his sister awkwardly on the shoulder, but then disengaged himself from her embrace.

'My calling here does not mark a change in my opinion, Rachel. I am here because this is in the nature of an emergency. I haven't changed my mind. I stand by what I said to you.'

The words were worse than a blow. Rachel lifted her chin, smoothed down her skirts and asked as calmly as she could, 'I understand, Tom. Please explain your visit.'

Tom hesitated, and then burst into a flood of incoherent speech, telling her of Jed Casey's visit and the theft of the cash-box.

'Now what am I to do, Rachel?' he demanded wildly. 'There is the child's part in it! She acted only from fear of her uncle, but the law will not see it so. If I report the matter, both Casey and the child will be in the dock! But I must recover the school's money. It's not as though it were my own cash and I could be free to decide about it. And there's Casey, a rogue if ever there was one—is he to be allowed off scot-free because I want to protect Sally? I've not slept a wink all night,' continued Tom bitterly, striking his hat against the newel-post at the bottom of the stair. 'It's the devil of a situation!'

It was the strongest language she had ever heard from Tom. 'Keep calm,' she told him. 'Being distressed won't help.'

'I let you bring that child to the house,' said Tom. 'I'm not reproaching you, Rachel. I agreed at the time. It seemed that taking her away from a bad home was reason enough. But the bad home has followed her, that's the result of it! If we don't get the money back soon, there's won't be a penny-piece left. Casey will have spent it. On drink, no doubt!'

Rachel thought feverishly. But the word 'drink' had sparked a memory. 'Captain Harland is a friend of Mr Grantham, the magistrate. We should consult him, Tom.'

'The magistrate? He's bound by his duty! He'll arrest the child and the uncle when he can lay his hands on him.'

'No, I mean, consult Dan—Captain Harland. Just wait a moment, Tom.'

Rachel hurried to the dining-room and, with a hasty knock at the door, burst in upon Dan at his breakfast.

A close observer might have thought Captain Harland had as little appetite as his son upstairs in the nursery. He sat before a cold plate of devilled kidneys, with his elbows on the tablecloth and a cup of black coffee in his hand. He set this down as soon as he saw her and got up, pushing back his chair.

'Rachel,' he began awkwardly, 'I've been trying to think of some way I can explain what——'

'Not now!' she interrupted vehemently. 'Do come! Tom is in the hall and something dreadful has happened at home.'

Harland's manner changed instantly. Indecision left it, replaced by calm authority. 'Well, then,' he said, 'let's see what may be done about it.'

The manner had its effect. Rachel immediately felt that all was not lost, after all, and somehow Dan would sort it out. Her spirits rose as she followed him back to where Tom waited impatiently.

'My dear fellow,' said Dan, cutting short Tom's confused apology for disturbing his household. He took his arm and guided him back towards the dining-room. 'Come and join me at breakfast and tell me what it is. Mrs Brereton! Bring some fresh coffee and another cup—two cups,' he added, glancing at Rachel.

They sat around the dining-room table and Tom repeated it all, together with all the possible complications of any course of action taken to recover the money.

'How much?' Dan asked bluntly.

'Nearly forty pounds—but how much of it is left now, lord knows,' said Tom despondently.

Rachel looked up. Forty pounds was a lot of money for the school to hold at any one time. Tom had been managing the fund-raising very well without her.

'If he's too free with his money, it will call attention to him,' said Dan thoughtfully. 'He'll spend some—but my guess is, he'll hide the bulk of it and wait to see what happens. Whether you come chasing after him, that is, or call out the law. He won't hide it in his own hovel, because that would be searched. He'll have stashed it somewhere only he knows of, and unless he chooses to lead us to it, I doubt we'll see it again. It is, quite besides being the school's money, material evidence. If he's not taken in possession of it, there is no proof other than the little girl's word.'

'Then there's nothing to be done,' said Tom in deepest gloom. 'I shall have to write to the trustees. They'll very likely remove me from my post.'

'I would counsel against your doing anything of the sort!' Dan said firmly. 'I should like it, Grey, if you would leave the matter with me.'

'What do you mean to do?' asked Tom suspiciously.

'Not go to Grantham, if that's what you fear. Look here, I was long enough captain of my own ship to get used to sorting out trouble for myself. My methods might be unorthodox on land—but I've not much time for the way things are done ashore, anyway. Will you trust my judgement, Grey, and give me free hand?'

'Yes,' said Tom doubtfully. 'But I wish I knew what you were going to do.'

'Better you don't. Look, old chap, you are a law-abiding citizen. The idea of not doing a thing by the book brings you out in a cold sweat. I'm not criticising you, believe me. But at sea it can't be like that. You're miles from anywhere in the middle of the ocean, you have to do what you can—if it's by the book, so much the better, if not, necessity is the mother of invention. It's like jerry-rigging a sail when is mast is down. So I won't tell you what I intend to do, because I swear it would only distress you. Let me stick my neck out. If it is chopped off, it's only mine and not yours. You agree?' When Tom nodded unhappily, Dan looked at Rachel and raised his eyebrows.

'I agree, too,' she said quietly. 'You know what to do in situations like this. We don't.'

'You have faith in me,' Dan said a little wryly. 'I hope it's not misplaced...' There was a little pause. Rachel looked into his face and then looked down. Tom glanced up curiously. Dan turned to him and went on briskly, 'Go back to your school, Grey, and let me handle it. Rachel...' He hesitated. 'You will stay with Pip? We can discuss other matters later. If you'll both excuse me?'

Left to each other's company, brother and sister stared at one another across the abandoned breakfast-table.

'Do you think he'll do it?' asked Tom.

'If anyone can!' she said confidently.

'Hmm—he seems a capable fellow...' Tom admitted grudgingly. 'I—I am pleased to see you looking well, Rachel.'

Well? Little did he know. She was the unhappiest she had been in years. She was spared the necessity of a direct reply, however, by a creak at the door. Pip put his nose through the crack and asked, 'What is all the fuss, and why has Papa gone running out of the door?'

'On some little business matter—do come in here, Pip, and meet Mr Grey, who is my brother.'

Pip sidled in and approached the stranger cautiously.

'Hello, young man,' said Tom, pulling himself together and visibly regaining some of his usual aplomb on being faced with a familiar situation—a problem child. That was something he could deal with. He held out his hand and Pip took it. 'So you are Philip. Miss Grey was telling me about you. You—er—are interested in ships, I hear.'

'I'm going to join the navy!' said Pip stoutly. 'As soon as they will let me. My papa was allowed to go to sea when he was only my age, twelve, but I have to wait. I don't think it very fair.'

'Twelve, are you?' said Tom thoughtfully, eyeing the slight figure of the child.

Pip's face reddened and Rachel's heart sank. But she need not have worried.

'Twelve?' said Tom. 'Why, I thought you must be already at least thirteen.'

She could have hugged him. But he was getting to his feet and preparing to leave. 'Well, then, Rachel, I must be on my way. The children will be running about the streets on finding the school locked up. I— I shall wait to hear from Harland. It has been a pleasure to meet you, Philip.'

'I like him,' pronounced Pip, when Tom had left. He swung on the banister, his spirits restored, fell off and landed in a heap on the floor, none the worse.

'Yes,' said Rachel a little sadly. 'I like him, too.'

Jed Casey sat in the corner of his favourite tavern and buried his face in a tankard of ale to hide the smile of satisfaction he knew was on his unlovely features—and which would cause the regulars to ask, 'What's put that smirk on your face, then, Jed?' It was a question he was anxious neither to hear nor to have to answer. He had hidden away his ill-gotten wealth in a place of supreme safety, and had nothing to do now but sit here and speculate on the spending of it. Jed grew expansive and almost generous at the thought of thirty-seven pounds and ninepence, the amount it had come to when he had counted it out. Less, of course, the money he had already spent on drink. But he might even tip a pound or two to the missus. She'd want to know where it came from—and if there was any more, that was the trouble. And there was Eliza, his sister-in-law, Sally's mother. If she heard that Kitty had money in her pocket from Jed, she'd be around to demand her share.

That's the trouble with wimmin, thought Jed with taproom-corner philosophy. They're always wanting money. Money fer this, money fer that. Reckoning potatoes cost more'n a penny a pound and the kids is hungry. Ruddy kids is always hungry, but a clip round the ear gener'ly deals wiv it. Then it's the landlord what gets to hear money is about, and he's round quicker than you can bat your eye and demanding back-rent, as if a body can pay out two shilling a week just like that. Two shilling,' muttered Jed into his beer. 'For a stinking room wiv rotten floorboards and rats, and a privy in the yard what's always overflowin' so's you've got ter put down planks of wood if you wants to walk across the yard wivout getting your boots soaked in Gawd knows what.'

All in all, things considered, it would be better to keep the money away from Kitty and Eliza. Best tell them nothing of it. Only cause trouble. Kitty was carrying again, too. As if they hadn't enough brats. Grumbling and complaining all the livelong day, she was. He'd blacked her eye only last night for it, but it didn't make any difference. Eliza was a bit better company, but a couple of days ago she'd told him she reckoned she was carrying as well. And me bruvver in the nick, thought Jed. Never going to believe it's his—him having been put away a year since. She'll have to take the kid down to the workhouse on the quiet and leave it outside the door. Reckon Kitty will have to do the same wiv hers, though she'll set up a screeching and carrying-on about it. Someone will take it in. They always does. Not that they does anything else for a body. Wimmin is always getting themselves in a family way; it fair destroys a man's peace of mind. Life gets that troublesome for a fellow, he don't know which way to turn, it's a fact.

As Jed reflected on the shortcomings of the parish and the sad lot of a decent working man, he spied, through the upturned glass base of his empty tankard as he drained out the last drop, movement in the bar. Two new customers had come in. Jed set down his tankard and leaned back with an idler's persistent curiosity in goings-on around, to see who it was. Strangers, and off a ship, most like. Two of them, with rolling gait, skin like leather and the colour of walnut and hair in pigtails. Jack Tars, he'd put a guinea on it. And he'd got guineas now, hadn't he? The thought amused Jed and he chuckled to himself.

The two seafarers had bought themselves tankards of ale and, rather to his surprise, they made for his corner and sat down, one on either side of him.

Jed did not like this much, but there again, they were two, and a handy-looking pair with broken noses and bulging muscles showing through their striped jerseys. No beauties, either of them.

'You look a happy fellow, matey,' said one to Jed.

'Oh, aye,' mumbled Jed.

The other sailor raised his tankard in salute. 'We just got paid off, shipmate, and don't like to see a man with an empty pot. Over here, tapster, and bring this bully-boy here another jug of ale!'

'Very civil of you,' said Jed cautiously. Sailors ashore with their pockets full of money very often were given to bouts of generosity. But usually when already in their cups. These two were stone-cold sober as yet. But it didn't do to refuse hospitality. Not when it was offered by a couple of pug-uglies like these two.

'Ah,' said the first, smacking his lips over his ale, 'it's always good to reach harbour again. You ever been to sea, matey?'

'No,' said Jed with ill-disguised horror. Catch him— what, salt pork and rolling about in gales and yellow fever and all the rest of it? Think he was mad?

'We rounded Cape Horn,' said the other.

Jed hadn't the faintest notion where that might be, nor did he wish to, but he nodded sagely.

They had drained their ale and they called for another—also for another for Jed. Jed was torn between wanting to get away, and a desire to enjoy free beer. The desire won. He downed his second free tankard, and was easily persuaded to follow it up with a tot of rum, in order to drink the Queen's health and the Royal Navy's, and to the memory of Admiral Nelson and numerous shipmates of his two companions, all gone below to Davy Jones' locker, and a lady in Rio de Janeiro possessed, if words were to be believed, of incredible stamina and invention. It took several tots of rum to achieve all this, and Jed rather lost count.

At last his two friends rose to their feet and announced to Jed's secret relief, that they intended to try out another public house. They asked Jed to recommend one. Jed, rather muddled, recommended the Red Lion, two streets away.

'We'll set course for that, then,' they said, and somehow caught up Jed between them and took him out of the tavern with them. Jed's legs were not quite steady and his brain less so, but it was clear they thought he wanted to come along too. He tried to explain that he didn't, but they would not take no for an answer. He was marched along the street, rather uncomfortably because they held him one by either arm, but instead of ending up at the Red Lion they turned down a number of alleys.

'This ain't the way!' protested Jed.

'Trust us, matey,' said one of the seafarers.

Trust them was just what Jed did not do, and he was less inclined to trust them by the minute. It occurred to him that they were far more sober than he was—their heads and stomachs being inured to rum. A flicker of unease, which had afflicted the pit of Jed's stomach ever since they had first joined themselves to his company, now became positive alarm.

'Here!' he exclaimed, trying in vain to disengage himself. 'You ain't the Press?'

'The Press?' exclaimed one of his captors scornfully. 'There ain't been pressed men on board ship since my old dad went to sea.'

Jed was marginally comforted, but not much. 'What do you want of me, then?' he demanded.

'Us, matey? Not a thing. But there's a gen'leman would like a word with you. In here!'

Jed was thrust through a doorway and found himself in a store of some kind. Boxes and barrels were stacked on all sides, together with coils of rope and various murderous-looking implements, all of which suggested a ship's chandler's warehouse. But Jed's eye was taken by a man sitting on a barrel and waiting patiently, with a cigar smouldering between the fingers of his right hand.

'Here he be, cap'n!' said the first sailor. 'No trouble finding him. He's well-known, he is. He don't hold his liquor too well.'

The two sailors propped Jed against a stack of boxes and stood back—but not very far back. He could not escape.

'Casey?' asked the man, seated on the barrel, affably. He had a beard and a nautical look about him, but was dressed like a swell, and Jed could not for the life of him imagine what he wanted. But with the smoke of the cigar swirling about his head, and his black beard—and a very cold look in his eye at variance with his friendly tone—he resembled nothing so much as Old Nick the Devil, popped up from his fiery kingdom below to recruit a stoker or two for hell's furnaces.

'I don't know you,' said Jed, both mystified and frightened out of his wits. He wondered if he might not be dead, after all, have bypassed St Peter and been taken off straight away down below by a couple of the Devil's minions. This bearded fellow looked quite as if he might open up a recording ledger at any minute and read out a list of Jed's sins.

As if to confirm this, the bearded man said sternly, 'No matter. I know you, Jed Casey, and that you're a rogue. But you've bitten off more than you can chew this time. Where's the money from the Ragged School?'

Jed was so astounded that his mouth dropped open. When he could speak, he stammered, 'I dunno nothing about it.'

His two sailing friends—not so friendly now—moved closer to him.

'Here!' said Jed, alarmed. 'What's it to you, anyway?'

'Now, look here, Casey,' said the bearded man, in the same affable tone. Jed did not like the tone nor the look of the man at all. Smiling away like he'd still be laughing to see a fellow hung. Fair made Jed's flesh crawl. Jed had never heard the legend of Faust and Mephistopheles, but he would have believed it instantly, if he had been told it after this. 'I'm not the law. But I am a law, understand? A law to myself. Now, you'll take these two fine lads here to fetch the money, or as much or it as is left, and bring it here to me. Or, depend on it, you'll be knocked on the head, and taken down to the harbour tonight in a sack and dropped in the ocean for the fish to feed off. Mackerel, most likely,' added the bearded man thoughtfully. 'Mackerel are partial to a drowned corpse.'

Jed tried to swallow, but could not. He felt sick. He tried not to remember that he'd eaten soused mackerel for supper the previous evening. 'Supposing I don't know nuffin?' he croaked unconvincingly. 'Suppose you got the wrong bloke?'

'Overboard you go, anyway. No loss to anyone, I imagine.'

'Best thing is,' said one of the sailors, 'we crates him up in one o' these chests, Cap'n. Loads him aboard and takes him out to sea—then there will be no likelihood he'll come floating back on the tide.'

'Well said, bos'un,' said the bearded man approvingly. 'It's the gases,' he explained kindly to the quaking Jed. 'They blow up a dead body and bring it to the surface. I've seen many a drowned sailor bobbing away on the waves.'

'Aye,' said the other seaman. 'And all swollen and nibbled at by the fish. A ghastly sight, matey.'

'I'm going to throw up,' mumbled Jed, ashen-faced.

'Take him out,' said the bearded man brusquely. 'The money, Casey! Or you're a dead man, my solemn word on it!'

'God rot your innards!' said Jed viciously. But he knew when he was beaten, and was by now so desperate to get out of here and the presence of his bearded tormentor that he was almost ready to offer to barter the money for his freedom.

'Going to show us where you got it hid, are you?' asked the nearer sailor. 'You leave it to us, Cap'n Harland. We'll be back before you've got your cigar smoked.'

Harland...the name lodged in Jed's churning brain. Captain Harland, was it? Well, Captain Harland, he thought venomously as he was hustled through the alleyways towards his hiding-place, you ain't heard the last of Jed Casey! I'll be revenged on you, see if I ain't. I'll find you when you ain't got your pug-uglies to do your bidding!

CHAPTER SEVEN

'SOME of it will have gone in the grop-shops, but most of it appears to be here.' Dan put the grimy canvas bag on the dining-room table. 'You had better count it, Grey, and if you will let me know by how much it's short of the original, I'll make it up.'

'I'm much obliged to you,' Tom said in a subdued voice. Without warning, he sat down heavily on the nearest chair and remained there motionless, staring at the bag of recovered money.

Dan studied him thoughtfully, then turned aside towards Rachel, who stood a little behind him. 'It seems to have shaken him badly, this little adventure,' he murmured. 'Give him a moment to pull himself together. Does he take everything so much to heart?'

'Yes,' she replied quietly, 'I'm rather afraid he does.'

Tom stirred and pulled out a handkerchief from his coat pocket and began to mop his forehead. Rachel moved towards him and gently put her hand on his shoulder. Dan went out of the room and left them together. If this business served to soften Grey's obstinacy, then Jed, by his actions, had achieved what no one else could have done. Dan hoped sincerely that the quarrel between brother and sister might be healed. He knew how much it hurt Rachel, and his own responsibility weighed heavily on his conscience.

In the dining-room, Tom made an effort to recover his presence of mind. He put away the handkerchief and repeated more firmly, 'I'm much obliged. Tell Harland again . . . It's uncommon good of him. I did not really think, you know, that he'd be able to get back so much as a penny-piece.'

'He found Casey before he could spend it,' said Rachel. 'I wish I knew how he got it back from him.'

'I don't!' said Tom frankly. 'Harland said it would be better if we didn't know it, and I'm sure that's so.' He hesitated again, then asked diffidently, 'Will you not check it with me, Rachel?'

'Yes, Tom, of course.'

She took a seat opposite him. Tom tipped up the bag on to the polished table-top and they counted out the money. 'Thirty-five pounds and ninepence. Casey spent two pounds of it. Well, I still cannot really believe it, Rachel. We shall be able to whitewash the schoolroom, after all.'

'Tom,' Rachel said slowly, 'naturally I am very pleased to see that the school is so well in funds. You say "we"—have you been able to find a suitable lady teacher to replace me?'

'Yes.' Tom looked a little embarrassed, but added in a more resolute tone, 'As a matter of fact, I have. It is Mrs Davies, a clergyman's widow and quite suitable in every way.'

'Oh,' said Rachel, unable to suppress a touch of resentment at the thought of another doing what she still thought of as her job. A clergyman's widow. Her heart sank. 'And is Mrs Davies very elderly, Tom?'

'Elderly?' exclaimed Tom, looking quite startled and his face gaining a reddish flush. 'Most certainly not! I mean, I believe her to be in her middle thirties. You can hardly expect me to enquire a lady's age, Rachel!'

'Indeed not,' said his sister, eyeing him with some curiosity. He was aware of it, and his complexion darkened to a dusky pink. He pushed a hand over his forehead as if he were perspiring, and began to thrust the money back into the bag. 'The school is doing very well, Rachel, you'll be pleased to know.'

'Obviously—since it possesses thirty-five pounds and ninepence.'

Tom ran a finger around the inside of his high-pointed starched collar. 'To tell you the truth, Rachel, Mary—I mean, Mrs Davies—had the capital idea to go back to her late husband's parish and appeal to his old parishioners to help the school. He is well-remembered there and they proved very generous. The appeal brought in all of this,' he touched the bag, 'almost forty pounds.' A faint, somewhat self-conscious, smile touched Tom's face. 'Passing the hat round, Mary called it. She is of an—um—amusing turn of phrase.'

'Is she, indeed?' asked Rachel, startled and thinking that this particular clergyman's widow sounded livelier by the minute.

'Yes, and she is just the sort of girl to get people to turn out their pockets for the school!' said Tom enthusiastically.

Girl? Presumably not only in her middle thirties, but passable good-looking and youthful in her ways as well!

'And does she still wear her widow's weeds?' asked Rachel, fishing furiously.

'No,' admitted Tom, shifting on his chair. 'After all, he's been dead two years or more, and frankly, Mary thought that the children would be put off by too much black crape. So she put it aside when she began at the school. She dresses very quietly, of course.' Tom seemed torn between assuring his sister that Mrs Davies was of utmost respectability and doing the lady justice. 'But in excellent taste. Mary has very good taste. She's very musical.'

'In what way?' asked Rachel faintly.

'She plays the flute,' said Tom. 'Very charmingly. And the piano. She has a piano of her own, in her home where she lives with her invalid mother. Mary thinks,' Tom was by now quite purple, 'she thinks I ought to learn to play the piano——'

'Tom!' cried Rachel, half-aghast at the promised transformation in the process of being worked by the redoubtable Mrs Davies, and half suppressing gales of laughter at the image which leapt into her mind. Tom solemnly ploughing his way through 'The Bluebells of Scotland,' accompanied by Mary Davies on the flute and all chaperoned by an aged but eagle-eyed invalid parent.

'You don't think it would be frivolous?' Tom asked anxiously.

'By no means!' said Rachel firmly. 'I think it an excellent idea. I should very much like to meet Mrs Davies.'

'In fact,' said Tom, 'Mary has expressed a similar wish—to meet you. I told her——' Tom broke off and his expression resumed something of its old obstinacy and his voice lost its enthusiasm. 'I told her not while you remained under Harland's roof!'

'Oh, Tom . . .' Rachel said wearily. 'Must you still cling to that? Even after Captain Harland helped you?'

'I have nothing against Harland himself,' Tom said urgently, leaning across the table. 'It is the confounded equivocal situation!' Suddenly he reached out and took her hand. 'Rachel, I wish you would come home with me—now, today.'

'But I can't—I can't leave Pip...' Rachel recalled belatedly that she had been contemplating doing just that before Tom had arrived with his news of the theft. That, in turn, recalled her reason for planning to leave. 'I thought you said you would not have me back, Tom,' she said a little sharply.

'I did. But Mary has persuaded me I was hasty. Mary says, you should have a refuge should you need it. And frankly, Rachel, I have been hoping that you had seen the error of your ways.'

Rachel pulled her hand from his and leapt up from the table. 'The error—— What on earth are you suggesting, Tom?'

'Myself, nothing!' he said stubbornly. 'But not everyone sees your coming here as—as quite proper, Rachel. Several of our neighbours, when they learned of it, expressed great surprise and—and some criticism.'

'They should learn to mind their own business!' said Rachel vigorously.

'Rachel, you must appreciate that, as schoolmaster of the Ragged School, my own household must be seen to be above reproach,' he protested.

'Kindly tell those busybodies who are fabricating slander about me, that I am gainfully employed in a respectable household!' Rachel stormed across the room in a rustle of skirts, and took up a position by the window, hiding her face from his sight.

There was a silence. Tom rose to his feet. 'Perhaps you'd care to visit the school and meet Mary? I think that would be in order.'

A compromise. From Tom's point of view, a considerable modification of his original position. From her own, only a confirmation of her nebulous situation, part way between acceptability and social ostracism. A miserable hole-and-corner, a furtive kind of semi-acceptance. But Tom meant it well.

'Yes—I—I will, Tom. One day.' She spoke in a flat, expressionless voice and did not turn round.

He contemplated her averted figure for a moment, then said, 'I had better go back and tell Mary the money is safe.'

'Do so,' said his sister in a muffled voice, without looking at him.

He walked past her, and then turned back and came to stand beside her. 'We shall see you in the school one day, then?' He hesitated, leaned forward and kissed her cheek. 'Goodbye, my dear.'

'Goodbye, Tom.'

She was able to wait until he had gone, but then gave way to her emotion, sitting down at the table and bursting into tears. After a moment or two she could control her sobs, mopped her eyes and blew her nose and tucked away her handkerchief. As she did so, a hand touched lightly on her shoulder. Rachel jumped.

'What's wrong?' Dan asked, bending over her in concern. 'Is it Grey? I know—he still doesn't approve of your being here.'

'Oh, Tom would come around, but he is beset by people who think I'm a ruined woman!' said Rachel fiercely.

Perhaps, thought Dan. Though I fancy Grey exaggerates to provide himself with reason for taking his sister away. He is jealous, and who can blame him? Not I.

Dan took his hand from her shoulder, pulled out a chair and seated himself beside her, his expression a mixture of concern and anger.

'Rachel, if you are in this scrape, it's my fault. I should have thought about this when I asked you to come here. It was selfish of me. I played on your kind nature, knowing you'd not refuse to help Pip. I caused a rift between you and your brother which I know has grieved you very much—and even now——' He made a gesture of frustration with his hand. 'This is unspeakable! We are a society of canting hypocrites or of people who are too confounded terrified of the opinion of others to act as they wish!'

'You must not mind Tom,' she said. 'You cannot make up his mind for him. He does that himself. Tom isn't a hypocrite. He wants to do what is right. He has difficulty deciding what's right, that's all. But when he has decided, he sticks to it and won't be budged.'

'Even so!' Dan slammed his hand on the table. 'I for one have had enough of all this shilly-shallying around the heart of the matter. It's time for some frank speaking, Rachel. I—wanted to talk to you anyway this morning, about last night . . .'

'Yes, I know.' She looked away, her unhappiness printed on her pale face.

'You feel, no doubt, that you should leave here,' Dan said more quietly, watching her. 'I don't blame you. I can only say I was drunk, which doesn't excuse it. But I can promise that it won't happen again, which it won't. It was unforgivable. I—I am thoroughly ashamed of it. I only ask if for the child's sake, you'll overlook it and not go flouncing off in high dudgeon, as you have every right to do, of course...'

'I will be honest with you, since that's what you wish,' Rachel said, meeting his troubled gaze. 'Before Tom came, I was preparing to come down and give you my decision to leave. But now Tom tells me,' Rachel voice rose and she burst out in a fury, 'Tom tells me I am the subject of all kind of malicious gossip! I will not have my actions dictated by the wagging tongues of others! If I leave now, after so little time as Pip's governess, there will be smug smiles all round and people saying, I told you so. They will have won a sordid little victory and gloat over it and me in their mean little minds. I shall stay on a little longer, Captain Harland, if only to give the gossip time to die a natural death. It will, I'm sure. A nine-day wonder, you know. I should like to stay at least until your marriage.'

Dan got up and walked away a little. 'I dare say you find my choice of Charlotte Ellis less than altogether suitable.'

It was a frank and unexpected statement. Rachel was taken aback, but at last managed to say, 'It's not for me to say. I confess that I'm not sure she and Pip—— But you've known her a long time. And her husband was your friend.'

'Yes, yes—Ellis was a good fellow. Rachel, I would like to try and explain some things to you. This isn't at all a proper sort of conversation to be having. Tom would pass out with horror if he knew of it. I don't say I embark on it lightly or find it easy, and I by no means intend to distress you—but you're a sensible sort of girl and I don't think you shock easily. I would like to put what happened last night into context. To explain why—not to excuse it, only explain it. May I?'

'Go on,' she said in a low voice.

'The fact is, a man without a wife is in something of a fix,' Dan began, and at the same time started to turn restlessly up and down the room with his hands clasped behind him. 'If, like me, he is a widower, there are certain obvious substitutes. A good housekeeper can run his household, a competent nursemaid or governess can mind his children...'

'It's not the same as a mother,' said Rachel, quietly but firmly.

'No, no, I agree. And one reason for my seeking to remarry was always to supply Pip with the mother he never—which he doesn't have. There are other minor inconveniences, such as no hostess to preside over his table...which a widower such as myself solves by re-marrying, but the whole thing really is not about that at all...'

He fell silent. Rachel folded her hands on the table-top. 'I think I do understand what this has to do with last night. You don't need to explain it, Captain Harland.'

'I wish you would call me Daniel,' he said soberly.

'You know that's impossible.'

'Yes, I do know it.' He sighed. 'A man needs a woman in his bed, Rachel. Don't rush away screaming to Tom to come back and save your honour! I don't intend to go stumbling about, making a fool of myself as I did last night!'

Rachel flushed and her interlaced fingers tightened until the knuckles showed white through the skin.

'Some of the things I said to you—all of them un-forgivable—they were perhaps a foolish error on my part. I simply assumed you would—would be concerned with the things which worry me, as a man, I mean. I am not good at understanding women. I was probably wrong.'

No, you weren't wrong, thought Rachel miserably. And you do understand women, or at least you understand me.

'I don't know how women—I suppose it's different for women,' Dan was saying. 'I've always been led to believe so. Although, my first wife didn't hesitate to take a lover when I was away at sea, so perhaps women are not so uninterested in the matter as they like to pretend!'

Who knew why poor, silly Bella Harland had taken a lover? In the eyes of all her contemporaries she had been a scarlet woman, unfit to remain in decent company or to have care of her own child. To her husband she appeared faithless, deceiving, treacherous, someone who had brought scandal on his name and on his son. But what of love? Had she loved the man who had ruined her? Or, when she had held her lover in her arms in the darkness, had she pretended she held the absent husband, achingly longed for but so seldom there?

I don't know, thought Rachel. She had her baby to occupy her and that ought to have been enough, or so most people would say. But they say women often behave oddly and unlike themselves after a baby is born. They become low-spirited and mope about the place when they ought to be happy. Perhaps Bella was downhearted and not herself when along came this other, offering her a kind of comfort.

To Dan she said softly, 'Perhaps you judge her too harshly. Perhaps she was only lonely and young and, I suppose, pretty.'

'Very pretty, in a pallid sort of way. Feather-brained, and what brain she had was easily turned. I don't suppose he found it all that difficult——' Dan broke off. 'Anyway, that's over and done with. What I am trying to say is that men are sadly prey to their physical natures, and that's the way of it. Now, I am not the sort of fellow who cares to visit those establishments where such needs are catered for. You must know such places exist.'

'Yes,' Rachel said, almost inaudibly. 'And of an evening, and sometimes during the day, the girls loiter in the streets around the Ragged School and accost the men. Some are very young. One can't ignore them.'

'I knew that school was no place for you to be!' said Dan, diverted and speaking with some satisfaction, as a man proved right. Then he shrugged. 'Well, I dare say, Tom and your other critics would say that this house is no more a place for you to be. Perhaps rightly. The reason I settled upon Charlotte as a possible wife is partly because she's very charming and she has many excellent qualities. I don't expect you, Rachel, to admire those qualities in her which attract a man. Nor do I suppose you see eye to eye with her in other matters. In fact, watching the pair of you circle round one another and trying to out-stare one another was like watching two cats square up across a scrap of garden,' Dan added disastrously.

That roused his companion. 'It was most certainly not!'

'Allow a mere male to make his own observations! What I'm trying to say, and doing it very badly, is that Charlotte, having been married before, has some understanding of a man's—a man's needs. She knows my situation, I mean. She understands it.'

'And hers?' asked Rachel sapiently, unable to stop herself.

'I suppose so.' He looked, if possible, even more embarrassed among his grim determination.

Rachel rose composedly to her feet. 'I understand what you are trying to say, Captain Harland. But it occurs to me that if a couple are planning to spend a lifetime together, there had better be a greater understanding between them than a mutual desire to rush upstairs and lock the bedroom door!'

'Rachel,' he said gravely, 'you are the most splendid girl. You never cease to surprise me. But you underestimate the nature of the beast. To rush upstairs and lock the bedroom door, as you put it, is the cornerstone of a marriage. If things are not right in the bedroom, they have precious little hope of being right elsewhere.'

She bit her lip. 'You must marry Mrs Ellis if you think it right. I shall stay, if you agree, until you do. I know Mrs Ellis—or Mrs Harland, as she will be— will not want me to remain after that. Now, if you'll excuse me, I'll go and find Pip, who should be doing his lessons and is probably floating paper boats on a bowl of water in Mrs Brereton's kitchen!'

She hurried out of the door and closed it quickly before he could reply. As she went up to the schoolroom she was hard pushed to prevent the tears returning. It was all very well to talk of his situation, and of Mrs Ellis' situation... But what of mine? asked

Rachel of herself miserably. Even Tom now has his Mary. Is life to pass me by?

Jed Casey had had time to recover from his fright, but his fury was, if anything, redoubled. He lurched through the streets with swinging arms and clenched fists, murder in his heart and in his expression, so that all who saw him quickly got out of his path. At last, he arrived at his own hovel. The sight of it did little to improve his mood. Rubbish was scattered about the miserable yard, on three sides of which rose ramshackle tenement buildings. The fourth side was occupied by a slaughter-house. They were killing today. The lowing of the beasts echoed mournfully on the air and the gutters ran with blood. The stench of it permeated the air and mixed with the other odours which always hung about the yard in an evil miasma. In addition, the blood-patients were here. These were the consumptives and anaemics for whom their doctors had prescribed the drinking of blood. They came to the slaughter-house on days like this and stood in patient, depressed queues, their bodies wasted by disease, their eyes hollow, clasping pottery mugs in which the blood of the freshly slaughtered animals was caught and downed warm.

Jed glowered at them, but they, unlike others, seemed oblivious of him. They shuffled forward as the queue moved up. Those who had already received and drunk their quotient came stumbling out of the slaughter-house door, their clothing stained with spilled blood and their mouths marked horridly with scarlet stains. They presented a horrifying sight, and even Jed's stomach would not take it, especially following on the fright he had already had. He hurried away and kicked open the door of his own mean dwelling.

As luck would have it, the only person there was Joey, who jumped up and, taking one look at his father's face, prudently got behind the table.

'Why ain't you in the school?' demanded Jed menacingly.

'Schoolmaster wasn't there,' returned Joey. 'Only new lady schoolmistress and I ain't going to be taught by wimmin.'

'Schoolmeester...' muttered Jed thickly, reminded of his loss. 'Schoolmeester were behind this, long-faced misery that he is! Not content wiv teaching brats to read and write and make out they are better'n them as brung them into this world! Know your letters, don't you?' demanded Jed, lurching forward and making a grab for his son, who dodged nimbly out of the way. 'Well, you ain't going to that school no more. I say so! What you needs to learn, I'll teach you! You come here, you little tow-rag——'

To Jed, all his misfortune and discomfiture now centred on the one person he could see, Joey. Neither Harland nor the schoolmaster could be reached for the moment. But Joey was there and Joey could be made to pay. To Joey it was an all too familiar situation. He ducked beneath the table, scrabbled across the floor, shot out the other side and was out of the door before his father could lay hands on him.

'You come back here!' roared Jed, lurching clumsily after him.

But Joey was across the yard, had burst through the queue of waiting blood-patients and was out in the street. When Jed lumbered up in pursuit, he became entangled in the queue. He began to push and shove his way through, and two hulking fellows in rubber aprons appeared, stained head to foot with gore, and ordered him to 'wait his turn'.

Jed swore at them and stumbled back. At that moment, the queue moved forward and bore Jed along with it into the slaughter-house. There he found himself in a scene worthy of a medieval hell. All around were the sick, stretching out their wasted arms for their share of the blood and staring with their wild, dark-circled eyes in deathly white faces. And, as in some satanic ritual, the blood flowed out, splashing and staining everything and everyone. A great wet, warm crimson mark suddenly appeared on Jed's shirt above his heart. He let out a great yell, and, turning, fled, the coarse laughter of the slaughter-house assistants echoing in his ears.

Pip reflected that there seemed to be a great deal of coming and going in the house these days. Not that he minded. It was interesting. Some of it he didn't like. He particularly did not like Mrs Ellis, and felt somehow threatened by her. Pip called her, in his own mind, 'the lady with the spiky nose'. He liked Rachel. He hoped that Rachel would stay forever. But sometimes Rachel and his father quarrelled, or it sounded like quarrelling to Pip's ear. They had quarrelled a few days after Rachel had taken Pip to Purbrook to see his mother's grave. Pip had lurked outside the door and unashamedly eavesdropped. He often did this because it was the only way he ever found out anything. No one told him anything. This time he had been rewarded by hearing his father shout 'Adulteress!' which was a new word in Pip's vocabulary. It had sent him scurrying upstairs to look it up in the dictionary. The dictionary spoke of 'infidelity in the marriage-bed'. Pip looked up infidelity in its turn, and found out that it meant unfaithfulness. Pip knew what unfaithfulness was, but he had no idea what a marriage-bed was, and supposed it some particularly splendid piece of furniture which people got for a present when they married. But how anyone could be unfaithful in it was a complete mystery.

Pip wandered down the garden, mulling over this and other matters. He was supposed to be taking fresh air. He took himself off to the furthest corner, where he could not be seen from the house and where he had a private den. It was a disused gazebo, but no one had sat in it to admire the view for years. The gardener had used it to store his tools for a while, but since the gardener had acquired a shed, some eighteen months ago, the gazebo had been left entirely for Pip's use.

He had furnished it carefully with old cushions and affixed pictures of galleons to its walls. Through its latticed windows, Pip kept watch for the Spanish Armada. Vigo Bay, Trafalgar and the Battle of the Nile had all been refought from the gazebo. 'England expects that every man shall do his duty' had been signalled many a time through a hole in its roof.

'Ho, there, master-gunner!' cried Pip aloud as he approached his vessel, entering early into the spirit of the thing. 'Man-o'-war on the port side!'

He flung open the door and stopped short in consternation. There was another boy in his den. On board his ship! A rough-looking boy with ragged clothes and a pinched face. He had been sleeping on Pip's own cushions. Piracy!

'What are you doing on my bridge?' demanded Pip, furious.

The intruder stared at him. 'This ain't a bridge, it's an old shed.'

'It's not an old shed!' shouted Pip indignantly. 'She's a ship of the line of eight hundred tons' burthen. She's my flagship.'

'Go on,' said the other, impressed.

Pip was mollified by his awe. 'It doesn't have to be. Sometimes it's a raft and I'm shipwrecked. Like Robinson Crusoe, you know. Or I get cast adrift like Captain Bligh.'

'What is it today?' asked the boy, propping his chin in his hands.

'I was thinking of being Blake and sailing to attack the Barbary pirates in Tangier Bay,' confided Pip.

'Can I come?' asked his new companion. 'Me name is Joey Casey.'

Pip was enchanted. 'You can be my second-in-command, or you can be a Barbary pirate, whichever you want. Only, if you're a pirate, your ship is over there in that apple tree.'

'I'll sail with you,' said Joey, 'and see how I get on.'

'Welcome aboard, Mr Casey,' said Pip solemnly, and they shook hands on it.

'There's something very strange going on,' said Rachel to Dan a few days later. 'Don't ask me what it is, because I don't know, but I feel I ought to mention it.'

'In the house?' He looked puzzled.

'I suppose in the house...' She sounded doubtful. 'Yes, in the house. Only little things have been happening, but they add together, or I think they do. To begin with, Mrs Brereton says there is no keeping up with the fruit bowl.'

'What?' he exclaimed, and burst into laughter.

'Be serious! She says, she is always filling it up, but apples, oranges, nuts—whatever she puts in—it vanishes.'

'I've not been eating more than usual,' said Dan.

'Nor I, nor does the kitchen-maid pilfer, and Pip has so little appetite, it can't be his doing. But now Mrs Brereton says bread is disappearing, too.'

'Mice.'

'No! Not nibbled away. Whole slices cut off and gone!'

'Oh, for goodness' sake,' said Dan. 'It's the kitchen-girl. Is she hungry?'

'She swears she's not responsible, and Mrs Brereton says she's a very truthful girl. And there's a blanket unaccounted for. Just gone from the linen cupboard. Mrs Brereton swears it was there last week, because she moved it and noticed particularly. It's all very odd.'

Dan sat back in his chair and gave a low whistle. 'Know something, Rachel? We've got a stowaway aboard!'

'Oh, nonsense!'

'Put my last guinea on it.' Dan paused. 'Pip has some kind of den in the old gazebo. I don't go down there because it's his, you know... private. I know he's taken odd bits and pieces down there. He might be kitting it out for a long voyage.'

'Whatever do you mean?' she asked, bewildered.

'I fancy he imagines it's a ship.' Dan got to his feet. 'Let's take a little stroll in the garden, Miss Grey. We'll soon find out if Pip has been loading extra stores.'

When they got into the garden, Dan offered her his arm. She accepted it with a little smile and they walked sedately down the gravel path. 'I'm no gardener,' said Dan, surveying the somewhat sorry state of the garden around him. 'The old chap who comes in and keeps the place tidy does no more than he has to. He cuts the grass and trims the hedges, but if he doesn't turn to and do something about these weeds, we shall finish in a jungle.'

'You should hire a boy to help him. The gardener is very old and he has rheumatism. He can't get down on his knees, he tells me, or he can't get up again.'

'You see, you know so much more about my household than I do! Ah——' Dan halted and pointed. 'There's Pip's ship.' He raised his voice, 'Ahoy there! Request permission to come aboard!'

There was a great scurrying and scrabbling from within the gazebo, and some whispering. Pip appeared, red-faced, and announced, 'You can't. We've got the cholera aboard and I'm just going to run up the fever signal.'

'I'm the port authority surgeon,' said his father determinedly. 'I want to count your sick.'

'You'll catch it,' said Pip desperately, barring his path.

'Believe me, young man,' promised Dan, 'you will most certainly "catch it", if you don't let me by!'

He walked past the crestfallen Pip, and put his head through the door.

'Well, well,' said Dan, 'bless my buttons. Come here and see, Rachel. We have been entertaining a guest, or Pip has. It's Joseph, I do declare!'

They all reassembled in Dan's study. The two little boys stood side by side, Pip defiant, Joey wary.

'Right,' said Dan, 'Joseph first. How did you come here and how long ago was it?'

'Since our dad come home wanting to half-kill someone and it was going to be me!' said Joey. 'I ain't staying there to get knocked all over the room. He's broke me arm afore now. And I ain't going back no more, so there! I've run off. I come here, because I went first to see our Sally and she said Miss Grey was here. I thought I might see Miss Grey, but it was late and I found this old place at the bottom of your garden——'

Pip shuffled his feet, opened his mouth, caught his father's eye and closed it again.

Joey, alerted by some telepathy, added quickly, 'I didn't know then it was a ship of the line, like I do now.'

'How long ago was this?' asked Dan. Joey thought it was about a week since. Dan glanced at Rachel. 'I fancy we can guess what put Jed in such a foul temper.'

'I ain't going back!' repeated Joey obstinately.

'See here, young man,' Dan told him, 'of course you must go home. I'll come with you and explain matters. I fancy I have some influence with your father.'

'No!' shouted Pip so loudly that they all stared at him. His face had grown alarmingly red and his thin chest heaved with emotion. 'He's my friend. He's the only friend I ever had—ever! I never had anyone to play with before. And now you want to send him away! You shan't!'

'Hold your tongue, sir!' ordered his father angrily. 'I won't be spoken to in such a way. If you cannot mind your manners, you shall wait outside until you are able to conduct yourself properly!'

Rachel saw with alarm that Pip was working himself up into what would undoubtedly finish in one of his nervous crises. She put her hand on Dan's shoulder warningly.

But Pip flew at his father with clenched fists and roared, 'You shan't! I never had anyone. He's my friend and I want him to stay!' He began to pummel his father's broad chest with both fists, while Rachel could only watch in utter dismay.

Dan picked his son up bodily, carried him struggling and shouting to the door, and deposited him in the hall. 'You too, Joseph!' he ordered. Joey scuttled out to join Pip, who sat purple-faced on the floor with tears in his eyes, and Dan shut the door on the pair of them.

'He's upset,' said Rachel. 'It's understandable. You can't send the boy Joey back to his home, Jed will mistreat him dreadfully and you can't prevent it.'

'Now, look here, Rachel,' said Dan, wiping his brow. 'I don't intend to have Joey here. Even you won't suggest that he's a suitable companion for my son, I hope?'

'They seem to get along very well. Pip does need other boys around him——' she began.

'Not that one! Are you mad? Joey is a gutter urchin of the worst type. The effect on Pip of his company has already been lamentable. I know Pip can throw tantrums, but never like that. Besides, look what was the result of taking the girl Sally into your household with Tom! One can't separate these children from their backgrounds, Rachel. The families are poor and criminal, and can only be expected to try and profit from their children's good fortune in some way!'

Rachel stamped her foot. 'I thought you had gained a more liberal attitude, but I see you're as stiff-necked as ever you were! I told you before, if I thought like you, I'd never try to do anything! No one would! Are children like poor Joey just to be abandoned?'

'No!' he shouted. 'I'll speak to Casey. The man is a bully, but like most of his type a coward at heart. To put the fear of death into him is not difficult.'

'Nor is it an answer!'

'The child is going out of here today!' Dan said obstinately, and she saw that he meant it.

Outside the room, Pip removed himself from his station with ear pressed against the door-panels and faced Joey, who sat on the bottom stair with his elbows on his knees and his chin in his hands.

'They mean to send you away,' said Pip in a trembling voice.

'I ain't going home,' repeated Joey. 'I shall run away, somewhere else.'

Pip's face lit up. 'We shall both run away! I don't want to stay here if you go. We'll run away to sea, Joey! We'll be ship's boys! It will be a fine adventure!'

Joey lifted his gloomy face from his hands and brightened visibly. 'Here, that's a good 'un, that is. I'd like that fine, to go to sea. I mean, your ship in the garden, it's fine enough, but it ain't a real—I mean,' he amended hastily, 'it ain't got water round it. I'm a real good swimmer,' added Joey. 'When the weather's hot, fellers hang round the waterfront smoking pipes and chucking pennies in the water for the kids to dive and find. I've made more'n a shilling a day in summer, diving. So if you was to fall overboard, I could rescue you easy.'

This clinched it. 'Only,' said Pip, 'I should leave a note for Miss Grey. It would only be polite, you know.'

'If you sez so,' said Joey, bowing to Pip's superior knowledge of such social niceties.

Pip hunted in his pockets and found a stub of pencil, and there was an envelope lying on the hall table. He turned it over and wrote on the back, 'We have run away to sea. I shall not be in for my dinner.' This missive was tucked carefully under the pottery lion-dog, so that it should not fall on the floor.

'Ready then, is you?' asked Joey.

'Aye, aye!' said Pip enthusiastically and, pausing only to fill their pockets from the fruit bowl, they scurried together to the rear of the house and out of the back door, while Mrs Brereton's back was turned, and through the garden gate.

CHAPTER EIGHT

As soon as they were alone, Rachel presented every argument she could think of to try and persuade Dan to change his mind. But he was not to be moved. Even the picture she painted of the nervous crisis Pip was sure to suffer as a result of his distress at having his new-found friend wrenched away from him failed to soften his father's resolve, usually so vulnerable to any suggestion that Pip might be made unhappy. The discussion in the study, run upon the rocks in this respect, turned in another direction and disintegrated into an acrimonious and pointless squabble. The fact that Joey had been a week on the property, and no one the wiser, fuelled Dan's obstinacy and his anger, and he turned the latter on to Rachel.

'You were supposed to be watching over Philip!' He glared at her accusingly.

'Do you mean I am to follow him about all day?' she retorted, flushing. 'You also knew he had a den in the garden. You thought he ought to be left in privacy there—so did I.'

Dan, thwarted in this argument, turned on his heel and glowered out of the window. 'And you had no idea that urchin was on the premises?'

Rachel's chin tilted defiantly. 'Am I to understand, Captain Harland, that you are accusing me of some complicity in bringing Joey here and hiding him?'

Dan turned round, saw her expression, and sighed. 'No, no, Rachel . . . Not even you . . . Well, let's get it over with.' He strode to the door and flung it open. The hallway beyond was empty. Dan looked in the rooms opposite, muttered, 'Confound those young imps, now where have they scuttled off to?' and shouted, 'Philip!' at the top of his voice.

Standing a little behind him, beside the hall table, Rachel's eye fell on the envelope pushed beneath the lion-dog. Pip's handwriting, scrawled across it, sent her heart to the pit of her stomach even before she picked it up and read it.

'They have gone back to that wretched den of Pip's!' said Dan irritably, turning back towards her. He caught sight of the envelope in her hand and asked, 'What's that?'

Silently, she held it out towards him.

He hesitated, took it and scanned it quickly. 'Good grief, this is ridiculous!' He crushed the envelope in his hands. 'I think Pip's head must have been completely turned by that imp's company! He would never have done this alone.'

He reached for his hat, which was hanging on the stand by the front door. 'I'm going after them. They can't have gone very far. It is all some stupid trick, in any case. Ten to one, they are hiding about the house or garden. You look here, Rachel, and I'll go around the neighbourhood. I promise you, this time Pip is not going to escape retribution!' He shook his finger at her to emphasise his words.

He looked so angry that Rachel darted forward and caught at his sleeve. 'Wait a little—try and understand!' she pleaded. 'Pip was right when he said he never had a friend before! He's distraught——'

Dan twitched his sleeve free. 'We've just been through all this, Rachel! The whole business has got quite out of hand! When I come back, we'll discuss it further. Obviously Pip needs greater supervision than he's had to date!'

He slammed out of the front door and could be seen striding down the path towards the gate. Rachel sighed. Dutifully, she searched the house and garden, aided by both Mrs Brereton and the kitchen-maid, but no trace of either boy was found—as she had expected. Dan might think Pip was playing some trick, a threat intended to sway his father's decision, but Rachel was sure the child was in deadly earnest.

When Dan returned alone, she knew she was right. His expression had changed. Instead of angry, he now looked worried. When she greeted him with a shake of her head, signifying her own search had been useless, he struck a clenched fist into the palm of his other hand in frustration and swore softly.

'Then they've set out for the waterfront. It's still daylight and Pip will be obvious, even if Joey isn't. There are plenty of ragged urchins about down there, but few boys well-dressed like Pip.' He turned back towards the door again. 'Tell Mrs Brereton not to prepare any food—I've no idea how long I shall be.'

'I'll come too,' Rachel said hastily. 'Only give me a minute to fetch my bonnet and shawl.'

'There's no need——' he began.

But she interrupted, 'I'm coming, anyway! You will do something foolish when you find them!'

'If you mean by that, I'm likely to box the ears of both of them, you're quite right!' he said grimly.

What she meant, thought Rachel as she ran up-stairs to fetch her bonnet, was that, left to deal with it alone, Dan's efforts to recover his son would cer-tainly result in a dreadful scene with Pip screaming and shouting as he was hauled away home. What was needed was for the child to be persuaded home tactfully... but it was no use trying to get Dan to see it just at the moment.

The harbour was at its busiest. A ship which had been in dock to be refitted was ready to sail again and loading stores. The imminent departure of the vessel and its crew meant that a horde of women and children had appeared about the dockside area, and to seek a pair of little boys among all this throng was like looking for the proverbial needle in a haystack. Nor were all the children running about the quayside urchins, as Dan had prophesied. Several of the officers' wives had come to bid farewell and brought along children turned out in their best to wave goodbye to 'Papa', so there was no shortage of clean and tidy little boys in new pantaloons and tasselled caps.

'Could they have got aboard unseen?' asked Rachel, seeing the bumboats pushing off from shore, laden not only with stores but with wives and children. 'Two little boys could attach themselves easily to a family group. The sailors would think nothing of it and the women would each think the children belonged to one of the others.'

Dan frowned. 'I'll go aboard and make enquiry. You had better wait here, Rachel.' He cast a glance about him. 'You can't stand about alone. You had better wait at the Vigo tavern. Go and find Abel. He'll remember you. Say you want to wait for Captain Harland and ask if you can have somewhere private.' He touched her arm and then, spotting a bumboat about to push off, put his fingers to his mouth, let out an ear-splitting whistle and sprinted towards the boat.

Rachel pulled her shawl about her and made her way towards the tavern. As she went, she searched the faces of the crowds, but although once or twice she saw a little boy who closely resembled Pip, and any number who could have doubled for Joey, of the two runaways there was no sign. Obviously, however, she could not search about here alone. Not all the women here were wives. The prostitutes of the town, seeing the departure of a number of good customers was imminent, had arrived in force to do what business they could before the ship sailed. They paraded up and down singly and in couples, with garish bonnets and silk dresses, despite the chill wind blowing off the sea; and, as the crew was equally aware of this being a last opportunity, business seemed to be brisk. Once or twice Rachel was herself accosted, and it was with relief that she reached the safe haven of the Vigo.

Abel, dispensing vast quantities of ale and spirits, red in the face and perspiring, clumped about on his wooden leg doing a roaring trade. When a ship came in or went out, he explained to Rachel, 'twas always the same. She should wait in the parlour.

The parlour turned out to be a small, dark, inconvenient nook, furnished out with ancient pieces most of which dated from the reign of George III, if not earlier, and not very well-dusted. Rachel refused the offer of gin and water and sat down on a uncomfortable chair beneath a grimy message worked in faded coloured silks and announcing, "If the Lord will be your pilot, you'll be guided safe to shore. If not, you'll run upon the rocks, lost forever more."

If eternity was called to mind by this pious instruction, then eternity seemed to be what Rachel suffered as she waited. At long last voices were heard outside the door, one of which she thankfully recognised as Dan's. But as soon as she saw his face, as he stooped beneath the lintel and entered, she knew his search had been in vain. She sank back on to her chair, white-faced.

'Confound it,' he said wearily. 'Not a sign of them. Though one or two fellows say there've been a couple of youngsters about the place, pestering the bumboatmen. But then, that's not to say they were Pip and Joey.'

Abel appeared in the doorway, wiping his hands on his apron. 'Permission to come alongside, Cap'n? What you needs is a search party. I'll have one made up in no time. You sits there with the lady and takes a glass of best Jamaica, and I'll have a dozen lads out lookin' for your deserters!'

'I'm obliged to you, Abel,' said Dan, wiping his hand over his brow. 'Yes, by all means, carry on...'

'Aye, aye, Cap'n!' said Abel, turning nimbly on his wooden peg. 'Look alive there! Volunteers for search party! You two over there, for a start, up on your pins and look lively!'

'They may have gone home again,' said Rachel doubtfully.

He roused himself. 'Yes, let's hope so... I think there is nothing more to be gained by staying here. I've enquired everywhere, including in the chandlers' shops and shipping agents, and left word that if there is any news, I'm to be informed. They know me here... they'll certainly tell me if there's anything to tell. I'm sorry you have been so long imprisoned in Abel's parlour...' Dan glanced up at the motto above her head and snorted. 'It will take more than that exhortation to save a few sinners in these parts! Come along.'

For Pip and Joey events had moved rapidly, but not in a fashion anticipated by either Dan or Rachel, and much less by the runaways themselves.

To begin with, they had quitted the immediate neighbourhood of the house more quickly than expected, because Joey had spied a horse and cart waiting for its driver. Clearly, something had been delivered to the house outside which it stood, 'and it's got to be going somewhere else,' said Joey with simple logic.

He swarmed up the tailboard of the cart like a spider, Pip following as best he could. They crouched down among boxes and crates, and pulled a piece of sacking over their heads. After a moment they heard the driver return, whistling. The cart lurched and they were on their way.

It was some time before it stopped again. 'Hang on...' said Joey, the street-wise. He peered out. 'All clear!'

They jumped down from the cart and found themselves in strange streets. 'Where do we go now?' asked Pip, both excited and appalled at their success so far.

Joey glanced about him. 'This way...' He set off at a jog-trot. 'We look out for another cart, the same...' he instructed Pip.

Their next ride was hitched on the back of a bread cart, and this time the roundsman spotted them and they had to run for it. But they had made good progress and there were clear signs that they were now near the waterfront. This was Joey's territory. He led Pip through a maze of evil-smelling alleys until at last they came out on a stretch of cobbled quayside.

'Look!' exclaimed Pip, grabbing Joey's sleeve and pointing excitedly.

In the distance, a ship rose and fell majestically on the swell. 'She's going to sail!' cried Pip, jumping up and down. 'Look at her flags!'

'Us will never get aboard her, not out there,' said Joey.

'Oh, come on!' urged Pip, not to be put off now. 'If she's going to sail, she may be short of crew.'

Joey was inspired by Pip's optimism, and they set off along the harbourfront.

Alas, it quickly proved not so easy to volunteer as Pip thought. Mostly, they were told to 'Clear off out of it!' and the one or two people who were persuaded to listen to their request burst out laughing.

Discouraged, they sat on a couple of barrels and ate the fruit purloined from the house before they had left.

'What I reckon,' said Joey indistinctly through a mouthful of apple, 'is that we wait until tonight, when it's dark. Them bumboats will still be going out. Ship won't sail till the morning. Look at the stuff what is going aboard. She's only half-loaded. Tonight, we'll do the same as we did with the carts. We sneak aboard, hide under something, and no one will know. When we get out to the ship, we climb up that rope ladder. Easy.'

'All right,' said Pip. He was not so sure it would be that easy, but if you were going to go to sea, you had to show a little determination.

Without warning, Joey jumped down from his barrel and exclaimed, 'Run!'

'Why?' asked Pip, alarmed, and joining him on the ground.

'It's your pa and Miss Grey! I seen 'em for sure! They come looking for us, but they've not seen us yet! This way!'

Fear of discovery lent wings to Pip's feet. He followed blindly behind Joey, not knowing where he was being led. Instinctively, Joey made for his own territory. When they at last stopped, panting, and looked behind them, they were safe but, as Pip saw, in a very insalubrious area of town altogether.

'I say,' he said nervously, 'I think we ought to go back, Joey. Back to the waterfront, I mean. There were more people there—I mean sailors and so forth. I don't like this place much.'

'Oh, 'tis all right,' said Joey carelessly. 'I know it. I live round here.'

Pip sniffed. 'What's that awful smell?'

'The slaughter-house,' said Joey. 'It's the blood. Always stinks, specially when the weather is hot.'

'I shall be sick if I stay here!' said Pip firmly. 'Do come on, Joey.'

Joey, seeing his friend was turning an interesting shade of bilious green, agreed. 'Come on, then,' he said. 'Very likely your pa and Miss Grey will have gone by now.'

They turned to go, but at that moment a pair of calloused hands grasped Joey's shoulders and a coarse voice roared, 'Got you, you little devil! Run off from me, would you? Where've you bin? Speak up!'

Pip looked up aghast and saw that Joey was held prisoner in the grip of the most desperate-looking villain Pip had ever seen. 'Run!' yelled Joey to his friend.

Pip obeyed for a few steps, but then, realising that Joey was being dragged away by the ogre who held him fast, turned and ran back to help his friend. He attacked the man from behind, kicking at his legs in an effort to make him release the struggling and squirming Joey. Jed roared, turned and, before Pip could escape, he too had been seized fast.

'Now, then!' growled Jed. 'What we got here?'

'Let me go!' yelled Pip.

'Oh, a fine young bantam-cock, eh? And tricked out pretty smart, too.' Jed's eyes ran over Pip's clothing. 'What's your name, eh? And what you doing down this way?'

'Don't tell him!' gasped Joey.

But too late. 'I'm Philip Harland!' shouted Pip furiously. 'If you don't let me, let us both, go—my father will come and make you!'

'Ah . . .' said Jed softly. 'You father wouldn't be a seafaring gentleman by any chance, with a black beard?'

'Yes!' squawked Pip.

Jed threw back his head and burst out into laughter. 'Bless me, ain't that a bit o' luck? I got a bit of business with your pa, unsettled, my fine young shaver. Now, you just come along with me!'

He set off along the street, dragging along his prisoners held fast one in either ham-like first, hauled them into the yard of the slaughter-house and thrust them through the door of his own grimy dwelling.

The woman there looked up. She evinced no surprise or emotion at the sight of her son, but, seeing Pip, demanded, 'What have you got there, Jed?'

'Our fortune, Kitty,' said Jed with satisfaction. 'This young feller here is going to make our fortune.'

Kitty came forward and snatched off Pip's cap. She examined it on all sides, then muttered, 'I can sell this to old Lumb the second-hand clothes' dealer.' She glanced up and added, 'But you're barmy to bring that kid here! He'll be missed!'

'So he will,' agreed her loving husband. 'And them as misses him will be glad to pay a little to get him back.' He released his captives and gave both a hearty shove. They stumbled back and fell together in a heap on the floor. 'You'll have to watch 'em, Kitty.'

'I ain't got eyes in the back of my head!' she snapped.

Jed considered, his eyes roaming around the room. Then he grabbed the two boys again and thrust them towards a corner and into a dingy, foul-smelling cupboard. The door was slammed on them and a bar dropped across it.

'That should do it,' said Jed with satisfaction. 'Don't you go opening that door, woman, or I'll black the other eye for you. I got my plans for them two, I have.'

Pip and Joey crouched inside the cupboard with barely room to move a muscle and little air to breathe for what seemed to Pip to be hours. He could hear all kinds of movement outside. Some other children came in, a lot of them, and the woman Kitty began to shout, scold and slap and the children to wail and cry and squabble. Every so often, Jed would burst out, cursing ferociously, and the children would cry all the harder. To Pip, whose family life had been lonely but cherished, all this was a revelation. Then, as if the smell in their cupboard prison was not bad enough, it got worse because outside in the room there was cooking going on of some kind and nauseating odours seeped through the cracked panels of the door.

'It's awful,' whispered Pip. 'What is it?'

'Ma will have got a pennyworth of bones from the slaughter-house,' Joey muttered. 'She's boiling up soup.'

'We shan't have to eat any of it, shall we?' asked Pip in dread.

'Fine chance,' said Joey gloomily. 'Our pa locked me in this here cupboard for a whole week once, and they only remembered to feed me twice.'

Pip silently weighed starvation against the sort of food likely to be dished up by Kitty, and thought perhaps starvation might be preferable. Sounds of the family dining on the other side of the door had a remarkable effect, however, on his stomach, which began to feel very empty. What was more, he was suffering from cramp and had a horrid feeling this cupboard was full of spiders.

Without warning, there came a clatter at the door of the cupboard. It was wrenched open, Jed reached in, grasped his son by the scruff of his neck and hauled him out. Pip was not sure what he was supposed to do, but the chance to stretch his aching limbs was not to be missed. He crept out cautiously and stood watching.

The room had emptied again. Kitty could be heard outside shouting amid a clatter of tin plates which indicated she was doing the washing-up at the communal pump. Jed pulled out a chair and pushed Joey down on to it at the table. Before him lay a piece of grimy paper and a pencil.

'Now, you knows me, don't you, Joe?' said Jed, bending over his offspring and twisting his ear by way of stirring up a prompt answer.

'Ow!' protested Joey. 'Yes, I knows.'

'You knows if you cross me, I'll skin you alive, won't I?'

'Yes,' said Joey resignedly.

'Fair enough.' Jed tapped the paper. 'Since you're so clever and you knows how to write your letters, you write there that if Captain Harland wants to see his son again, all in a piece, he leaves a hundred pound cash in a bag in the hole in the wall, by the back door of the Red Lion. He leaves it after dark and he don't try to pull tricks. He gets the boy when them as has got him gets the money. You write all that, Joe.'

'He won't have a hundred pounds!' exclaimed Joey. 'Who's got a hundred pounds, 'cepting the Queen or a money-lender?'

Jed cuffed his head. 'He's got the money. Think everyone is poor like us? He's got that and more. Mebbe I ought to ask fer more.' He scratched his nose. 'No . . . we asks for a hundred first, and then, when he's paid that, we asks for another.'

'That ain't fair!' said Joey vigorously. 'That's cheating!'

'That's business, that is,' returned his parent. 'Just you write it—and don't go writing anything else. Only what I said.'

Joey cast an agonised look towards Pip, picked up the pencil and obediently printed out the message.

Jed scrutinised it mistrustfully. 'You sure this only says what I told you?'

Joey nodded and snuffled miserably.

'It better had—because if you've put anything else, like where to find the brat—it will be the worse for you! Now, you get back in that cupboard—and you!' added Jed, pushing Pip roughly back whence he had come. The door was slammed on them and they found themselves back in their former dark, cramped, malodorous prison.

'I'm real sorry,' whispered Joey. 'I had to write it—he means what he says, our pa. If he says he'll half kill you, he will.'

'It's all right,' said Pip generously, 'it's not your fault. Do you think your mama might let us out, when your father has gone?'

'No,' said Joey simply. 'She's afraid of him. We all is.'

So was Pip, but he reflected that a British seaman never shows fear and resolved to be British to the last, only it would be easier if he had a drink of water and his feet were not tormenting him so with pins and needles.

Rachel and Dan returned home in silence. It had grown dark, and to search further for the boys was useless.

'It is only to be hoped that they—or Pip, anyway—come back of their own accord.' Dan threw himself down on the sofa in the drawing-room. 'Lord knows where they are.'

Rachel untied her bonnet and took it off. Holding it in her hands and standing before him, she said quietly, 'I suppose it is my fault. I am with Pip most of the time and I should have realised something was going on. He has seemed very excited and happy of late.'

Dan stirred and stretched out his legs. 'The boy is lonely. I've always known it. I should have paid greater attention to it. Found him a suitable companion of some sort. I didn't think he could be so attached to a friend, especially one like young Joseph.'

'Children judge by other criteria than adults.' Rachel let the bonnet fall on to a chair with a weary and despondent gesture.

'Here...' Dan said gently and stretched out his arm.

Rachel sat down beside him and leaned against his shoulder, and he put his arm round her shoulders and gave them a comforting squeeze. She knew that by accepting this gesture of intimacy she was burning her boats irrevocably behind her, but it no longer seemed to matter. She said desperately, 'Oh, Daniel...' and put her head on his chest.

'Hey, now, don't despair! Little boys are indestructible—like corks. They bob up again every time.'

'Joey perhaps, because he's a child of the streets. But Pip has scarcely left this house, and never unsupervised!' she said wretchedly.

He kissed the top of her head lightly. 'You are tired, Rachel. Tomorrow everything will sort itself out. Our runaways will turn up, never fear. Nor must you blame yourself, for it is my fault if it is anyone's. I filled Pip's head with seafarer's tales and ideas of adventure.'

She twisted in his arm to look up into his face. 'You are always so calm when there is trouble. You lose your temper at other times, but not in emergencies.'

'Temper is no good in the face of a storm.' He picked up her hand which lay on her lap and closed his fingers tightly around it. 'You are very fond of the child, aren't you?'

'Yes, indeed,' she whispered. And of the father. It was impossible to say whether the loss of Pip or her feelings for his father made her feel the most unhappy.

'Rachel...' he said quietly, and when she looked up into his face he stooped and kissed her mouth.

She ought to resist, to protest, to jump up and run away, but she did none of these things. Rachel Grey, sensible Miss Grey, put her arms around his neck and surrendered herself to an emotion she had never felt before and a physical contact she had never experienced. She had sometimes imagined it, but the reality was something not only more robust, it was both exciting and frightening, and it was a step along the path on which there was no turning back. When they drew apart a little, she stared up at him with an expression which was at once so puzzled, so wondering and so enquiring, so like that of a disturbed wild creature which did not know whether to bound away or stay and take a closer look at the man who had disturbed its privacy, that he lifted his hand and touched her parted lips with his finger and whispered, 'Don't be scared...'

She shook her head and said uncertainly, 'I'm not afraid...'

If she was a little, it was not of him but rather of herself and what was happening to her, of feelings she did not understand and a confusion both sweet and painful at the same time. She allowed him to push her gently back on to the cushions and he whispered again 'Rachel...' in a way she had not heard him say her name before and which set her heart pounding wildly.

He bent over her and kissed her again, but this time differently, more roughly and in a way which was more demanding. She knew what he wanted and knew that she too wanted this, more than anything. His fingers plucked at the buttons on her bodice, springing them loose, and then his hand slid beneath her under-chemise and rested on the bare skin of her breast. As his fingers pressed into the soft flesh, she moaned and thrust herself against him as if they might be fused together under the heat of their own mutual passion. She knew it was madness, that this could only bring bitter regrets, but just at this wild moment regrets seemed of no importance. Nothing could equal this or matter more. If a lifetime of regret was what it brought, then it was a price she wanted to pay all too willingly.

Dan muttered in her ear, his voice hoarse, his breath rasping and obstructed, 'You don't know how I've wanted you, Rachel. Since you came into this house—you can't know what torment I've suffered because of you. Once they would have burned you at the stake for the spell you've cast over me, and I would have run through the flames to drag you back again or perish with you.'

She whispered, 'Oh, Dan, it's been the same for me . . .'

His fingers were clawing at her skirts, wrestling with the layers of petticoats. She wanted to help him and snatched herself at the recalcitrant underlinen. But at that very moment there came the sound of a voice in the hallway and a tap at the door.

Dan swore heartily and thrust himself away from her. He leapt to his feet, tucking in his disarranged shirt-linen and moving swiftly to obscure the view of Rachel from whoever should open the door.

It was Mrs Brereton. 'Mrs Ellis is here, sir.' The housekeeper's eyes caught sight of Rachel, who had scrambled to her own feet and was attempting to smooth her hair and straighten her skirts. 'I beg your pardon, sir. I'm sure I had no idea——'

Rachel heard him mutter, 'Damn...' but then Mrs Brereton had been manoeuvred aside and Charlotte Ellis swept into the room.

'My dear Daniel!' She held out her hand. He took it automatically and bent over it, but did not kiss it. Charlotte's gaze flickered past him towards Rachel, froze momentarily, then her face resumed its first expression of sympathetic enquiry. 'I called this afternoon and was told the news. I came back tonight just to see if the little boy was found. But Mrs Brereton says he has not come home.'

'No, Charlotte, we—I—have looked all over the waterfront.'

'You will excuse me,' Rachel muttered awkwardly. She fled from the room, knowing that she looked confused and guilty and that unless Charlotte was both blind and stupid—and she was neither—it must be obvious what had been interrupted.

Behind her, as the door closed, Dan began, 'Charlotte, I must explain——'

'My dear Daniel,' she put her hand on his arm. 'You need to explain nothing. I quite understand. It's only natural. The girl is very pretty and has a very forward way with her. I can tell you now that I expected something of this sort. I saw from the start how it would end. But I am not blaming you!' She tapped his sleeve to emphasise her words. 'I have been a married woman and I understand how lonely a man can become. I am neither shocked nor am I reproachful. But it must stop. It must stop now, at once! I don't ask how far it has gone...but the result can only be a scandal. Your reputation will suffer. It will reflect upon the child, upon me... and as for the girl, she will be quite ruined. I'm sure, you wouldn't wish that?'

'No, no...' he muttered. He turned aside, wiping his hand over his brow. 'Charlotte, I really...'

'I know I told you I needed time to think over your proposal of marriage,' Charlotte said, sweeping over his sentence. 'But I have done so and I accept it.'

'You—accept?' He whirled round and stared at her wildly.

'Yes!' She pursed her lips at him in a *moue* of amusement. 'You look so astonished. I had thought you might look pleased!'

'I—yes, of course I'm honoured...' A man drowning was said to see his former life pass before his eyes. For Dan, it was less his former life than his future one which suddenly appeared in alarming detail. Was it possible? In the name of heaven, he was engaged to this woman! He could not get out of it. To say that she'd sue for breach of promise was the least obstacle. In all honour, he simply could not take back an offer of marriage made to a respectable woman. It would be seen as jilting her. He had made his offer—she had accepted it. A lady might be permitted to have second thoughts. A gentleman could not, did not.

'The girl will have to leave the house at once,' said Charlotte serenely. 'But don't worry about it. Obviously she did not take proper care of the boy or this would not have happened. A boy should be in the charge of a man, a tutor, not a governess! I shall find you a tutor who can take over immediately, as soon as the child is found. Then, later on, we can discuss some more permanent arrangement.'

He only half heard her. His mind seized by one thing she had said, he exclaimed, 'I have no wish to do Rachel any harm!'

'Of course you don't! But she must go at once or harm will be done whether you wish it or no.'

'I do assure you, Charlotte,' he burst out, 'that nothing has taken place which——'

She patted his hand. 'My dear Daniel—I do understand! We shall be married as soon as possible. That will take care of everything.' She smiled sweetly at him. 'Now, then, the boy will turn up. That child lacks discipline, Daniel. This must not be allowed to happen again!'

She was gone before he could find any answer. Alone in the drawing-room, Dan sank down on the sofa again and buried his head in his hands.

As Mrs Ellis' brougham clattered away from the house, it rolled past Jed Casey, hiding in the hedge. Jed had waited until dusk before setting out with his ransom note. He had found a hiding-place and settled down to watch the house, waiting for a suitable moment to deliver it. There was still a light in a downstairs room and it continued to show for some time. But at last it was extinguished and the lower floor of the house was in total darkness. Jed emerged from his hedge, crept across the lawn and pushed his note under the front door.

Rachel sat on the edge of her bed and tried to control the fit of trembling which overtook her. The arrival of Charlotte Ellis had done more than prove an embarrassment. It had starkly recalled her to her situation. She had given way, in a moment of madness, to a love which could never be admitted. What Dan felt, she did not know. But Charlotte would not relinquish her hold and he, on reflection, would realise that there was nothing to be gained by an irregular affair with a governess, and everything to be lost.

Rachel pulled down her portmanteau and spent much of the night packing her things and writing a letter to her employer. It was difficult to know what to say, but in the end she wrote simply:

> 'I should have wished to stay until Philip was found but, in the circumstances, we both know I cannot. I hope that Mrs Ellis will not have taken too much offence, and that your understanding with her has not been damaged. I wish you every happiness for the future and would be grateful if you would send some word to tell me when Philip is safe. Otherwise we should not, cannot, meet or correspond in any way again.'

Rachel sealed it up and left it on the dressing-table where she knew Mrs Brereton would find it. She then dozed fitfully, lying fully dressed on her bed, until dawn broke. She awoke stiff and sad at heart, washed her face, tied on her bonnet and taking up the portmanteau, crept down the staircase. The front door was the easiest to unbolt. She stretched out her hand towards it and, in doing so, saw the crumpled piece of paper lying by it.

Rachel stooped and picked it up. 'Oh, no...' she whispered in horror. She read it again, and this time a frown crinkled her forehead. The writing was strangely familiar.

'Why!' she exclaimed to herself. 'Joey has written this!' But could Joey be holding his friend a prisoner? 'No!' muttered Rachel. 'Jed Casey! This is Jed's doing. He has found the boys and somehow discovered whose son Pip is. This is his revenge!'

She clasped the paper to her bosom and glanced wildly towards the staircase. Should she awake Dan and tell him? But no, Joey had written this and, feeling the way he did about Joey, Dan would more than likely believe Joey a willing accomplice.

I must get Pip back! Rachel decided. She pushed her portmanteau out of sight behind a curtain, thrust the note into her pocket, and let herself out of the house as quietly as she could. There were few cabs about so early, and she had to walk some way until she reached a mews where the cabhorses were stabled. The drivers were engaged in grooming the animals and in harnessing up, and some in standing about in groups and gossiping. Rachel approached the nearest man and asked if he could not make ready straight away and take her to the waterfront.

He looked surprised but said, 'Yes, miss—if you'll wait five minutes. I'll have the mare ready.'

A nearby church clock struck six. Rachel pulled her shawl round her. She did not yet know what she was going to do, but at least surprise was on her side.

CHAPTER NINE

THE cab set Rachel down on the waterfront. It was now about seven in the morning and the district was already busy. She shielded her eyes with her hand and squinted awkwardly out to sea. The light was so bright, it almost seemed a white translucent curtain cast over everything. The sea sparkled with diamond points which hurt her eyes and the horizon was lost in an opaque haze. The waves slapped and gurgled against the jetty, mischievously releasing their own curious odour of salt, uprooted seaweed, sodden wood, pitch and dead fish. Tiny dead crabs floated on the surface, the cause of their mass demise a mystery. The ship which had floated at anchor the previous day had now sailed, leaving a curious air of emptiness where she had been. She had done so without Pip and Joey, and for that—in a curious sort of way—perhaps Jed Casey was to be thanked.

Rachel turned her back on the dancing sea and made her way into the dark, dirty streets where the Casey family lived. She knew the addresses of all the school's pupils, and she had visited several of their homes at different times for a variety of reasons. But the Casey household was one she had never visited, although she had passed by the yard many times. She stopped before it now.

They were scrubbing out the slaughter-house. The men whistled cheerfully as they worked, and the noise of the brooms, the clatter of buckets and the splash of water sounded on the air. A horse and cart clip-clopped slowly by her, a mongrel dog running along behind. It was deceptively peaceful. But, for all its early morning normality and cheerfulness, this was a dangerous place at all times. Its community was close-knit. They supported one another in their villainy, and it would be no use asking about Jed Casey or the boys. She would be told nothing, but Jed would learn of it and the danger to herself would be real.

Rachel threw her shawl over her head, covering her bonnet, and crossed the street. She ignored the good-humoured if ribald banter of the slaughter-house workers, and peered into the yard. Women were gathered around a pump in the centre of it, awaiting their turn. They stood with hands on hips, dirty petticoats pinned up above the mire, gossiping. Among them Rachel recognised Mrs Casey. She would have to wait until later in the day, when the yard was emptier. She turned away and set off back to the waterfront.

For all its untidiness, it appeared a much more salubrious and healthy spot by comparison. Rachel made her way to the Vigo tavern. Abel stood on his doorstep in a spotless white apron, and directed a shock-haired youth who was on his hands and knees, scrubbing the step.

'Call that swabbing down?' demanded Abel fiercely. His underling began to work furiously at twice the pace. ''Tis a disgrace! Put your back into it, you idle landlubbing fish bait!' He glanced up as Rachel approached and screwed his eyes in the early morning sunlight. 'Ahoy there! Cap'n's lady, or I'll be a Chinaman!'

'I'm not the captain's lady,' said Rachel, the words sounding sharper than she had intended. 'I'm Miss Grey. I see you remember me, Mr Abel. I—I have some private business in this neighbourhood and I wonder if I might wait in the Vigo?'

'Come aboard, ma'am!' said Abel hospitably. 'Come into the galley and have some vittles.'

He pegged his way back into the tavern, followed by Rachel, and the lad with the bucket and brush heaved an audible sigh of relief and stopped work, squatting back on his heels and wiping his brow.

The galley—as Abel called his kitchen—was a much brighter and jollier place than his gloomy parlour. A fire burned brightly in the hearth. Copper pots and kettles gleamed like gold, and on the wall hung a variety of items. They included a stuffed swordfish in a glass case. Nearby, a picture of Admiral Nelson bedecked with black crape caught Rachel's eye, surrounded by other drawings of ships, sailing ships mostly. The age of steam had come too late for Abel's seafaring days. There were also two ships in bottles hanging from the rafters.

'I have heard of those,' said Rachel, diverted. 'But never seen one! It's very clever how it's done.'

'Aye,' said Abel, looking pleased. 'I'll make'ee one, ma'am, for your parlour.' He pulled out a chair for her. 'Now, then, how would you fancy a pair of kippers for your breakfast? Boiled cockles, dug fresh? No mud nor grit in 'em. I got smoked eel and I got seabass as I can fry up in five minutes. They're hanging up out back to keep cool. That is,' added Abel thoughtfully, 'if that danged cat ain't got to them.'

Rachel declined all these kind offers hastily. Abel looked so downcast at being unable to provide any 'vittles' that she finally agreed to allow him to send the boy for coffee to the coffee-shop down the street. The boy proved the same one who had been cleaning the front step. Viewed upright he was of gaunt but towering frame and slightly vacant eye. However, he brought back the coffee and Abel directed him immediately to roll up a barrel or two from the cellar. He shambled away, looking gloomy. Rachel enquired whether he was Abel's son.

Abel looked horrified. 'Dang me, but I never had no hand in spawning that! His ma was a bumboat-woman and his pa was making port of call, as you might say. That bumboatwoman, she could drink a bottle of rum straight off faster than a ship's surgeon. Ah, you never saw anyone so powerful fast with a knife as a ship's surgeon in the old days. Take off an arm or a leg neat as anything in under two minutes, and all the time roaring drunk. They don't have 'em like that any more. They have fancy doctors on board ship nowadays! Seafaring ain't the same.' He stomped away, shaking his head mournfully.

Rachel waited impatiently in the kitchen until mid-morning. Then she returned to the yard. It was empty now except for a grimy child or two playing in the dirt. Rachel crossed it and knocked at the door of the Casey dwelling. No one answered. She tried the handle and, to her surprise, it gave beneath her touch and the door swung open. Rachel took a deep breath and stepped inside.

She immediately saw why it had not been locked or fastened in any way. Jed Casey was still at home—but lay on an iron bedstead in the corner, snoring loudly on the unwashed sheets. An empty bottle on the floor by the bed suggested a reason for the soundness of his slumber. Rachel looked about her with disgust. The place was filthy. It was not altogether Kitty Casey's fault. Rachel knew her for a downtrodden creature who did her best in lamentable circumstances to provide for a large family with little or no help from her husband. There was only the one bed in the room, a table and some chairs and in the corner, a large cupboard. Tattered blankets piled on the floor indicated that this was where the children slept.

Jed uttered a loud grunt and tossed over on to his other side, the bedstead creaking alarmingly. Rachel started and stepped back towards the door, but Jed did not awaken. There was no sign of the little boys and her heart sank. She had been so sure they would be here somewhere. Perhaps in some other room in the rambling tenement building? She could not gain access to them all.

But, as she stood there wondering what to do, her ear caught the sound of a faint scrabbling from the cupboard. At first, she thought it was a rat, but then it was repeated and followed by a muffled whisper. A child coughed. Rachel's heart leapt into her throat. They were prisoners in the cupboard!

Trying to keep one eye on the slumbering Jed, Rachel tiptoed across the room. The cupboard was made fast with a wooden bar dropped into two brackets. She lifted it out and leaned it carefully against the table. Then she opened the door.

Two small, grimy faces peered up at her, blinking in the light. Then Pip's eyes lit with recognition and his mouth opened to cry out. In the nick of time, she darted forward and put her hand over his mouth, shaking her head furiously. Joey, ever practical, leaned forward and twitched at his friend's sleeve, then pointed at the bed. To emphasise the danger, Jed let out another loud snore.

The boys crawled out of their prison on hands and knees. After a long night cramped in such a confined space, both of them stumbled when they tried to stand up, and Rachel had to grasp them tightly by an arm a-piece, usher them past Jed and out into the yard.

'Quickly, now!' she urged.

They scurried across the yard, past the slaughter-house and set off full-pelt through the streets. To Rachel running was a difficult business, trying to hold up her skirts, clutch at her shawl, and support Pip and Joey. Her heart pounded in her chest and her bonnet fell off and hung perilously by its ribbons. Pip was gasping and panting miserably, but Joey had breath enough to demand, 'Where're we going, miss?'

Where, indeed? The obvious nearest sanctuary was to be found at the Vigo. Rachel piloted them in that direction.

Behind them, Jed continued to snore on the bed. But Rachel, in her haste to get away, had neglected to fasten the outer door properly. It began to swing to and fro. The draught blew across the bed and Jed's face. That and the creaking of the hinges caused him to stir and mutter. Then, with a clatter, the wooden spar which Rachel had propped against the table fell down.

Jed sat upright, stretched, scratched his chest and snorted. He swung his legs off the bed and glanced idly towards the cupboard. Its doors gaped open, revealing it empty.

A great roar of fury burst from Jed's throat. He lunged towards the cupboard in disbelief, then turned and stumbled out into the yard.

'Kitty! Where the devil are you? You come here, woman!'

From a nearby doorway, Kitty put out her head. 'What is it?'

'You come here!' he repeated. 'You come here and look!'

She approached cautiously and peered through the door. Jed seized his wife's arm and dragged her inside. 'You done it! You let 'em out! I'll teach you to go against me!'

He began to shake her violently as she begged, 'Do let me go, Jed. It wasn't me did it—I swear! One of the kids must have let them out! It wasn't me!'

Jed released her and she fell on the floor. He aimed a desultory kick at her and lurched out of the door. There was a slaughter-house worker in the yard. Jed hailed him.

'You seen a pair of brats run past here? One of them dressed up swell?'

The man frowned. 'A woman with a pair of brats come running past, five or six minutes ago.' He pointed up the street. 'Went that way.'

Jed swore heartily and set out in pursuit. He was hampered by the maze of streets and no knowledge of where his quarry was heading. But by dint of asking and looking everywhere he eventually arrived at the harbour and there, in the distance, spied Rachel and the children hurrying along between the boxes, barrels and coils of rope. He set up a great roar and dashed forward, sending others sprawling out of his way.

''Tis Pa!' cried Joey in terror, glancing back.

The Vigo was only steps ahead. Rachel burst through Abel's door with her charges and leaned against the doorjamb, speechless and with bursting lungs, her hair hanging in dishevelled locks about her scarlet face. She closed her eyes briefly and drew a deep, pain-racked breath; opening them, she saw with horror Abel approaching in businesslike manner, armed with a knife.

'What are you going to do?' she stuttered, pushing herself away from the wall.

'Cut them staylaces!' said Abel. 'You'm gasping like a codfish fresh landed!'

'No, I'm not! Please——' She warded him away. 'May we hide in your kitchen, Mr Abel? We're being pursued! These are the little boys were were looking for—Captain Harland's son and a friend...'

'I remember this whipper-snapper,' said Abel, peering down at Joey. 'And don't you go fretting anyone will come in here and do you any harm, miss! Just to go and sit yourself wherever you fancy. Here, you fellows over there, take a look outside, and if you see anyone looking like he fancies a fight, toss him in the drink!'

'That young man,' continued Rachel with some difficulty, putting her hand to the painful stitch in her side, 'your servant—could he be sent to Captain Harland to ask him to come here directly and fetch Pip?'

''Tis as good as done!' said Abel serenely.

Dan arrived within the hour. He dashed into the kitchen with his coat unbuttoned and his hat on the back of his head, and came to an abrupt halt.

'Papa!' yelled Pip, and hurtled into his father's arms.

Dan clasped his son tightly for a moment in silence with his head bowed. Then he looked across the kitchen to where Rachel sat with her arm round Joey. 'I am obliged to you...' he said hoarsely.

She smiled uncertainly at him. Her hair was still a mass of untidy black curls and her face rather shiny. Although on the way there he had thought of little but finding them all safe and had urged the cabman to a pell-mell race against other road-users, the sight of her now brought him to a kind of mental halt, accompanied by a sensation akin to a blow in the chest. He repeated, 'Yes, obliged...' in a muffled voice and turned aside.

Rachel, watching, took his emotion for one of relief at the safe return of his child. It occurred to her that, once he had recovered from it, his feelings might well turn to anger against the two young culprits.

'This has been Jed's mischief!' she said urgently, scrambling to her feet and coming towards him. 'They would have come back before, had they been able.' She glanced at Joey and bit her lip. Then she delved in her pocket and handed over the ransom note.

Joey, recognising it, sank down in his chair and muttered, 'Our pa made me write it. Suppose I'll get the blame. I allus do. I ain't going home no more. Pa will kill me.'

Dan scanned the note and his face set in harsh lines. But he folded it up carefully and put it in his pocket. 'This is a criminal matter. The law will deal with it. The note is material evidence and will settle Casey's hash.'

'There is the child...' She glanced again at Joey.

'Don't worry about him—I'll see to it!' Dan drew in a deep breath. 'You two, just go and sit in Abel's parlour and don't touch anything!'

When they were alone, Dan took off his hat and rubbed his hand over his tousled hair, before tossing the hat down on the table. 'You should have told me what you intended, Rachel. You could have fallen into Casey's hands! The man is a desperate villain, quite capable of anything! Good lord, my blood runs cold at the thought of what might have happened...' He spoke quickly and in a thick voice, as if he had some impediment in his throat.

'I know, but I thought you might suspect Joey. But poor Joey was as much prisoner as Pip.' Rachel twisted her hands together. He wanted to reach out and take hold of them and hold them fast in his, but there was something else.

'I would have wished you might have shown more confidence in me.' Dan hesitated. 'Mrs Brereton found your note. I was just reading it when Abel's messenger came.'

Rachel said, 'Oh..' and looked down.

He reached out now and gripped her shoulders tightly. 'Before God, Rachel,' he said huskily, 'I swear I wish this could have ended differently. I had no intention, when I brought you to my house... You can't stay there now, as you quite rightly wrote. There will be some malicious scandal—Charlotte would make sure of it. She certainly wouldn't rest until your reputation lay in tatters.'

'You must not blame her,' Rachel said quietly. She hadn't the courage to look up at him. She could hear her own voice shake and made a desperate effort to control it. 'From her point of view, the situation must have looked very odd, and of course she objected to it. You—you will be married to her, I suppose?'

'She's accepted me...' He made a gesture of resignation. 'What will you do, Rachel?'

'Go home, to Tom. He says I may. I don't know what I shall do after that. Seek some other post as governess, I dare say, in a household of which Tom approves.'

'If there is anything I can do...' he began awkwardly, and stopped.

'Yes.' She looked up into his face now. It was furrowed in concern. She thought with aching heart that she could never love any face more, nor could any man ever be to her what he was. He was far from perfect. He was irascible and obstinate and plunged from one mistake to another. But he was entirely honest, and no man wanted more to do what was right or tried harder. 'Make some arrangement about Joey. He really can't be sent home.'

'I'll keep the boy. I promise you. Pip needs a friend about the place, and it seems as though Fate has decreed that I'll finish with Joseph on my hands! Grantham shall sort it out. But kidnapping and demanding ransom is a serious business, and Casey shall pay for it—by Harry, he will!' Dan added fiercely. In a quieter voice, he went on, 'I shall come with you to explain to Grey——'

'No!' she interrupted quickly, and put out her hand to stop his speech. 'It's better not.'

He seized at last the hand she held outstretched, and in a low, angry voice burst out, 'This is intolerable! It's worse, it's dishonest! Rachel, I will speak my mind——'

'No, no! Don't!' she begged. 'Please—don't. You will be sorry afterwards—we shall both be sorry.'

She tried to free her hand, but he caught her round the waist with his other arm and pulled her towards him. She realised he meant to kiss her and turned her head away, gasping, 'No, no—it can only make things worse!'

His grip slackened and then he released her, although he still clasped her hand. They stood for a moment in silence, Dan's face twisted with pent-up emotion.

Rachel gently withdrew her hand from his, and this time he made no move to stop her. 'You must take the boys home with you now.'

'Let me at least first take you as far as Grey's house!' His voice was taut with his inward struggle.

'No, I shall take a separate cab. I left my portmanteau in Southsea and will send for it later.'

He turned abruptly aside, snatched up his hat and strode to the parlour door. 'You two—look lively!' The two boys appeared and peered up at him like two watchful puppies. 'In the cab!' he ordered. 'The pair of you—yes, you too, Joseph.' They scurried away. Dan turned back towards Rachel. 'You will not forget I am your friend. If ever I can be of service . . .'

'Thank you,' she said quietly.

He hesitated, then made her a bow and hastened out of the door. She watched him jump up into the waiting cab, and it clattered away.

Outside, Jed had lurked, waiting his chance. His quarry was holed up in the Vigo and he could not go in after it, but sooner or later they had to come out. But, when he saw Captain Harland arrive and leap out of the cab, he began to change his mind and to think more rationally. Harland knew him and had found him once before. It was not a pleasant memory for Jed, who still regarded the captain with superstitious awe. In addition to that, he knew very well that the crime he had now committed was far more serious than his theft of the cash-box. The kidnapping and the attempt at extortion might well carry the penalty of transportation, still on the statute books and occasionally handed down as a punishment; if not, certainly a lengthy prison sentence. It was time to make himself scarce. Jed set off back into the dingy streets, cursing his ill-luck.

Rachel had not realised it was Saturday. With all the events that had happened, which day of the week it was had seemed quite immaterial. But it mattered now, because Tom was at home when she got there. He jumped to his feet when he saw her and exclaimed, 'Rachel!'

She said desperately, 'Oh, Tom——' and ran into his arms.

'What the devil has happened?' demanded Tom, grasping her by the shoulders and holding her a little away from him so that he could see her distraught face. 'Speak up, Rachel! I want to know!'

'You shall, you shall know... But it is no one's fault, at least, it is not Daniel's, it is not Captain Harland's fault.' She sat down and managed to tell him the whole tale of the two runaways, and Jed's part in it and the rescue.

Tom listened in impatient silence. When she had finished, he jumped up and began to stride up and down the room, his face flushed and his hair tumbling over his forehead. 'Confound it, Rachel! If you could not confide your plans to Harland, at least you might have come to me and I would have confronted Casey.'

'I never thought of it,' she confessed.

Tom stopped in his tracks. 'Well, that's blunt enough!' he said stiffly.

'Oh, Tom dear—don't be hurt. But sometimes when one gets into a muddle, one must get out of it oneself.'

'And Harland?' asked Tom after a moment, in a quieter but still tense voice. 'Am I to overlook that he has been playing fast and loose with my sister's affections?'

'He hasn't!' she exclaimed.

'It seems very like it to me!' Tom's jaw jutted aggressively. 'I can hardly call his behaviour that of a gentleman. I knew this would happen! But there——' Tom snorted '—I shall say no more about it. I only hope that another time you'll listen to me!'

'He didn't mean it to happen,' she said almost inaudibly. 'Neither of us meant it. I never thought I could be so unhappy, Tom. I know he is unhappy too. He will marry that woman—and she will make him even more wretched. It is all such a—such a mess!'

Tom sat down and scratched his head furiously. 'We shall go and see Mary, that's what we'll do. You need a woman to talk to. As far as there is anything to be done between men about it, I'm sure, if it were left to me, I'd go to his house and punch him on the nose!'

'Tom!' Rachel gasped, startled.

He set his lips tightly. 'If I had not my professional reputation to consider... but there—ah!' exclaimed Tom with an explosion of frustrated fury, and he struck his hand on the table-top. 'Let him show his face here, that's all!'

Dan, for his part, sat disheartened in his study and stared at the empty hearth. The two boys had been handed over to the capable Mrs Brereton and marched away to be bathed. He had written to Grantham, enclosing the ransom note, and explaining briefly what had occurred. Grantham would see that the law took its course. Now he was left alone and could do nothing—nothing that he wished to do.

Dan stirred and leaned back in his chair. 'Well, Bella,' he said softly aloud. 'Wherever you are now, my dear, if you have ever harboured a wish for revenge, you are pretty well revenged on me now.'

Wheels grated on the road surface outside, and the sound of horses' hoofs was clearly audible. Before his gate, they came to a halt. There was some noise at the front door, and Mrs Brereton put a flushed face through a crack in the study door.

'Mrs Ellis, sir.'

'Well, Daniel!' said Charlotte, coming briskly into the room. 'So all is well that ends well! I take it the child is not harmed?'

'No, thank God,' he said.

'His behaviour was intolerable,' she said severely. 'He must be punished for it, Daniel, and there's no two ways about it. You see where petting and spoiling the child gets you? He has no discipline. I saw it the moment I set eyes on him. However, I've already taken measures to remedy that.'

Dan, who had walked away a little towards the window with his hands clasped behind his back, turned on his heel and stared at her. 'What measures, may I ask, Charlotte?'

'My dear man, I've found a tutor. I told you I would.' Charlotte looked extremely pleased with herself. She sat down and arranged her skirts about her. She shook a gloved forefinger at him. 'You cannot possibly object, Daniel—so do, please, abandon that quarter-deck manner! Mr Dashwood is a very experienced tutor. He has worked for three families of my acquaintance and is currently between situations. This is very convenient, because we shall only need him for a few months.'

'Why?' asked Dan curtly.

'Because then Philip shall go away to school!' She spoke as if the situation was quite settled.

'Now look here, Charlotte,' Dan said energetically, 'there seems to be some misunderstanding. I don't object to your looking out a tutor. Miss Grey has left—and someone is needed. But there is no question of Philip being sent to school.'

'Why ever not? It's the recognised thing. You must not mollycoddle the boy, Daniel.'

'I don't intend to!' he said impatiently. 'But I don't believe boarding-school is suitable for Pip.'

Charlotte surveyed him, then rose elegantly to her feet and came to put her hand on his arm. 'Please don't think me unsympathetic, Daniel. Why, I want to do the best for the child, every bit as much as you do! But he is twelve years of age and must learn to get along among the rough and tumble of other boys.'

'That can be done without his being sent to school!' Dan said sharply.

'Mr Dashwood will tell you the same,' said Charlotte firmly. 'And Mr Dashwood knows about educating boys. Shall I fetch him in? You can discuss it with him.'

'He's here?' Dan asked, taken aback.

'Waiting in my carriage. I'll send your housekeeper out for him.'

Mr Dashwood proved a pallid young man, rather puffy about the eyes and with a receding hairline. He wore a checked coat and trousers, and had a floppy black silk bow about his neck in lieu of a cravat. At the sight of him, Dan's expression darkened.

Urged by Charlotte to present his credentials, the tutor addressed Dan in a high-pitched monotone. 'I am well-qualified to instruct in the Latin and the Greek, sir. Together with mathematics and geography, history ancient and modern and the rudiments of modern chemistry.'

'Chemistry?' snarled Dan. 'Do you want him to set fire to the house? Or blow us all to smithereens?'

'Properly supervised, sir, there is absolutely no danger,' Mr Dashwood assured him. 'And none of the chemicals used is poisonous.'

'I'm pleased to hear it!'

'I understand,' said Mr Dashwood, undeterred, 'that the young man has no Latin. I can guarantee to take him through his primer in three months and have him on to Vergil.'

'Hmm...' Daniel leaned back. 'You would be required, however, to teach two boys. And one of them is a little rough round the edges. He can read and write—he learned his letters in the Ragged School!'

'In the Ragged School!' exclaimed Mr Dashwood, starting back as if mention had been made of the Black Death.

'My dear Daniel, what are you talking about?' Charlotte demanded.

'Simply that I have brought another child into the house, to keep Pip company. I told you I had taken care of the question of companionship. He's a street urchin, but a bright child. Quite a challenge to your talents, Mr Dashwood.'

The tutor opened and shut his mouth silently, and cast a look of silent appeal to Mrs Ellis.

'Mr Dashwood,' said Charlotte leaning forward, 'perhaps you would be so good as to wait outside in my carriage?'

When the tutor had taken himself off, Charlotte made a visible effort to compose herself and asked, 'May I ask your reason for this extraordinary decision, Daniel?'

'Ask away. Pip has struck up a friendship with him. He's a bright little lad. He'll be no trouble.'

'Daniel,' Charlotte said in suppressed tones, 'you don't expect me to agree to your filling the house with—with boys? Especially boys of that sort? A street-urchin? He'll steal the silver and teach Philip coarse language and have fleas!'

'Nonsense, Charlotte!' he said.

She stared at him as if she had never seen him before. 'But I don't agree, Daniel. This child, whoever he is, must go—at once!'

'That's quite impossible. You see, I promised Miss Grey.'

'You—promised—Grey?' Charlotte whispered, turning pale.

'Yes,' Dan said calmly, 'I did.'

*   *   *

Tom's Mrs Davies proved a jolly young woman with a great deal of frizzy brown hair and rosy cheeks. The three of them sat in a neat little parlour, and Mary poured tea and listened to Rachel's story. From time to time, a furious knocking sounded on the ceiling above their heads.

'Take no notice,' said Mary serenely. 'It's only Mama. I'll send the girl up with some tea and cake, and then she'll leave us in peace.'

'I shall have to look for another place,' said Rachel in a small, resolute voice. 'I must go right away from here. Someone must want a governess. It's the best thing.'

'I don't agree,' countered Tom obstinately. 'What do you think, Mary?'

'I think it always a great mistake to rush into things.' Mary set down her teapot and pursed her lips. 'Especially when matters are unfinished, so to speak.'

'They are finished as far as Harland is concerned!' Tom said pugnaciously.

'But not as far as that awful man Casey is concerned. After all, no one knows where he is, do they?'

'He must be arrested!' declared Tom. 'Harland said he'd see to it.'

'All the same,' pursued Mrs Davies, 'until he is, I think Rachel should stay here with me. One can never be sure of persons of Casey's type. They are both very stupid and very cunning by turn, you know, and one never knows whether they will do something foolish, or rather clever.'

CHAPTER TEN

AT first Rachel did not see how she would survive the first week. Just to come through the waking hours would need not only the help of Mary Davies, but every last drop of resolve dredged up from the depths of her own being. If a human being had hope, even a tenuous hope, it was possible to fight off numbing despair. But she had no such secret comforter, and although Rachel did her best during the long, wearisome days to keep a fairly cheerful mien in front of Mary it did not reflect what was in her heart. She could have raged against Fate, but that would not have helped. There was a kind of calm in acceptance of reality. The truth was, as Rachel told herself over and over again, that Dan had expressed his intention to marry Charlotte Ellis long before Rachel's own arrival on the scene. However badly timed or badly thought out his plans, once they had been set in motion neither she nor Dan himself could alter matters. 'There it is!' said Rachel to her mirror every morning, and again every night. But it didn't help.

She did not know whether Mary was deceived by her outwardly composed manner. She suspected not. But Mary, who had suffered an early widowhood, understood the value of time and its healing power and the need for a person to be left in peace to come to terms with a personal disappointment. So, although she observed Rachel's pale face, lack of appetite and listless manner, she very wisely said nothing, though her own kind heart sighed in sympathy.

As for Casey, he had not yet been found, but Mr Grantham—who called in person to express his admiration of Miss Grey's heroism, and also his misgivings at her rashness—was confident he would be found soon.

'Without money or shelter,' said the magistrate, 'he'll be forced to return sooner or later to his old haunts and acquaintances. It is the way of these rogues. They return to their slum refuges as surely as homing pigeons, and as the place is well-watched, we'll know of it.'

In this way Rachel came through the week and, like many another possessor of a broken heart, discovered that life did go on. The sun continued to rise and set. The world did not, after all, stand still, and the practical considerations of life meant that one just had to get on with it, however disinclined one might be. A change of surroundings was, in any case, always worth a bottle of physick, and Mary's idea that Rachel should stay with her was proving an excellent one. Mary's home was a comfortable and cheerful place, a solace for bruised emotions, and this despite constant commotion on the part of old Mrs Aylmer, Mary's mother.

The old lady held sway from the middle of an enormous four-poster bed, and insisted on being kept informed of 'what's going on!'—leaning out of bed at a perilous angle to strike the floor with her stick if information was slow in coming. From time to time Mrs Aylmer tumbled out of bed altogether with a resounding thump, and would be discovered by the alarmed household, sitting on the floor with her lace cap over her eyes and ordering shrilly, 'Put me back! Put me back at once!'

'You,' said Mrs Aylmer, peering at Rachel from the impressive stack of pillows which supported her, 'you are the sister of that fellow who's come courting my daughter, hey? Speak up!'

'Yes, ma'am, so I believe,' confessed Rachel.

'I like to be told,' said Mrs Aylmer pettishly. 'He's got a long face, but at least he ain't a clergyman. The last one was a clergyman. Don't you have a follower?'

'I beg pardon, ma'am?'

'A follower!' repeated Mrs Aylmer testily. 'A beau! Good-looking gal ought to have some fellow making a fool of himself over her!'

'No, ma'am,' said Rachel quietly.

Mrs Aylmer looked glum. 'Dull business, life, these days. Not when I was young! I was presented to Queen Charlotte when I was a girl, and to the old king.'

'King George the Third?' hazarded Rachel.

'He was mad,' reminisced Mrs Aylmer thoughtfully. 'Lot of folks were mad in those days. But at least they weren't dull!' Her boot-button eyes sparkled at Rachel. 'I miss the mad ones the most,' said Mrs Aylmer. 'That and the fellows. I miss the fellows. I might be old. I am old! But I ain't forgotten everything!'

And I miss Dan, thought Rachel. I miss Dan and Pip, too, and there's a hole in my life which can never be healed up, not if I live to be as old as Mrs Aylmer. She at least has some memories. Disgraceful ones, I shouldn't be surprised! But better than none at all!

The end of the week arrived, and with it a spell of fine, sunny, if cool, weather. It was Sunday afternoon, and Tom was due to arrive for tea. Rachel leaned on the windowsill and looked out at the garden path which lay beneath a carpet of red and yellow fallen leaves. The beauty and the melancholy of the late autumn scene appealed to her mood. She felt a longing to join it.

'I think I might just go out for a walk, Mary. You don't mind? I shall be back before Tom arrives, or very shortly after.'

Quite some time after was what she intended. Her own love affair might be thoroughly blighted, but there was no need to cast a blight on Tom's. He and Mary must be given some time alone together over the scones and sponge fingers. Tom was clearly working himself up to propose, but was never going to do it unless he got the chance.

'Take my umbrella,' advised Mary, scurrying past with the cake-stand. 'There's no trusting the weather at this time of year, even if the sun is shining.'

Rachel collected the umbrella from the stand in the hall, pinned up her skirts and set out.

While Rachel had been spending her time that week learning how to come to terms with love's unkind tricks in Mary's serene home, equal peace and quiet had not, unfortunately, reigned in the villa at Southsea.

'Those children,' shrieked Mr Dashwood, gripping the mantelshelf in the study for support, 'are fiends! Fiends, sir!'

'Oh, come along, man,' said Dan curtly. 'Pull yourself together. What have they done? Played some boyish prank?'

The tutor advanced on him and swept back his long hair from his high forehead with a trembling hand.

He was perspiring freely. 'In ten years as a private tutor, I have never—never... That urchin—that urchin ought to have been despatched to Botany Bay! And your son, sir, is not slow to follow a bad example! In the past twenty-four hours, they have painted my hatband with soot, put dead mice in my bed, salt in the sugar basin on my breakfast-table and mixed some foul-smelling substance, the nature of which I have not been able to ascertain, in my hair pomade. You informed me that I was not to chastise the children physically. But in the circumstances, I must insist—insist, sir—that I am permitted to use the cane!' A grim note entered the tutor's voice, and a determined glint his glittering eye.

'I am extremely sorry, Dashwood,' said Dan. 'You certainly seem to have suffered. I'll put a stop to it at once. They shall apologise. No, you may not thrash them. Either of them.'

'It is quite impossible to control boys without the use of the rod!' howled Mr Dashwood.

'Miss Grey managed it.'

The tutor wrestled for self-control. Finally, he drew himself up and hissed, 'I am accustomed to teach the sons of gentlemen! Not Ragged School brats! And if the methods of a schoolmistress are to be preferred to mine, then I cannot stay. I should wish to oblige you and Mrs Ellis—but it's impossible.'

Dan got to his feet. 'Then you had better go, Dashwood.' He opened a drawer of his desk. 'Will fifteen guineas see you compensated for your time—a rather short time—under this roof?'

Mr Dashwood—who had been visibly checked on hearing his resignation accepted with such alacrity—

rallied and brightened. 'Well—very generous, sir, very generous of you.'

'Believe me,' Dan told him, 'the money is well-spent.'

Mr Dashwood looked at him mistrustfully, as if he would have suspected some double meaning, had Captain Harland not been a gentleman.

Charlotte, when she arrived that Sunday afternoon, looked at Dan with perfect comprehension. 'Dashwood came to me and explained what has happened. I find it hard to believe the whole thing was not set up on purpose! Don't deny it, Daniel. You encouraged those boys to torment poor Dashwood!'

'A tutor worth his salt would have been able to handle the situation. I was glad to see the back of him, Charlotte.'

She advanced on him in a swirl of silk petticoats. 'That child—the ragamuffin—must be sent away, back to the streets he came from, today! And as for Philip, there is nothing for it but school immediately. The one I told you of in Yorkshire——'

'And I told you, Charlotte,' said Dan quietly, 'that I wish my son to be educated at home. I intend him to stay here, and young Joseph as well.'

She hesitated. Then she touched his arm in a coaxing gesture and offered persuasively, 'I had thought we should be alone here, Daniel, when we married. You know it's what I should like!'

'As Cromwell told the artist to paint him warts and all, so I'm afraid you must take me together with Pip,' Dan said, unmoved by her pleading tone and the flutter of her eyelashes. 'Dash it, Charlotte, you knew from the first I was a widower with a child. You can't expect simply to blot the child out—like a mistake on a page!'

Her face mottled alarmingly and she snatched back her hand. 'If you imagine, Daniel, that I intend to be plagued by badly behaved children, half-wild little boys, you are quite mistaken! If you will not take the action I wish with regard to them both, then I certainly have no intention of marrying you!'

'I am greatly disappointed, of course,' he said calmly. 'But as you wish, Charlotte.'

Her mouth opened, but then snapped shut. She was not an intelligent woman, and she had so long been accustomed to get her own way that she was slow to recognise defeat. But she recognised it now, and realised too, belatedly, that she had quite misunderstood and woefully over-estimated her influence over this man. With lips pressed tightly together, she snatched up her parasol. Eyes flashing, she said icily, 'Good day to you, Captain Harland! Our acquaintance is at an end!'

The door slammed. Dan winced. He went to the window and watched the brougham rumble away from the house. As soon as it had turned the corner, he strode to the door of the study and wrenching it open, yelled, 'Mrs Brereton! Send that girl out for a cab at once—and bring my hat!'

In Rachel's old home, Tom was preparing to set out for the Sunday afternoon tea-party. He accepted his hat and coat from Hannah, and debated earnestly whether a button-hole might be in order, as he was calling on ladies, or whether it would be seen as totally unseemly. He was not, reflected Tom resignedly, a fellow much given to cutting a dash. Nor had

Hannah's attentions done much to improve the state of his coat or his hat. Tom stood before the parlour mirror and contemplated his general appearance with much misgiving.

He was distracted by the appearance of Sally, who piped loudly, 'There's a gent come ter see you, sir!'

'Gentleman,' corrected Tom automatically, turning away from his own reflection without regret—though he did not much care to be delayed at this particular moment. 'Who is it, Sally?'

Sally disappeared, and there was a murmur of voices. She reappeared and pronounced with much careful aspiration of the ''H'', 'His name is Captain Harland, and he'd be obliged if you could spare a minute.'

'What?' shouted Tom, and Sally jumped back in alarm. 'Show him in!' ordered her employer grimly.

A step behind her heralded Dan, who barely had time to duck his head beneath the lintel of the door before Tom hurled aside his ill-brushed hat and leapt towards him aggressively, red in the face and looking, thought Dan wryly, less like a schoolmaster than a determined contender in the prize ring.

'How dare you show your face here?' howled Tom, clenching his fists. 'Today, sir, is the Lord's Day, and I am prevented therefore from doing what I should like to do—but not from expressing my opinion!'

'Hold on, Grey,' interrupted Dan, holding up one hand placatingly, 'I'm aware of your opinion, and I don't disagree with it much. The fact is, I'd called hoping to see Rachel—Miss Grey—but the little girl says she is not here.'

'No!' snapped Tom, 'she isn't! And I'm extremely glad of it. What have you to say to my sister?'

Dan drew a deep breath and informed him.

There was complete silence for a moment. Then Tom, as whitefaced now as he had been scarlet before, demanded through clenched teeth, 'Is this some joke on your part? I understood you to be intending to marry some other lady—or have you seen fit to play fast and loose there, too?'

'No, I damn well haven't!' exploded Dan angrily. 'The situation has changed. Look here, I've come here to put matters right between Rachel and myself. It's probably as well that I've seen you first. Rachel has a good deal of respect for your opinion and you are her only male relative. I ought, to do the thing properly, to ask your permission.'

Tom looked alarmingly as though he might choke. Colour flooded back into his face and he uttered a series of incoherent noises. Eventually he gasped, 'You're out of your mind! I shall certainly never give it!'

'If it will make you feel any better, punch me on the jaw by all means,' offered Dan. 'Get it off your chest. If I were in your shoes, I'd do the same.'

'Don't tempt me!' snarled Tom.

'You're a good fellow, Grey,' said Dan appreciatively, 'and I hope we shan't always quarrel. Where's Rachel?'

'Staying with—a friend . . .' Tom leaned against the edge of the table behind him and folded his arms, glowering at his visitor. 'I'm about to call on them, as it happens.'

'Then allow me to come, too. I'll explain matters as we go along. I have a cab outside. Come on, man, be fair! I'm the first to admit I've managed to get just about everything wrong from start to finish, but I'm doing my level best to set things right.'

This appeal for justice set up a visible struggle in Tom between his inclinations and his conscience. At last he said belligerently, 'Very well. But don't imagine you are going to have any time alone with my sister! Whatever you intend to say to her, you'll say in my presence.'

The streets had a Sunday afternoon calm about them as Rachel walked along. Occasionally she passed a small family outing, but otherwise the area seemed deserted. She was glad of the peace and quiet, and for not meeting anyone to whom she must talk.

Her footsteps eventually brought her to a little park, enclosed by trim privet hedges. She turned into it and walked past its flowerbeds and lawns. From the tangled shrubbery on the right-hand side of the path came an occasional rustle which caused her once or twice to look in that direction. But she saw nothing, only the occasional leaf quivering as if the twig to which it was attached had been disturbed, and she supposed that a squirrel or a bird hunted through the undergrowth.

In the middle of the park, surrounded by lawn and trees, was a small pond. A few goldfish swam in it lazily around a central fountain—not working—of a boy astride a dolphin. Rachel stood on the edge and watched the gold and silver shapes flicker in and out of the weed in the pond's greenish depths. Overhead the sky was blue and cloudless and there was no breeze. The surface of the pool, dotted by a few fallen leaves from surrounding trees, was like a mirror. And in that mirror, behind her shoulder, appeared a face.

For a moment, a kind of superstitious incredulity rooted her to the spot, for the face seemed to peer up from the pool at her, ugly and grinning, a satyr at large in this urban and artificial scrap of nature. Then a fish darted though the image, shattering it, and shattering with it Rachel's paralysis. Her heart gave a great leap of fear and she spun round and beheld Jed Casey.

He looked even worse than the last time she had seen him. His clothing was stained with mud and the greenish marks of grass. His face was unshaven and there was a wild glitter in his eyes.

'Ah,' said Jed mockingly, seeing her alarm. 'Didn't expect me, did you?' He saw her throw a desperate look about her and chuckled. 'There's no one for you to call to! There ain't a soul here. We got the place to ourselves.' He scratched his unshaven chin and eyed her. 'Took me a while to find you, missy. But find you I did. I bided my time, watching that house where you've been staying. I knew you'd come out alone sooner or later, and I got you now, I reckon!'

'What do you mean to do?' whispered Rachel.

He scowled. 'The Peelers are out looking for me. I can't go home and I've been sleeping rough. All thanks to you!'

'Not to me!' she protested. 'You brought it all on yourself. You stole the school's money and you snatched Philip Harland off the street!'

'Only want my due!' growled Jed sullenly. 'I needed the money. I'd have the money, too, if it wasn't for you and that devil with the beard. He owes me them guineas! Well, he can't help you now! No one crosses Jed Casey and gets away with it! No one, see?' He thrust his face into hers, grimacing at her with yellow teeth. She was reminded of a snarling wild animal, and there was indeed something truly wolf-like about this shabby, hirsute creature, hardly human in its primitive rage.

Rachel recoiled. But a sensation of nothingness behind her stopped her instinctive movement backwards. She remembered that she stood on the very edge of the pool and could not step back. She was effectively trapped. He saw her dilemma and grinned evilly, stretching out a huge, unwashed paw to seize her. Rachel instinctively struck out with the umbrella, her only weapon. Jed cursed her and threw up his arm to deflect the blow. Seizing her only chance, Rachel ducked down and dodged under his raised arm.

She knew she could not outrun him. But her one hope of salvation was to reach the park gate and the main road. God willing, someone would be walking along the pavement and she could cry out for help. Fear lent her feet wings, and she was almost there before Jed's brawny arms encircled her waist and lifted her bodily from the ground. Feet kicking, she jabbed back one elbow and struck him across the bridge of his nose. Jed swore and dropped her. Free for that vital second or two, Rachel stumbled out of the park gate and looked wildly up and down the road.

A cab was trotting towards her. She opened her mouth to call out to it, but at that moment Jed grasped her again and began to drag her back into the park. Rachel screamed as she had never screamed in her life. The power of the effort tore at her throat and sent a pain shooting through her lungs. Jed tried to stop her by putting his grimy hand across her mouth, and she bit him. It left a revolting taste in her mouth, sweat and dirt and freshly drawn blood. Cursing, he snatched his hand away and Rachel screamed again.

The cabbie hauled on the reins and the mare reared up. The cab rocked violently and one of the two men in it put out his head and shouted, 'What's amiss?'

''Tis a female screeching fit to bust, sir!' came the reply.

'My God!' cried Dan. 'It's Rachel!'

Jed had perceived his danger. Dragging Rachel with him, he retreated into the park and came to a halt, panting, before the pond where he had first come upon her. He swung round, holding her before him as a shield, her arms tightly imprisoned in his cruel grip. As Dan raced up followed by Tom, Jed faced him, snarling over the head of the powerless Rachel, taunting, defiant and dangerous, a wild beast at bay.

'You just stay right there, gents!' Jed shouted. 'I'll break the lady's arm, I swear I will, if you comes a step nearer!'

'Dan!' gasped Rachel incredulously.

He held up one hand and said loudly but calmly, 'Stay quiet, Rachel. Casey! You're a fool if you harm her. You'll be transported, and if she's seriously injured you'll hang!'

'If she be injured, it'll be your doing!' returned Jed hoarsely. 'You just stays there, Cap'n Harland. You, too, schoolmeester.'

'He cannot watch us both at once,' muttered Dan to Tom, who had arrived, panting and hatless, at his side. 'Move round to a position where he can't see you. It will take his eye off me for a moment.'

'Stay there, schoolmeester!' howled Jed, seeing what the plan was. 'I swear, I'll break her arm!' By way of underlining his threat, he twisted Rachel's right arm viciously and she could not help but shriek out in pain.

But Tom had achieved Dan's purpose. He was now out of Jed's direct line of sight. Casey twisted his head to see what had become of him, and that split second was all Dan needed. He leapt forward, wrenched Rachel bodily from Jed's clasp and threw her to one side and clear. Then he struck Casey a mighty blow with his fist on the nose. Bone and cartilage crunched, and blood spurted out and ran down Jed's cheeks and chin. But he had fought in many a taproom brawl, and it took more than one punch to floor Jed Casey. With a great roar like a tormented bull, he lunged forward.

Sometimes, in the mean streets around the Ragged School, Rachel had come across men brawling. But she had never seen anything to compare with this for ferocity and naked hate. She thought they must kill each other, and pressed her clenched fist against her teeth to stifle her cries of alarm when she saw Dan fall, only to roll over in the dust and scramble to his feet just in time to escape the kick aimed at his jaw from Casey's hobnailed boot. And then Dan struck Casey in the midriff, causing him to gasp and double up, and followed this with a swift uppercut to Casey's jaw. Jed's head snapped backwards. He stumbled, teetered on the edge of the pond and fell full-length backwards, sending a great spray of water over them all.

There was a sudden silence, a deathly stillness. Jed lay sprawled motionless in the water, a thin trail of crimson from his shattered nose seeping in a slowly spreading stain across the water through which the goldfish darted in fright.

Rachel let out a long, low sigh and collapsed in a dead faint into the arms of Tom, behind her.

Faces, blurred and indistinct, swam before Rachel's vision, and she seemed to hear voices, but from very far away, so faint she could not distinguish any words. She tried very hard to concentrate, though it hurt her head, and there was another insistent throbbing pain shooting through her right arm. Gradually, the faces stopped spinning around in Catherine-wheel-like circles and became stable and familiar. There was Tom, pale and anxious, and Mary, frowning with concern, and Dan—yes, Dan—rather dishevelled still and with a rapidly blackening eye, who sat on the edge of the sofa on which she lay and held her hand. Seeing her gaze clear and a frown pucker her brow, he leaned forward over her and whispered tenderly, 'Rachel?'

Through the pain pounding at her temples, she mumbled, 'You...' and felt his fingers tighten their grip on hers. Then she remembered that other face, not here but just as real, and imprinted forever on her memory. She gasped, 'Jed?' and tried to sit up. Stars shot across her vision.

'Steady,' Dan said, pushing her gently back on to the cushions. 'It's all right. He won't trouble you any more.'

With difficulty she managed to form the words, 'Is he——?'

Dan was shaking his head. 'No. We pulled him out just in time before he drowned in five inches of water. Tom and I pumped him out and now he's safely under lock and key! For my part,' said Dan grimly, 'I'd happily have let him drown—but Tom here is of a more saintly disposition than I, and felt that as it was the Sabbath, we ought at least to try and save him!'

Mary clicked her tongue, but whether in disapproval at this slightly flippant reference to the day, or because she regretted Jed Casey's resurrection, was unclear.

The pain in Rachel's head subsided. 'Thank God,' she said weakly. 'He's an awful man, but I wouldn't want——' Her eyes focused on Dan again and she frowned and asked, bewildered, 'What were you doing in the cab with Tom?'

'Harland came——' began Tom, behind them, but was not allowed to finish.

Mary took hold of his arm. 'Come along, Tom, I need you in the other room, to move the piano.'

'What—now?' exclaimed Tom.

'Yes, now!' said Mrs Davies firmly, hauling him away.

Dan smiled faintly as the door closed, leaving them alone. 'Tom has met his match.'

'She's very nice...' said Rachel in a small voice. 'And has been very kind.'

'And I'm a fool!' exclaimed Dan with sudden vehemence. 'I should have watched over you like a hawk until Casey was found. I thought he might come after me or Tom, but not after you! Rachel, if that brute had done you any harm, I think I should have killed him with my own hands——' He broke off suddenly and clasped her tightly in his arms.

Unhesitatingly, although her bruised right arm ached from Casey's rough handling, she put both arms round his neck and clung to him, exclaiming from the depths of his waistcoat, 'I still don't understand how you came here, but I am so glad you are!'

'Oh, lord, Rachel, I love you,' he groaned.

There was a silence. Rachel disengaged herself from his linen and looked up at him. 'And I love you,' she said rather dismally. But what's the use of it? echoed unspoken in her head.

'I came here to ask you to marry me, Rachel.' He heaved a deep breath. 'That is, I went to Grey's house, but you weren't there. After some argument, Grey agreed to bring me here with him. That's how we came to be on the road in that cab—and thank heaven that we were!'

'What—what about Mrs Ellis?' stammered Rachel, hardly able to believe her ears and thinking she must still be only half-conscious.

'Threw me over. I explained it all to Grey on the way here. There was this fellow, Dashwood, a tutor she had unearthed somewhere.' Dan's expression changed momentarily to one of bemused indignation. 'Lord, Rachel, if you could have seen the popinjay! He was dressed like a poet and wanted to teach Pip to mess about with chemicals. I promised Charlotte I'd give him a trial, but he only lasted twenty-four hours and took himself off. I think it was Joey,' said Dan thoughtfully. 'I think it was Joey he couldn't cope with. Or maybe both. I think they conspired to give the poor fellow a wretched time. He went running with his grievances to Charlotte, and she appeared earlier this afternoon, insisting I get rid of Joey and pack Pip off to some school or other at the other end of the country, in the middle of the Yorkshire moors. I refused both suggestions. She then told me she had no intention of spending her life surrounded by half-wild boys! The marriage was off!'

'Then it's my fault, because I asked you to take Joey,' said Rachel, adding honestly, 'But I'm not sorry.'

'I feel like a condemned man who's been reprieved from the scaffold!' Dan told her bluntly. 'I don't know how I got into such a—such a ridiculous situation, when I knew in my heart I'd fallen in love with you. I did so when I first met you and you were fighting to save Joey from the just clutches of the law! I don't know why it took me so long to realise the obvious. There you were, as pretty as a picture and as brave as a very small lion, jumping up and down, all pink in the face and with curls bobbing... My heart said to me, "That's the girl for you, Dan Harland!" Only I think my brain must have got pickled in seawater at some stage, because it was rather slower off the mark!' Dan paused. 'Forgive me, Rachel.'

'There's nothing to forgive,' she said, leaning her head on his chest.

He lifted his hand to stroke her hair. 'And you will marry me, won't you?' he asked a little anxiously.

'Yes, of course I will!' said a muffled voice sturdily.

Dan twisted his finger in one black ringlet. 'That's all in order, then, and ship-shape! Do look up, sweetheart, I want to kiss you!'

'I've found out what a marriage-bed is,' said Pip, seated upon the cushions in the gazebo. He sounded both smug, as the owner of a piece of special knowledge, and rather disappointed. 'It's just the same as an ordinary bed. I thought it would be special. The only difference I can see is that Mrs Brereton has gone and put new sheets on it with lace trimmings. I think that dictionary got it wrong. Nobody could be faithful or unfaithful in it. Nobody even sleeps in it, and it seems to me a complete waste. But I dare say it's the fashionable thing to have, you know, like a piano.'

Joey frowned. 'What do you mean, no one sleeps in it?'

'They don't. The bed is all ready in the best bedroom and no one even goes in there except Mrs Brereton with flowers.'

'You're a right noodle,' said Joey loftily. 'It's been got all ready for your pa and Miss Grey after they're married and come back from the church. Then they sleep in it.'

'I don't think,' said Pip reproachfully, 'that ladies and gentlemen get into the same bed.'

'Yes, they do, only they gets married first. A real slap-up do with carriages and folks in their best clothes and bottles of wine. I seen 'em. I used to hold the horses while folks was waiting for them all to come out of the church. They throws rice over 'em, which seems real daft when you could cook it up and make a pudding. I used to wait till everyone was gone and pick up the bits of rice and take 'em home to Ma. That's the sort of do your pa and Miss Grey will have. Not like poor folks,' said Joey, 'who don't allus bother to get married unless the girl is carrying.' Joey sketched a swollen abdomen with his hands, and Pip reddened and tut-tutted. 'Sometimes,' said Joey, warming to the subject, 'they don't get married at all. Our Lily, that's my eldest sister, she's always getting into blokes' beds. She does it for a shilling.'

'Oh, a wager!' said Pip, everything now clearly explained. It had long been evident that Joey's family were all quite disreputable. Their antics both fascinated and shocked Pip. But whatever Lily did for a shilling had nothing to do with the imminent marriage of his father and Miss Grey. He turned his mind and the conversation firmly back to the subject. 'I've always thought they ought to get married. So that they could eat their dinner together. I mean, I like Miss Grey having her dinner with me, but I'm sure she'd rather eat it with Papa. And besides that, he could kiss her and it would be all right, you know—and they could stop quarrelling.'

'Getting married don't stop folk quarrelling,' said Joey, the authority, 'it starts them off. Married folks yells at each other all the time and they don't go kissing much.'

'What do they do?' asked Pip, feeling himself uninformed on this point, but sure Joey would know.

'Fights and scratches and argues about money,' said Joey. 'Then they goes out to the pub, gets drunk on gin, comes back and gets into bed and starts all over again fighting and kicking, only this time without their britches on.'

Pip was so horrified by this scenario that he fell silent and gazed at his friend, who seemed curiously indifferent to this shocking state of affairs. 'I'm sure they don't,' he said at last, in hushed tones.

'Yes, they does. Then they gets another baby.'

'Why?' Pip puzzled over this connection.

Joey, having been brought up in one room and having had the dubious privilege of a ring-side view of the procedure, informed him.

Pip thought it over. He supposed, since Joey said so, some people did this. But never, he was sure, his papa and Miss Grey. He came to the conclusion that it was only the rougher sort of persons who indulged in this quite uncivilised and indecent way to go on, and gentlemen and ladies had some other means of acquiring babies. He had no wish to hurt his friend's feelings, however, by suggesting that Joey's family were hopelessly committed to the lower orders and didn't know any better, so he said politely, 'Thank you for telling me,' and then changed the subject.

'I don't go much on being a pageboy, Joey.'

'Nor I,' said Joey grimly. 'I seen them new suits they got for us. Satin!' Joey's voice gained all the shock and disgust which Pip's had held on being acquainted with the facts of life. 'Girls wear satin! Lace collars and all.'

'We could run away again,' suggested Pip.

Silence fell while they contemplated this.

'It's not as easy as it sounds,' said Joey at last. 'Look what happened last time. I got a better idea. I reckons we spills something on them satin suits. So as we got to take them off and wear our ordinary clothes.'

But on the day Pip and Joey were crammed, protesting, into their pageboy suits. Under the eagle eye of Mary Davies, who was matron of honour to the bride, they went through their paces with solemn faces and without putting a foot wrong—largely because they suddenly found themselves near to the centre of a rather a lot of attention, and Pip had seen all the food Mrs Brereton had cooked and which they would eat as soon as the ceremony was over. They were borne away later, replete with glazed ham and fruitcake, to stay overnight at Mary's house, and Dan brought Rachel home to the villa at Southsea as its new mistress.

'Which I should have done at the very first,' he said. 'Because I knew when I first saw you that there could never be anyone else.'

Rachel unpinned her bonnet and put it down on the chair, smiling at him a little uncertainly. He put out his hand to touch her hair, and she caught at his fingers and held them against her cheek.

Dan stooped, caught her in his arms and whirled her around, her feet clear of the floor. Then he set her down and said wryly, 'I should tell you that Joey has been instructing Pip on the matter of marriage, and that Pip is quite convinced it is no way to behave.'

'Poor Pip,' she said, laughing, but flushing pink partly because of the look in his eye and partly because of having been swung around. 'He will be sadly disappointed in us when he learns the truth one day.' The crimson glow on her cheeks darkened, and she added, 'I hope you will not be disappointed in me.'

'My dear Mrs Harland,' said Dan firmly, 'you constantly enchant me. Besides which, I couldn't be disappointed in you—whatever you may mean by that—if I tried. Anyway, if you had any French, you would know that the French themselves—who are no mean experts on the subject—have a saying that there are no frigid women, only clumsy husbands. It is my belief,' he put his mouth to her ear, 'that we should put the matter to the test.'

She looked up into his face with her lips slightly parted, which was so much an invitation to kiss her that he did so. As his mouth closed over hers, he sensed her yield in his arms and broke away from her to mutter huskily, 'I want to take you to bed, Rachel... Now, let's go now.'

'Yes, now,' she whispered.

He smiled. 'We shall not be interrupted this time.'

'No,' Rachel said, and slipped her arm through his as they climbed the staircase together.

It was already late afternoon, and the days were shortening as autumn drew to its close. The fading rays of the sun had already crept away from the far side of the room, and shadows begun to cast their dusky veil across the lace-trimmed linen of the bed as if they would add their own touch of mystery. She could not pretend she had never dreamt about this moment, imagining Dan's fingers unhooking her gown, as they did now, and the touch of his breath on the nape of her neck as he accomplished his task and bent to kiss her bare shoulder. But the dream had been her most secret one, never admitted, hardly even to herself, because it had seemed it could never be realised. But it had been made real, and Rachel turned to face him and smile up at him, sliding her hand across his chest.

He added huskily and a little anxiously, 'You are not afraid?'

Rachel shook her head. 'I always used to feel as if there were two of me. An outside me, someone everyone knew and saw every day, and another me, hidden inside. But now I feel that everything is right. And that's how I want us to be, one person.'

'Rachel . . .' he whispered, and, picking her up effortlessly, carried her through the last golden splash of evening sunlight, to the waiting bed. And she knew that, for them, this was not a day ending, but a whole new life waiting to begin.

THE IDEAL TONIC

New Beginnings — ANN JENNINGS

A Stormy Partnership — KATHLEEN FARRELL

Misplaced Loyalty — JENNY ASHE

Over the past year, we have listened carefully to readers' comments, and so, in August, Mills & Boon are launching a *new look* Doctor-Nurse series – MEDICAL ROMANCES.

There will still be three books every month from a wide selection of your favourite authors. As a special bonus, the three books in August will have a special offer price of **ONLY 99p** each.

So don't miss out on this chance to get a real insight into the fast-moving and varied world of modern medicine, which gives such a unique background to drama, emotions – and romance!

Mills & Boon

Widely available from Boots, Martins, John Menzies, W.H. Smith, Woolworths and other paperback stockists.
Usual price £1.25

COMING SOON FROM MILLS & BOON

Your chance to win the fabulou

VAUXHALL ASTRA MERIT 1.2 5-DOOR

Plus

**2000 RUNNER UP PRIZES OF WEEKEND
BREAKS & CLASSIC LOVE SONGS ON CASSETTE**

SEE
♥ **MILLS & BOON BOOKS** ♥
THROUGHOUT JULY & AUGUST FOR DETAILS

Offer available through Boots, Martins, John Menzies, WH Smith,
Woolworths and all good paperback stockists in the UK, Eire and Overseas

THE COMPELLING
AND UNFORGETTABLE SAGA OF
THE CALVERT FAMILY

April	August	November
£2.95	£3.50	£3.50

From the American Civil War to the outbreak of World War I, this sweeping historical romance trilogy depicts three generations of the formidable and captivating Calvert women – Sarah, Elizabeth and Catherine.

The ravages of war, the continued divide of North and South, success and failure, drive them all to discover an inner strength which proves they are true Calverts.

Top author Maura Seger weaves passion, pride, ambition and love into each story, to create a set of magnificent and unforgettable novels.

W●RLDWIDE

Widely available on dates shown from Boots, Martins, John Menzies, W.H. Smith, Woolworths and other paperback stockists.

FRUIT SALAD WORDSEARCH
COMPETITION!

How would you like a years supply of Mills & Boon Romances ABSOLUTELY FREE? Well, you can win them! All you have to do is complete the word puzzle below and send it in to us by Dec. 31st. 1989. The first 5 correct entries picked out of the bag after that date will win **a years supply of Mills & Boon Romances** (*ten books every month - worth £162*) What could be easier?

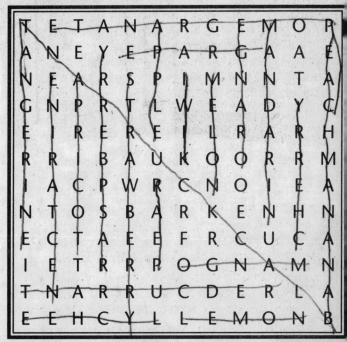

T	E	T	A	N	A	R	G	E	M	O	R	
A	N	E	Y	E	P	A	R	G	A	A	E	
N	E	A	R	S	P	I	M	N	N	T	A	
G	N	P	R	T	L	W	E	A	D	Y	C	
E	I	R	E	R	E	I	L	R	A	R	H	
R	R	I	B	A	U	K	O	O	R	R	M	
I	A	C	P	W	R	C	N	O	I	E	A	
N	T	O	S	B	A	R	K	E	N	H	N	
E	C	T	A	E	E	F	R	C	U	C	A	
I	E	T	R	R	P	O	G	N	A	M	N	
T	N	A	R	R	U	C	D	E	R	L	A	
E	E	H	C	Y	L	L	E	M	O	N	B	

RASPBERRY	ORANGE	LYCHEE
REDCURRANT	MANGO	CHERRY
BANANA	LEMON	KIWI
TANGERINE	APRICOT	GRAPE
STRAWBERRY	PEACH	PEAR
POMEGRANATE	MANDARIN	APPLE
BLACKCURRANT	NECTARINE	MELON

PLEASE TURN OVER FOR DETAILS ON HOW TO ENTER

HOW TO ENTER

All the words listed overleaf, below the word puzzle, are hidden in the grid. You can find them by reading the letters forward, backwards, up or down, or diagonally. When you find a word, circle it or put a line through it, the remaining letters (which you can read from left to right, from the top of the puzzle through to the bottom) will spell a secret message.

After you have filled in all the words, don't forget to fill in your name and address in the space provided and pop this page in an envelope (you don't need a stamp) and post it today. Hurry - competition ends December 31st. 1989.

Mills & Boon Competition,
FREEPOST,
P.O. Box 236,
Croydon,
Surrey. CR9 9EL

Only one entry per household

Secret Message _____

_____

Name _____

Address _____

_____

_____

_____ Postcode _____

You may be mailed as a result of entering this competition
Please tick the box if you are a Reader Service subscriber ☐

COMP7